DAUGHTER OF DAMASCUS

Her Secret Life Will Shock the World

Hussin Alkheder

Copyright © 2023 Hussin Alkheder

All rights reserved

The characters and events portrayed in this book are fictitious. Any similarity to real persons, living or dead, is coincidental and not intended by the author.

No part of this book may be reproduced, or stored in a retrieval system, or transmitted in any form or by any means, electronic, mechanical, photocopying, recording, or otherwise, without express written permission of the publisher.

ISBN-13: 9798857164235

Cover design by: 99designs

She neither moved nor moaned when the belt buckle struck her back, biting into her skin, the first time, the second time, nor the third time. When she finally cried out, her three sisters in the room wept, not daring to inch closer. He didn't even stop when her cheap white cotton dress became stained with her blood. He only stopped when she finally fell to the ground, unconscious. Her sisters ran to her, shook her, and called her name. When she didn't respond, the eldest turned to him and screamed, "Murderer!"

CHAPTER 1

Tuesday, January 12, 2010

Mansoor noticed the police car double-parked in the narrow alley and sensed the issue was serious this time. It was unusual to see a black-and-white police car in these old Damascus neighborhoods. Years might go by before residents saw a police car or an ambulance. Not because they were immune from mistakes or exposure to health crises, but because these simple people considered calling the police or ambulance a scandal that must be avoided at all costs.

The alley was lined on both sides with rows of drab, gray, four-story attached buildings. Pedestrians might think it was one long building, but those who lived there knew that on each side were six buildings connected.

Despite the early morning hour and the freezing temperatures, the police car's siren lured almost all the residents from their apartments and out into the streets. With their hands deep in their pockets and stamping their feet on the ground, their steamy breath ascended as they chatted among themselves, speculating over the most likely reasons for the police being there. Those who couldn't make it down to the street stood on their rectangular, cantilevered balconies to observe the growing crowd. No less curious, passersby stopped and gawked at the buildings, wondering which family had the bad luck.

In these parts of the city, there were so many families who, despite their extreme poverty, seemed to never stop having children. The sheer number of clothes in a variety of sizes hanging from the clotheslines on each balcony made it apparent that more than one family lived inside most apartments. Each room in the apartments held a family, and each family had multiple children, who spent their mornings in public schools and their evenings in the street, playing and learning many nasty things. If the public schools had not been free, none of these families would send their kids to learn.

Detective Mansoor Chait worked for the Criminal Security Administration—CSA—on Fairooziah Street in Damascus. The CSA was the primary force tasked with maintaining the country's security. His temper mounted as he shouldered his way through the crowd till he finally reached the door of Building 11. The entrance to the building was doorless and unsurprisingly grimy. A short hallway led to the stairs. Two rows of filthy, old, electric meters hung at the top on both sides of the hallway. At the bottom of the same walls were three rows of rusty water meters. Water leaking from the meters guaranteed the floor would be wet and muddy all year long.

Detective Mansoor climbed the stairs, ignoring the clamor from the crowd in the street. He tried to ignore the thin, peeling walls, the spiderwebs filling every corner, or the cracked bottoms of the wooden doors. The squalor reminded him of his tragic childhood. On the third floor, he paused at a closed door, read the name on the tiny copper plate: Mazen Mis'ed, then pressed the bell and waited.

He concealed his surprise when a police officer opened the door, rather than Mazen or his father, Haj Adel. The policeman gave him a who-the-hell-are-you look. Mansoor pushed past him, resisting the urge to cover his nose to avoid the smell that assaulted him. It too was familiar, like his parents' house when he was a kid, with a combination of odors; rancid cooking oil, a sweaty heap of shoes, and the sharp smell of cheap cleaning products that his mother always complained about because they dried out her hands.

He noted the sparse furnishings, two sofas and a straw mat. The sofa on the left facing the doorless kitchen held a body covered by a brown blanket, and two police officers stood next to it with crossed arms. On the other sofa at the far end, between two closed doors, Mazen's four daughters huddled together, covered their bodies with bedsheets and their heads with scarfs. Their eyes were swollen and red. Their disabled brother sat at the far end of the same sofa, staring at the ground as if contemplating something invisible. His crutches leaned against the arm of the sofa.

The ceiling was noticeably high. The yellowed white walls' paint smudged with green paint spots as if a baby or a crazy person tried to paint them. It was not the first time he'd entered Mazen's apartment, but he could never get over the visible manifestations of poverty.

Why Mazen's family was living in this old neighborhood was a mystery to him. Mazen himself lived in Dubai and owned a trading company that generated a lot of money. His father, Haj Adel, was the very wealthy owner of an entire building for general trade in the Bozooriyah region.

Detective Mansoor struggled to control his expression, to conceal his displeasure from Haj Adel, who had called him at dawn, asking him to attend to an urgent matter. Haj Adel was an old man with connections to high-ranking government officials. The money Mansoor received every month from Haj Adel and men like him to wipe their records clean was more than he earned from his job in an entire year. The last thing he needed was to destroy his relationship with Haj Adel. So, he put the kindest expression he could muster on his face and shook hands warmly.

Haj Adel made a head gesture to follow him into the room behind him. Mazen came right behind them and closed the door. This room's condition was no better than the main room. It contained four rusty metal beds, with no sheets on their stained sponge mattresses, and a closet. Two large windows allowed natural light to come in but also allowed the din outside to pollute the silence. They stood in the middle of the room, since there were no chairs.

Haj Adel turned and spoke to Mansoor, "Mazen's wife passed away during the night. When her daughters found out in the morning, they began screaming. I don't blame them. But one of the nosy neighbors called the police, which puts me in a sensitive situation. I have an important position among the merchants and senior government officials, plus I am the wealthiest trader in the market. I have a shiny gold reputation to maintain. What will people say now? *The police went to Haj Adel's daughter-in-law's apartment on the same day she passed away.* People will think there was something wrong. That she didn't pass away naturally." Haj Adel raised his gaze to look at the ceiling. "Oh, Allah, what have I done to put myself in such a situation? It's extremely embarrassing, with hundreds of people gathering outside." He looked at Mansoor, his words coming from between tightly pressed teeth. "After I am done with this, I want you to find out who called the police. I swear I will make her regret it."

Mansoor's voice remained calm. "Leave it to me, Haj Adel."

Tears were glistening in Haj Adel's eyes, and a plea was in his voice. "Please, detective, save us from another scandal. The two policemen insisted on calling the ambulance to take the body of my daughter-in-law to be examined by a coroner. Oh, Almighty Allah, what will people say about me in the market? A police force and an ambulance in the same day coming to my son's apartment."

Mansoor put his hand on Haj Adel's shoulder. "Don't worry. I will handle it. Just calm down." Even though the policemen's reaction was logical, he didn't blame Haj Adel for his anxiety. The custom in this community was for the corpse to remain in the house so the corpse washer could perform the death ritual. The washer would wash the body with water and camphor and then enshroud it in white clothes for the grave. The shrouded corpse would be moved to the mosque, where a special prayer would be offered. After that, the family and the congregation would go to the cemetery to bury the body. All that would take place without the intervention of the police or a coroner unless someone called them, suspecting suspicious activity. But this was a private family matter, and the last thing Mansoor wanted was to interfere in the private life of someone like Haj Adel.

The three men left the room. Mansoor

introduced himself to the two policemen and quickly learned which precinct they were assigned to. It was the Fifth Territory police station, as he had expected. He knew their boss, General Zafer Abyad. He went back in the bedroom for privacy, called his assistant, and asked her to dispatch a telegram to the Fifth Territory police station to inform them that this case was now under the jurisdiction of the CSA. Then he left the room and rejoined the rest.

Haj Adel and Mazen immediately stopped whispering together when he appeared. The four sisters wept openly, gazing at the covered body. The brother was still in his meditation mode. It seemed like their father and grandfather were unmoved by the tragic scene.

Mansoor went over to the two policemen, who stood like statues next to the body, arms still crossed. He filled them in on the situation. Minutes later, one of the policemen's mobile phones rang, and after talking for a few moments, he informed Detective Mansoor what he already knew. They left without a backward glance.

Detective Mansoor looked around for a place to sit and start preparing his report. Mazen took notice and quietly asked his daughters to go into their room and close the door behind them. The girls, still draped with sheets, moved slowly and silently, like ghostly apparitions.

He took a seat on the still-warm sofa. Haj Adel and Mazen sat on each side. They paid no attention to the disabled brother at all, nor did they seem to take notice of his odd behavior.

Haj Adel handed him a folder with several sheets of paper and Detective Mansoor began writing as the two men looking on. When he was done, Haj Adel and his son signed the report, which he put in the folder to finish processing back at his office. As he prepared to leave, Haj Adel handed him a fat, white envelope. He slipped it into the inner pocket of his jacket and hurried out, resisting the urge to smile as he went.

The frigid air slapped him in the face outside the apartment, making him realize just how dense and foul the air in the apartment had been. Outside the building's gate, the crowd had thinned, and he no longer needed to push anyone with his shoulder to get through. He glanced around at the balconies. Almost all of them were occupied by those who continued to watch, hoping to witness something to gossip about. Detective Mansoor slid into his car, looked around, and when he was sure no one was watching, he slid out the envelope, opened it, took out the wad of money, and began counting it.

CHAPTER 2

Friday, February 26, 2010

Ahmad Kishat was exhausted after a long day working in his textile factory in the Hareeqa area of Damascus city. He loved to work on Fridays, even though it was the weekend. It gave him a chance to catch up on the overdue orders, which hadn't been completed during the week. His factory was one of the most expensive in the country, not because it was the biggest or the most modern, but because it occupied a vast basement in Hareeqa where the square foot price was higher than hundreds of square feet outside the city. He felt pride whenever he remembered the start of his business, when he'd only had one rented loom. Now he owns twelve high-tech looms.

He rubbed the back of his neck as he slid into his BMW. Lately, his neck had been very stiff, and he'd been having headaches. He knew he should see his doctor.

He drove towards Shagoor mosque to take part in the memorial birthday of Prophet Mohammad, the messenger of Allah.

Ahmad lived in Dommar, a remote area of the city of Damascus, where there were plenty of mosques, all of them celebrating this anniversary. But just now, he needed to meet the imam of Shagoor Mosque. What was his name? Taking out his mobile phone, he called Hani Alfarawati, one hand on the steering wheel and the other holding the phone to his ear.

"Hi, buddy."

"Hello, Ahmad." Traffic noise came as a normal background to his voice. Hani was a traffic policeman.

"What's the name of the imam of Shagoor mosque?"

"Mullah Abdullah. When are you going to meet him?"

"On my way now."

"Don't let him think you are hiring him to do a job. Even though he's been doing this business for years, he admits it to no one, and he'll deny it if you mention it and refuse to help you. Just mention my name, and he'll understand. Also, when you want to pay, never ask him how much. Just give him as much as you believe it's worth and tell him it's a gift for his help, no more, no less."

"What is his name again?" he asked, then lowered his mobile phone when he noticed a police officer beside his motorbike looking for his next victim. After he'd passed by, he raised the phone to his ear again and heard Hani saying, "... he loves to let people think he is different."

"Sorry, man. What did you say? I passed a policeman, waiting for his next bribe, like you." He laughed.

Hani retorted, "You wanker, don't waste my time."

"Oh, I forgot, your highness is prime minister now." They both laughed.

Ahmad was parking the car when Hani said, "His name is Abdullah Al-Allab. He calls himself Mullah. When you meet him, don't call him sheik or imam, just say mullah."

Hani had referred Mullah Abdullah to him as an unofficial private detective, who took advantage of his religious position to help people solve their problems.

The mosque was in Shagoor alley in the old part of Damascus, one of the oldest continually inhabited cities in the world. The buildings were over three thousand years old. The rich history of the place remained alive along the hundreds of narrow alleyways that crawled between the ancient buildings. Islamic culture was apparent in every corner and wall. Even traces of Roman and Byzantine cultures could still be seen in the old city.

In the alley, all the buildings looked alike from the outside. The old wooden door of the mosque looked like any other door in that part of the city. With no sign, and the door closed, no one would guess it was a mosque. This was in sharp contrast with the developed areas of Damascus city, where most mosques were built on specially allotted land.

As Ahmad entered the mosque, four chanters were reciting canticles in soulful tones. He walked across the worn red carpet, passing behind dozens of men sitting cross-legged on the floor appreciating the canticles. Easing himself down to the back, he leaned against the wall. Looking around at the other attendees, it wasn't difficult to locate the only man with a long beard. Dressed in a conservative, long white dish dash, he was sitting right out in front.

This wasn't the first time he'd seen Mullah Abdullah; he'd met him at his sister's funeral almost two months ago. The man had led the burial ritual, but Ahmad hadn't known his name then. At the funeral, he'd wondered why Mullah Abdullah wore a red fez wrapped with a turban; a rare head covering these days, having been most popular at the time of the Ottoman occupation.

How simple and humble this quiet and airy mosque was. Like most mosques he'd visited, the walls and the massive oak doors were all painted a yellowish white. When he was a small boy, he used to spend a lot of time looking up at the roof ... *Well, not really the roof, the ceiling ... Is it a ceiling?* It wasn't even a ceiling. It was just enormous tree trunks laid side by side, with gaps in between.

He used to wonder how the builders found all these trees, all the same size, same length, and why they'd never painted them. On top of the tree trunks, wooden planks were laid, also left unpainted. On top of the planks, a thick layer of dried mud mixed with straw kept the building cool in summer and warm in winter. Of course, nowadays, many mosques had ceiling fans for summer and a diesel furnace for winter. As far back as he could remember, the chandeliers, lit by electricity, had always been there, hanging from the tree trunks.

In front of him, bookshelves were filled with copies of the Qur'an for worshipers to recite from after their prayers. To his left was a door to the ablutions and lavatory.

Hundreds of worshipers from all around the neighborhood gathered daily in this mosque, each with his personal demands for Allah. He imagined these whispered requests hovering in the space within the mosque, some of them ascending to the heavens with high speed to be answered. Some reached the sky but went unanswered, maybe because Allah loved to hear their pleas every day and reward them for their patience in the Hereafter.

Some of those ardent pleas probably remained in the mosque, never quite making it past the ceiling for reasons only Allah knew. It seemed that the world where spirits gathered differed vastly from the earthly world. The spirits didn't need castles or palaces to be happy, they just needed a place such as this simple mosque where they could take refuge from the earthly temptations of daily life and rejuvenate to a purer form where only bliss reigns.

The ceremony ended, and four young boys distributed small foil-wrapped sachets of sugar-coated almonds to the attendees. He enjoyed the almonds while watching people greet Mullah Abdullah as they left the mosque. He waited patiently until there were only three people in the mosque apart from him and Mullah Abdullah. In front of him, an old man gazed at the worn old wooden pulpit, the rostrum from where Mullah Abdullah piously preached his sermons before the Jumu'ah prayers. In the left corner, two young men stood talking, until one of them left, and the other dragged out a beat-up old vacuum cleaner and started cleaning the carpet.

Mullah Abdullah finished his farewells, sat down, and opened the Qur'an.

Ahmad approached and sat beside him. "Peace and Allah's mercy be upon you."

Mullah Abdullah returned the greeting automatically as he turned to look at him.

"I am Ahmad Kishat. Hani has sent me to see you. Would you please grant me a few minutes of your precious time?"

Mullah Abdullah glanced around before saying, "Brother, usually I discuss these things outside because it's not proper to discuss non-spiritual matters in a mosque."

"Would you like me to come some other time?

Just give me an address…"

Mullah Abdullah interrupted, "No, no. Let me just recite a few verses of the Qur'an, then we can go to my house."

Ahmad assumed that Mullah Abdullah wanted to be the last one to leave the mosque with him. "As you wish. I'll sit in the back and wait for you."

He leaned against the wall; the only sound was the vacuum cleaner's monotonous whine. Fifteen minutes later, Mullah Abdullah stood and dropped his chestnut brown cloak over his shoulders. All religious men wore a cloak over their white dish-dash to distinguish them from the rest of the people as a servant of Allah. He rearranged the fez on his head and pulled his prayer beads from his pocket.

The young man shut off the vacuum cleaner when he noticed Mullah Abdullah preparing to leave and approached them. A broad smile spread across the Mullah's face as the young man approached.

"My son, Salah, may Allah grant you a beautiful wife in this life and a hundred in heaven." The three of them laughed. Salah stretched his hand to shake their hands. He appeared to be in his twenties, handsome, fit, with eyes sparkled with confidence.

"I am leaving now. Please don't stay too late cleaning. You need to wake up early and attend the dawn prayer," Mullah Abdullah said.

"Ok, I will just clean the lavatories before I

close up," Salah said.

Mullah Abdullah advanced towards the door and said, "I have never met anyone like Salah. He loves to serve this holy place. I always pray to Allah to grant me a child like him. He is the son every father wishes to have."

Ahmad looked back, but Salah was nowhere to be seen. His own two sons, Hasan and Hussain, were almost the same age as Salah, and he wondered if he could perhaps arrange for the young men to meet.

Mullah Abdullah and Ahmad walked among the hurrying inhabitants of the narrow alley of Shagoor as dusk fell. The alley was reasonably well-lit, though several streetlamps had been purposely broken by local teenage vandals, probably seeking cheap thrills on their way home from school. Shop owners on both sides of the alley were closing for the day. It was impossible to talk, as each passer-by in the alley kept on interrupting with their greetings to the well-known mullah.

They passed the butcher, the grocer, the frame maker, the old Turkish bath, and finally reached an old bakery with an ancient ball-like furnace made of mud.

They exited the noisy alley into an even narrower one, with only doors separating the ancient houses from the quiet alley. The Mullah's house number, 14, was engraved on a metal plate and fastened to the stone over the door. Nothing distinguished the brown door except for a metal hand holding a metal ball that served as a knocker.

Mullah Abdullah unlocked his wooden door, and pushed it open, the hinges creaking noisily. He shouted, "Ya Allah Ya Allah, ladies, we have a guest!" Ahmad could hear doors opening and closing, as the women scurried to their rooms, leaving the courtyard free for the males to inhabit. Only then did Mullah Abdullah lead him through the hallway to the courtyard.

The minute they entered the courtyard, they were struck by the aroma of the precious Oud wood on the incense burner. A cascading fountain graced the center of the open courtyard and hundreds of potted plants lined the walls. A grapevine climbed two walls, its leaves almost covering the windows. Framed Qur'anic verses decorated the exposed areas on the walls.

Like all historically traditional Damascus houses, the Mullah's house was square and reflected the family's social needs and Islamic traditions. The rooms were large, their windows looking out on the alley at the back and the courtyard in the front.

Many of the neighboring house's second floors protruded over the alley, often bringing them so close to the house opposite it made the alley resemble a tunnel in places.

Ahmad particularly admired the intricate hand-laid stones on the floor and the walls, with alternating strips of black basalt and white limestone that were very striking.

The liwan was an area between two rooms open to the courtyard. A stone arch marked its entrance. Its ceiling was made of the same tree trunks as the ceiling of the two rooms. Families spend most of their time in the liwan, especially in summer and spring.

"Let's sit in the liwan," Mullah Abdullah said as he led Ahmad towards one of the three sofas. "How do you like your coffee?"

"Please, don't trouble yourself."

"Brother, a guest in our house is like a guest of Allah."

"Thank you very much. In that case, black, no sugar."

"Good. Just give me a minute while I tell my wife," Mullah Abdullah said as he went into one of the rooms.

Soon the aroma of the Arabic coffee filled the liwan. Mullah Abdullah went to grab the tray from his wife when she knocked on the kitchen door to attract his attention. Setting the tray on a small side table, he filled the two small ceramic Turkish coffee cups and handed one to Ahmad.

"Thanks. May Allah protect your hands."

"You are most welcome. Now tell me, what you want me to help you with?"

"My sister borrowed a goodly sum of money from me and didn't pay it back for a very long time. When our father passed away, he left a vast tract of land as an inheritance for all of us. It was an opportunity for my sister to pay my money back, but she needed to sell her share of the property to do so. To make it easier for her, I told her she could just sign over her share of the land to me, and she agreed.

"So, I prepared the authorization letter and asked her to come with me to the notary office to sign and stamp it with her fingerprint. As you know, she can't go outside her house unless her husband allows her. She asked him about it, and he told her to wait until he came back from Dubai for a brief visit, you see."

Ahmad raised the cup of hot coffee to his lips, sipped carefully, set down the cup, and continued, "I was expecting her to call me when my brother-in-law came for his visit, but she didn't. Suddenly, one day, the bad news came that she had passed away."

"Who's your brother-in-law?" Mullah Abdullah interrupted.

"Mazen Mis'ed."

"Hadiya is your sister? I led her burial ceremony." Mullah Abdullah gazed up at the night sky and said, "May Allah show her mercy and make her destination paradise."

"Yes. I was at the funeral and saw you, but we didn't have a chance to talk."

"Mazen was one of my friends in school when we were young. Also, his son Khaled is one of my students at the mosque," Mullah Abdullah said.

Ahmad said, "Out of respect for her soul, I didn't speak of the matter until after the fortieth day of mourning. That was a few days ago. My wife, Rema, and I went to visit my nephew and nieces, just to be sure they were alright, and to talk about the matter. They claimed to know nothing about it, but they were behaving strangely."

Mullah Abdullah narrowed his eyes as Ahmad continued, "We met with Khaled, and his sisters, Farah, Marwa, and Ro'wa, but Zakiya, the youngest, was not with them. They said she was sick with a severe cold and fever. When we asked to see her, they told us she was sleeping and shouldn't be disturbed. We didn't insist on it, but I noticed that the three girls were not acting normally. They kept on looking at Khaled every time they spoke."

"I beg Allah to give guidance to Khaled to be patient," Mullah Abdullah said. "It's not an easy thing for a son to lose his mother at such an early age, especially since she is the one who raised him. He is a good boy with high morals and ethics. I've only seen good deeds in him since the old days when his father brought him to me and asked me to teach him the faith. He was very committed and didn't miss any of my classes at the mosque. He was also brilliant. One of our best students, especially in the Arabic language classes." Mullah Abdullah took a sip of his coffee.

"All Hadiya's children are smart," Ahmad said.

"Unfortunately, Khaled stopped showing up at the mosque after his mother died," Mullah Abdullah said. "He no longer comes for prayers or classes. I am still waiting for him to get over the emotional upheaval and return to his routine."

Ahmad stared into his coffee. "Something has changed in that boy since his mother's death."

"It is quite natural. It hasn't been two months

since she passed away. You need to give him time to recover from his loss."

"But that's not what bothers me," Ahmad said. "What's bothering me has to do with his sisters."

"What's the matter with his sisters? It would also be quite natural for them to feel depressed. They lost their mother, and their father is away all the time."

Ahmad put the cup on the tea table faster than usual. It struck the edge and spilled a little coffee on the table. "That is another issue," he said, taking tissues from his inner pocket and wiping up the spilled coffee.

"As far as I can remember, Mazen left for Dubai immediately after Khaled was born," Mullah Abdullah said, looking at the wet tissue, which was now deep brown.

"It has been almost sixteen years, and he does not come to visit his family regularly." Ahmad leaned forward, his eyes locking with the Mullah's. "I think he used to come for two weeks every few years. The last time he came to Syria was when my sister passed away."

"How amazingly patient she has been living by herself all that time. May Allah show mercy to her."

Ahmad sighed, "My wife and I are concerned about the girls, but we couldn't even reach them by phone to ask if Zakiya is feeling better."

"Why not?"

"They don't have a phone in their apartment, for one thing."

"What?"

"That's right, they don't have a phone or a computer. All they have is an old black-and-white TV. I'm not even sure if that still works."

"Khaled used to talk to me about their financial difficulties," Mullah Abdullah said.

"Their financial circumstances have been a problem since the day their father left for Dubai."

"It is written, our provision is guaranteed by Allah, and it might be that the father's income has been made insufficient by the decree of Allah."

"People who have seen him in Dubai are not blind. They tell me Mazen is a very wealthy man."

"Let's not judge him from the gossip of mere humans. Have you seen this with your own eyes?" Mullah Abdullah asked.

"I haven't seen it with my own eyes, but people I trust reported this to me," Ahmad said. "The only way to contact them was to visit them, so I asked Rema to visit the girls again, but no one opened the door. So, she went next door and asked the neighbor if she had seen the girls leaving the house. The neighbor seemed relieved to learn that Rema was the girls' aunt. She invited her in for a cup of coffee. She complained that Hadiya's children had always been noisy, but after Hadiya's death, the noise got worse. It often sounded like horrifying screams of pain."

"Did she know the reason for this?" Mullah

Abdullah asked.

"No, but she told Rema, many times she or her husband knocked on the door to ask what was going on, but the girls or Khaled never opened it. Her husband even went to meet with their grandfather, Haj Adel, in his shop and told him what was going on. The grandfather promised to check on them. But nothing has changed. She said if no one did anything about the screaming, her husband would go to the police."

"How sure are you of the truth of the neighbor's words? As you know, brother Ahmad, you can't believe all you hear, and before you judge. You have to listen to both sides of the story."

"But why would she lie?" Ahmad asked.

"I don't know, nevertheless you must hear from both sides."

"That's why I came to see you." Ahmad placed both his hands on the Mullah's right hand and pleaded, "Rema and I are very concerned for the girls. Please help us find out what is going on so something can be done about it."

"What about talking to their father in Dubai?"

"Mazen doesn't talk to me at all," Ahmad said. "He knows I asked my sister to leave him more than once." He stared at the plants around the fountain for a while, reliving painful memories. The Mullah's question brought him back to the present.

"Why did you ask her to leave him?"

"The biggest mistake my parents made was letting her marry Mazen," Ahmad said, not looking the Mullah in the eyes.

"Careful, brother, speaking badly of him while he is not present is an enormous sin."

Ahmad was annoyed, but he did his best to hide it. He understood Mullah Abdullah couldn't keep silent because his duty as a religious man was to defend accusations against an absent party.

"My sister is the youngest in our family. When she was born, my father considered her a gift and called her Hadiya. Among all of us, she was the one most often smiling and laughing. We grew up in a small village. My father owned a simple grocery shop and my mom supported him by making homemade yogurt and cheese to sell in the shop. We were not rich, but despite that, my father insisted that all of us continue our education during a time when it was considered a shame for a girl to go outside the house.

"Unfortunately, Hadiya was an exception. She left school after the ninth grade when Mazen's father asked my father for her hand. They both decided without consulting her. The engagement period didn't exceed three weeks, and she was not allowed to sit with him alone during that time. So, technically, her wedding night was the first time for her to be alone with him. It's not that he was ugly or had any physical deformities. On the contrary. He was a very handsome man. But since then, happiness has evaporated from her life."

"Why was she not happy?" Mullah Abdullah asked.

"Her misery in life was not only because of him. Her mother-in-law turned her life into a living hell. Hadiya lived with her mother-in-law in the same apartment until she'd had four children and it became impossible for six people to stay in that small room. But Mazen didn't have enough money to buy a separate apartment. I lent her the money to buy the apartment they live in now.

"It was a positive turn in Hadiya's life that she left her mother-in-law's house. But the happiness didn't last more than a year. In the same year, Khaled was born handicapped, as you know. Mazen's business faced challenges because of the sanctions against the Syrian government, and he lost all his money. So then he borrowed money and moved to Dubai to start a new business from scratch. I provided that money as well. She came to me and asked me to loan her money and not him. She knew I wouldn't help him. I lent her five million Syrian pounds and told him I was only giving him the money because of her. The money was enough to start up his business again in Dubai. I went to visit her about a year later and asked why he had not come back yet, even for a few days?

"She said he went to Dubai to earn enough money to pay me back, and he isn't able to come back to Syria every year. Despite all that, she was patient and overcame the obstacles of this life the best she could. She brought up the girls and Khaled in a decent lifestyle despite their tight financial circumstances.

"Because she was convinced he would come back to Syria to live with his family again after he paid back his debt. She wanted to be a good wife, so she didn't complain or nag him or ask him to return. She didn't even let him know how difficult her life was without him."

"Despite all of that, I don't see why you said that her marriage was a mistake?" Mullah Abdullah said.

What do you want to hear to be more sympathetic toward her? Ahmad once again hid his feelings and continued, "When Mazen lived in Syria, he spent all of his earnings on his sisters and their families. The last one he would think of was his wife. He would spend his entire day at work and after that, go to the gym for a few hours and later to the coffee shop with his friends to smoke hookah and play cards. He would return home late every night. She would wait up to serve him his supper and ask if he needed anything else before she went to sleep."

"It is the best kind of wife who is loyal, obedient, and patient. May Allah bless her soul and make her final destination heaven," Mullah Abdullah said.

It seemed to Ahmad that Mullah Abdullah thought he was exaggerating. He said proudly, "My parents brought up all their daughters on these concepts. They respect their husbands and serve them in the best way. Never have any one of their spouses complained about their wife's behavior."

"Those are the Islamic principles, and every woman must follow them," Mullah Abdullah said.

"Yes, true, but what about the Islamic principles that every man must follow? Are we men not required to treat women fairly and kindly? Doesn't the prophet order us to treat women as gently as possible because they are delicate creatures?"

"Yes, brother Ahmad, but everyone has a test in this life and Hadiya's test was her husband. From what you say, she passed her test successfully. And if what you say about Mazen is true, Allah will judge and punish him in the hereafter for mistreating his wife."

"I am hopeful he will be punished in this life," Ahmad murmured.

"Sorry, what did you say?"

"Can you help me with this matter?" Ahmad asked while rubbing his stiff neck.

"I will talk to Khaled and ask him what is going on. I don't think he will hide anything from me. He always comes to me whenever he needs to talk. Well, at least he did before his mother's death."

"Will you please ask him about the letter? I am sure my sister left it somewhere in the house," Ahmad begged.

"Are you talking about the proof of the loan for the apartment and the five million or is there some other debt as well?" Mullah Abdullah asked.

Ahmad removed an envelope from his pocket and put it on the small tea table in front of the

Mullah. "The apartment is not a problem. It is registered in my name. Technically, it is still mine. I am talking about the five million only."

Mullah Abdullah picked up the envelope, opened it slightly with two fingers, and glanced at its contents. The thick wad of money widened the Mullah's eyes.

"But of course, you have the documents to prove it?" Mullah Abdullah asked.

"Only a handwritten piece of paper without witnesses. Foolishly, I didn't insist on more." He sensed the Mullah's skepticism.

"In the Holy Qur'an, Allah orders us to keep a record of any debt under the eyes of witnesses."

"I was willing to do anything to make Hadiya happy."

"Still, you should have kept a record."

If I had the official documents, I would go to court and put Mazen in prison until he pays me back every cent of my money. "I made a mistake, and I came to you because I believe someone in your social position has enough influence to solve this." Then he pointed to the envelope and said, "This is a gift for your help."

"It is my duty to help. Also, I will give it one more shot with Mazen since I am going to Dubai next month."

"Really, what for?"

"I received an invitation from the union of Muslim religious leaders to attend their annual conference."

"That's great. I wish you a safe journey, and yes, it will be a great opportunity to meet Mazen and ask him about the money." He was not optimistic that Mullah Abdullah would have positive results.

***

Mullah Abdullah accompanied Ahmad to the outside door.

"I will call you as soon as I get back from Dubai," he said, with a firm grip on Ahmad's hand. Ahmad was in his fifties, clean-shaven, thin eyebrows, brown eyes with a kind look, and a pointed nose. The smell of cologne surrounded him, and every part of his outfit showed he was a rich man. Despite that, exhaustion was apparent on his face from the dark circles under his eyes.

He shut the heavy door behind Ahmad, causing its knocker to rattle. The knocking sound gave a sense of peace and tranquility descending on the home.

As he entered his bedroom, Mullah Abdullah took off his fez. He could hear his wife Amani busy preparing supper. He changed into the soft brown woolen dish-dash he usually wore at home. He pulled out his prayer beads, took a seat in the liwan, and started reciting, anticipating his long-awaited supper. He smiled broadly when his daughter, Zahra, appeared. She pulled the table nearer to the sofa where he was sitting, then she went to the kitchen and carried the dinner out on a large tray, placing it on the table. Her mother came behind, carrying a teapot and a plate of fresh bread, still hot from the oven.

The tray held a variety of traditional Syrian dishes. Scrambled eggs in the middle surrounded with creamy homemade yogurt soaked in olive oil. Makdous, — eggplant stuffed with red peppers and hazelnuts, — also drizzled with olive oil. Zaatar served with olive oil for dipping the bread. Black olives, green olives, braided cheese, hummus dotted with pickles, and Halloumi cheese were all served on beautiful white plates, much to the Mullah's delight.

They devoured the delicious meal in the tranquil atmosphere of their liwan. He knew their lifestyle would be impossible to maintain with the meager salary he received from the Ministry of Endowments. As he dipped the warm bread into the olive oil, he fleetingly remembered how much he'd wanted to be a detective when he was younger, but his father wouldn't allow him to join the security sector. Instead, he had followed his father's wishes and attended the Islamic Sharia College at Damascus University.

His father had told him a detective's career was not suited for faithful people, and he'd reminded him that the hereafter is our final destination where we will live like kings. That's why his father was always nearly destitute and died poor. His mother died giving birth to him, and his father had passed away when he was fifteen and still at school. He'd promised his father he would study the Islamic Sharia, but never promised that he wouldn't also work as a private detective. When he enrolled in the sharia college, he chose to specialize in personal and civil status, because these subjects were closer to the law than to the religious subjects. Things like marriage and divorce, eligibility, wills, inheritance and legacies, ethics and social order in Islam, plus legal and civil principles. These subjects enhanced the knowledge he needed to apply to his dream job.

He had graduated, naively believing that people would queue for his services. However, he wasn't very well known, and most people laughed when he told them of his ambitions. Not to mention, private detectives were illegal in that part of the world. He decided to apply to be an imam in a mosque where he could use his position to facilitate his ambitions. After four years of applying, he had almost given up when the imam of the mosque in Shagoor Street died of heart failure, and he was assigned to be the imam.

As he'd always hoped, people came to him for solutions to their problems and his position made it easy to solve them. Unfortunately, no one paid him for those services. They considered it part of his job to serve them. He quickly discovered it was overwhelming to take on these extra tasks for free. It was not an option to refuse people because it was part of his job to serve, and he was the only one they could turn to. After extensive brainstorming, he decided he needed a key person who would send him clients and instruct them to pay.

That was years ago. It was the actual beginning of his dream career, especially after Allah sent him Hani Alfarawati. Despite Hani's minor role as a traffic cop, he had an extensive web of personal relationships in both government and the community. For a percentage, sometimes up to 50 percent, he sent him plenty of wealthy locals who were either afraid or reluctant to go to the police for help, especially when the circumstances were delicate. Yet, he had still not received a case where he felt the thrill of being a detective. The last case Hani brought him was siblings fighting over their inheritance. The case before that was spouses who wanted to get divorced, but he had prevented that calamity. The most exciting case had been when Hani took him to a remote field to persuade a woman who practiced witchcraft to return the money to the field's owner after he realized she was a liar and couldn't extract an ancient treasure of gold from the ground after all. Alas, Ahmad's case seemed to be another boring one.

He considered all the gifts that Allah had granted him. Plenty of healthy food, a large house, an obedient and well-mannered daughter, a beautiful wife, and most importantly, a stream of clients willing to pay him handsomely for his services.

"Oh Allah, I thank you for these abundant blessings," he intoned. Amani and Zahra acknowledged his praise to Allah by chiming in, "Amen."

After dinner, Zahra rose and cleared the table with grace, then washed the dishes in the kitchen.

When she'd finished, she wished her parents goodnight and went up to her bedroom.

Now that he was alone with Amani in the liwan, he turned to her with a deep sigh, and said, "The guest who came here earlier is your friend Hadiya's brother."

"May Allah grant her mercy," she intoned with a serious face.

"He told me there is something strange going on in Hadiya's house. Something horrible is happening to Khaled and his sisters. Neither he nor his wife can figure out what is going on. They hear hints from other neighbors that the children were always fighting and screaming. He asked me to find out what's happening. But," he paused, searching for words, "What will people say if I march into their apartment, a home with four single girls and a parent recently passed away? The other parent is far away in Dubai, and their brother is physically handicapped?"

"You are on the side of truth, as always. Let people say whatever they want to," Amani said.

"Yes, right, but I still feel that visiting that apartment would not be appropriate."

"I remember how resolute their mother was. I used to love sitting with her. Hadiya would always be laughing and smiling, despite living on the edge of poverty in that decaying old apartment."

He frowned at her. "Decaying old apartment?"

"Yes, they were penniless," Amani said. A wave of pain passed over her face. "You can't imagine how the paint was chipping off the walls, and when she appealed to her husband for fresh paint, her mother-in-law bought the paint and went to Hadiya's house to repaint the walls. The problem was that only certain parts of the walls were repainted, and the color was different from the original."

"Ahmad mentioned Mazen seems to be wealthy in Dubai. But we don't know what the circumstances were that made the mother-in-law do such things. Let's not judge her, as we did not witness the incident ourselves."

"Oh, dear, but this is only one incident," Amani said. "The husband prevented her from visiting her sisters down the street or going to the mosque or even to go outside the apartment without his permission. Her apartment was nothing more than a prison."

Mullah Abdullah recalled that Hadiya hadn't gone with Ahmad to the notary office because her husband wouldn't allow it. He said, "I understand your sympathies towards her, but try not to exaggerate things you don't fully understand. Think well of her husband. Being an obedient wife is an obligation, a solemn duty under all circumstances, and such a faithful wife will have her big reward in the hereafter."

"You men will always stand by each other, but never for your women," Amani said.

"Beg Allah for mercy and forgiveness. You don't know or understand fully what men have to face."

"For Allah's sake, don't lecture me like one of your students in the mosque. What do you know about Hadiya and her husband?" she gulped.

Her eyes gleamed. He wanted to object, but she was right. What did he know about Hadiya and Mazen? nothing more than what Khaled used to complain about, which was mainly that they never had enough money, and now what Ahmad had told him earlier.

"Have you ever been inside their apartment?" Amani demanded. "Did you know she had only one change of clothes and one pair of shoes? Did you know she used to go to sleep hungry because there was barely enough food for her children? Did you know she used to go to the hospital every week with her son Khaled to see the doctor regarding his legs? Did you know that every year Mazen promised her he would come to visit them the following year, and he never fulfilled those promises? What more do you want to hear to stop justifying the actions of the monster who lives in Dubai and leaves his four girls alone with their disabled brother?" She was unable to continue as she choked back her tears.

He moved to sit beside her and put his arm around her shoulder. She covered her eyes with both hands and wept. Still holding her, he said in a faint voice, "How do you know all of this?"

Amani's whispered from behind her hands, "Hadiya used to complain to me. She used to tell me because I'm a religious woman, she felt comfortable talking to me. I know many minor details about her life, but I don't think she would forgive me if I told you any of them."

She wiped her eyes and turned to face him. He released her and moved back to give her his attention. "One of her neighbors said that on the night she died, they heard a horrible scream. A lot of police came to the apartment in the morning, and the street was full of police cars."

"Do you mean..."

Amani interrupted, "Yes, more than once I've heard whispers that Hadiya was murdered."

CHAPTER 3

Sunday, FEBRUARY 28, 2010

Using his handmade crutches, Khaled hobbled into his mother's bedroom. He could set his right foot on the ground, but only the tips of the toes of his left foot would touch it because it was shorter. A typical bedroom for a married couple, containing a queen-size bed, a four-door closet, and a mirror over a bureau. All of them were brown. The gray curtains on the right served only to cover the ugliness of the bare wall since there were no windows.

Closing the door, he approached the bed, leaned his crutches against the frame, and put his elbows on top of the mattress, which was chest high to his slight frame. He reached out and touched a mound caused by a pillow under the quilt. As his tears dripped on the quilt, he said, "I know you are happier now, but I miss you so much."

He buried his face in the mound and cried bitterly, repeating over and over, "I love you, Mom. I miss you, Mom."

Khaled was shorter than most boys his age because of osteogenesis imperfecta, a congenital bone disorder. The tension of his muscles on his soft bones caused bowing in his limbs. He also had an exceptionally large head relative to his body size. Because of the over-development of his cranial bones and the under-development of the facial bones, Khaled's face had a triangular shape.

Now, at age sixteen, he hadn't yet grown a full beard, only a few bristles scattered on his jaw. His ruddy complexion stood out like a flame from the sensitivity of his skin. His eyebrows were thin, and the normally white parts of his eyes were light blue, which made most people shiver just looking at them. His unruly mop of black hair was uncombed.

He had used crutches ever since he first started to walk, but never new crutches. His grandfather refused to give his mother the money to buy brand-new crutches for him, so she'd bought some wood from Zahi, the carpenter in Shagoor Street. She had a big scar on her left hand because she cut it while making the last pair of crutches for him.

As he leaned on them, his collarbone and shoulder blades became prominent. The bones in his hands stood out as if his hands belonged to an alien, a result of gripping his crutches so tightly. His usual attire was an oversized khaki shirt, untucked, over worn-out black pants, and black shoes, which he put on as soon as he got up. He only took them off again at bedtime.

He was the only one allowed to wear shoes at home, as he could not bend his knees to take them off. His feet always smelled rotten because of the long hours of wearing them, and his toes overlapped. Because he detested seeing the reflection of his distorted body, he had covered all the mirrors in the apartment.

When the doorbell to the apartment rang, he raised his head, wiped his tears with his sleeve, and said, "I am going out with Salah now, Mom. He's the only one who's looked out for me since you left."

He hobbled to the door. His four sisters Farah, Marwa, Ro'wa, and Zakiya were in their room sitting on their rusty beds, studying. The apartment comprised three rooms off of the main room. His sisters' room, his parents' room, well actually his mom's room since his dad had never lived in this house since they bought it. The third room was his alone, since no one but his mother could bear the rancid smell of his feet.

When he opened the door, he found Salah standing there, playing with his smartphone.

As their eyes met, Khaled inhaled deeply, putting on his brightest smile.

"What's wrong, my hero?" Salah asked and dropped to his knees, bringing his face down to the same level as Khaled's.

"Nothing, I was just remembering my mom," Khaled said.

Salah put his arms around Khaled's shoulders and hugged him. "Don't worry, she's in heaven now." Then pulled back and looked in his eyes, "My hero, what would you think about some shawarma?"

"Let's go before I start drooling," said Khaled, barely able to keep himself from smiling. Salah was the cool friend every young boy dreams of. All who knew him loved him without reservation, and yet Salah chose to be friends with a cripple.

When Khaled walked with others, he always looked down where his crutches were going. But with Salah, he looked up at him often, as if making sure Salah didn't vanish.

Khaled moved slowly, and Salah kept pace with his hobbling progress. They reached the market where the vegetables and fruits of the hawkers covered the ground, and their yelling filled the air. People passing by were unable to hide their true feelings. He could see it in their eyes. Wherever he went, he saw the same reaction from most people when they looked at him for the first time. He wasn't able to just ignore them. Every time he saw the horror on people's faces, he felt a sting in his heart.

The smell of chicken shawarma welcomed them long before they reached the restaurant. This restaurant, like all the shawarma restaurants in the area, had their upright rotisserie set up outside so the rich smells would draw customers in.

Khaled liked to watch the graceful movements of the chef in front of the big dripping cone of meat as he used his long-bladed knife to slice off thin shavings of meat as the cone rotated slowly.

The sizzling sound was another joy to Khaled, while he took in the delicious view. His father always said the eyes eat before the mouth.

A few of the waiting customers were staring at him, so he lowered his head and darted into the restaurant.

The restaurant's second floor was reachable only by stairs. It would be easier for Khaled if they stayed on the ground floor, but he insisted on going up. He didn't like people staring at him while he was eating.

Upstairs, all the tables were empty, which was just as he'd hoped. Salah pulled out a chair and helped him into it, then sat opposite him.

The drool-inducing aroma of the shawarma preceded the waiter as he placed it in the middle of the table. The still dripping, steaming shawarma lay in thin slices on a pita in the center, surrounded by hummus, garlic cream, fried potato slices, green chili with cucumber pickles, and a jug of yogurt to drink. Khaled and Salah attacked the food like starving wolves.

The scene of Salah devouring the food with his sleeves rolled up would make a great advertisement, Khaled thought and wished he had half of his charm.

"Here's your payment." Salah first wiped his

greasy fingers on his napkin, then passed him a wad of Syrian five hundred notes.

Khaled slipped it in his pocket. "You know I am not doing this for money."

"I know you want to be part of something great," Salah said.

"Yes," Khaled said, "But there is another reason." He dropped his gaze from Salah's eyes to his lips.

"Better than being part of something great?"

"For me, yes."

"Let me guess," Salah said. "You want to be my friend and spend time with me?"

"Am I that obvious?" Khaled asked, wiping his hands again.

"More than you think," Salah said, and they both giggled.

"If I hadn't agreed to join you, would you have taken me out every week for lunch all these months, even after I stopped going to the mosque long ago?"

"See, I told you, you want to be part of someone great," Salah said, and winked.

Khaled sighed. Deep down inside, he couldn't help wondering what someone like Salah saw in him, but he was scared if he pushed it, Salah would stop spending time with him.

"What about you?"

"I am just an exceptional guy," Salah said, raising his nose in the air like an aristocrat.

"Seriously, what was your reason for joining them?" The few seconds of Salah's gazing caused him to wish he could read minds.

"When I'm in school, no one is as clever as I am," Salah said. "At home, my dad and mom are old and nag at me a lot. In the mosque, all the people are illiterate. In my father's shop, the employees are hypocrites, always complaining and gossiping. I never felt I belonged anywhere until the day I joined them."

"I wish to have half of the admiration that people have toward you," Khaled said. "When I used to attend the mosque, I once heard Mullah Abdullah tell one of the old men, 'Salah is a model student with a bright future ahead of him, serving our religion and humanity.'" Khaled blew out a long breath, "At that moment I wished the praise was for me."

"Don't worry, you just follow my lead, and I will make you great." Salah burped without covering his mouth.

"I don't think you can change this," Khaled said and pointed to his own head.

Salah didn't say anything, just looked into Khaled's eyes.

"Sometimes I wish people would treat me in a bad way. You know, scold me, shout at me. Because that would mean they see me. As it is, people don't even notice I exist."

"You need only one person to treat you as the center of his life and everything else will be as unimportant as a shadow for you," Salah said.

"I think you would make an outstanding

leader," Khaled said.

"Yes, I know," Salah said. "So far, I am one of the best recruiters."

"Is there anyone new from the mosque?" Khaled asked.

"Young man, you never ask a question when the answer might hurt you," Salah said, his face dead serious.

Khaled just stared at him.

Salah burst out laughing. "You should see your face. It's okay Khaled. Off the record, Fathi is with us now."

CHAPTER 4

Wednesday, March 3, 2010

Mullah Abdullah returned a warm smile as the chief flight attendant bade him farewell. He was the only first-class passenger and thus the first into the tunnel connecting the plane with the terminal in the Dubai International Airport. He pulled a small, unpretentious, black carry-on bag behind him. At the end of the tube, a bright young female in Emirates Airline uniform waited for him, holding up a tablet with his name in a large Arabic font on the screen. She greeted him in perfect Arabic and asked him to come with her.

Like a man who has spent his life on a rusty bicycle being dragged into a Rolls Royce showroom for the first time, Mullah Abdullah gazed around at the airport's abundant luxuries, the likes of which he'd never seen in Shagoor Alley. Enchanted by the glossy wide pillars clad in shiny metal and the intensity of the lighting that gave luster to thousands of products he was seeing for the first time. As they passed through the displays of jewelry, sunglasses, and watches, he remembered the tiny, dusty shop that Majdi, the watch repairman in his alley, owned. If Majdi came to this place, he would have a heart attack. He smiled as he imagined Majdi putting a hand over his heart. After that came the electronics section. He was impressed with the flat-screen computers. They were very thin compared to his daughter's bulky monitor. A warm feeling crawled into his heart when he thought of his family. This was his first time traveling and leaving them behind. The last time he'd traveled was to Mecca for the pilgrimage, but then Amani had been with him, and Zahra had not been born yet.

Suddenly he stopped in the middle of a crowd of fast-walking passengers, turned his face to the left and, covering his eyes with his free hand, he repeated a few times.

"Oh Allah, I beg your forgiveness."

His escort came up and tried to peek between his fingers. "Are you okay, Mr. Abdullah?" Her words came out in a trembling voice.

"How come an Islamic country like Dubai sells all these forbidden drinks?" he asked.

The woman gazed at the long rows of shelves full of liquor with pursed lips. She exhaled, then just the hint of a smile crossed her face.

"Please, let me know when those forbidden drinks are no longer within my sight." He continued walking with his head turned to the left.

Around him, long rows of travelers mingled at the cafes and restaurants as the energetic staff served them. He contemplated the variety of nationalities all around him. It was his first time seeing such vast numbers of foreigners in one place, and he was amazed by the activity and the quick pace of so many passengers.

"This is a lot of people," he said.

"We now serve over 66 million people a year, flying them to over 260 destinations across six continents." She sounded like a machine spitting out information.

He looked outside through the large diamond-shaped terminal windows. So many huge planes lined up in parallel rows, like sleeping dragons waiting to be awakened. *No matter how great these massive vehicles are or how powerful their engines are, they cannot fly except by the will of Allah.*

The Immigration Hall contained numerous counters, with hundreds of passengers waiting in long queues. He thought how great Allah is, who conceived us all so identical on the inside, yet so different on the outside.

Behind the immigration counters, both males and females wearing official uniforms; men wearing the long white dish-dash and women wearing long black dresses with their heads covered. He smiled, remembering the discussion with his wife and daughter about the powerful impact and the pervasive role of Arab women nowadays.

A limousine was waiting for him outside the airport, and the driver jumped out and opened the door the minute he glimpsed him with his elegant escort. Before he knew it, he found himself settling into a plush, velvet-covered seat. The air inside the car was freezing, the windows were blacked out to block the blazing heat of the sun. The driver sped through Dubai's wide, traffic-clogged streets.

"My son, why are you driving so fast?" He had never been in a car at this speed in his life.

"My apologies," the driver answered with his Egyptian accent, and slowed down a little.

Mullah Abdullah was shaken by how fast the cars whipped past them. He noticed that most of the vehicles were grand, four-wheel-drive vehicles.

The roads were lined with construction on both sides. Tall buildings rising as if by a giant's hand.

"We are now on the famous Sheikh Zaid Road," the driver announced.

Gigantic skyscrapers lined both sides of the street. He lowered the window and marveled at the grand design of the towers and the incredible brightness of their exteriors. Never had he seen such mirror-like qualities as in these buildings. He craned his neck until it ached, trying to see the top of one towering building that captivated his attention. The difference between Dubai and Damascus was startling. Dubai was a young, modern, and rich city, while Damascus was an ancient city built upon thousands of years of tradition and the passing of many civilizations.

He shivered as he whispered to himself, "I seek refuge in Allah from the accursed devil." He allowed his soul to drift into the temptations of this life, a stab of desire to possess more, and his heart yearned for an opulent lifestyle. He closed his eyes and repeated, "Oh Allah, please erase the desires for this life from my heart."

The five-star hotel on the Jumeirah Palm was built like an Indian palace, with the sea stretched out before it. Two slim women greeted him at the door of the hotel. They wore short skirts and tight white shirts, which accentuated their perfect bodies. He fixed his gaze on the marble floor of the lobby until they reached the concierge. There he was greeted by two more women, equally attractive, also wearing seductive clothing and broad smiles.

He was relieved when he eventually reached his suite on the seventeenth floor. From the entrance of the hotel all the way to the seventeenth floor, he'd avoided looking at many gorgeous women, which was difficult because they seemed to be everywhere.

He peeled off his travel clothes and threw himself on his back on the king-size bed with his arms thrown wide. The mattress bounced several times under his considerable weight. He gazed up at the ceiling and noticed the green arrow with the word "Mecca" printed next to it. He slapped his forehead, remembering he had not prayed the afternoon prayer.

*****

Mullah Abdullah was on an invitation from the union of Muslim religious leaders in Dubai to lecture at the union's annual conference, slated for International Women's Day on March eighth. The conference title was, "Muslim Women Between a Traditional Past and the Contemporary Present." He was euphoric because he was not only a guest, but he would lecture at length about Muslim women in the Middle East during a period of enormous transition and confusion.

He smiled, remembering his conversation with Amani and Zahra when he informed them about the invitation, the topic, and his lecture. When Zahra understood the grandness of the occasion, she could not contain her enthusiasm. She jumped up and said, "Papa, tell them that women perform a most crucial, critical, and useful role in the Syrian community. She has myriad achievements which should give her remarkably high esteem from menfolk as her counterparts. One finds women employees in the government, doctors, pharmacists, engineers, businesswomen, and even policewomen and soldiers."

He pretended a mild annoyance to provoke her a little, pushing her to talk more about the topic. "What are you talking about, my dear? A woman must stay at home and serve her husband, not go outside and mix with men." Naturally, he provoked a reaction from her.

"Papaaaa, what is this?" Zahra said and flopped back in her chair. "Is it possible that you really think this way?"

"So, you don't like my way of thinking? Do you think women have the right to work outside their homes?" He looked attentively at her, curious to hear her answer. He hoped to understand his teenager more at a critical time in her life. Especially since her behavior had changed recently. She had become noticeably moody and silent more often.

"Women must be dependent to a certain extent and yet able to rely on themselves without the absolute need for a man," Zahra said. "All my classmates' mothers are working either in government or private companies. This is in stark contrast to your days when women weren't allowed to work at all and would be held prisoners in their own homes like goats."

He laughed loudly at this description. "But in the early days, the women did work..." Mullah Abdullah began.

Zahra interrupted, her voice full of conviction, like an attorney defending all the oppressed women in the world. "Papa, in the old days, women were not allowed to go anywhere without their husbands' permission. And then a male family member had to accompany her if she wanted to walk in the street. They were forced to cover their bodies from head to toe with a black abaya. It's pitiful how they used to walk like blind people because they couldn't see clearly because of the thickness of the abaya." Her face flushed pink from her fervor.

He chose to overlook Zahra's unfair and humiliating description of the old days for the time being. He decided it would be better to discuss it with her at another time. Perhaps he could convince her to be more neutral in her judgments. He knew everyone has his or her unique circumstances, and time and place can often affect ones' lifestyle.

"My dear Zahra, in the old days, women used to work, but only at particular types of jobs. Moreover, most of the women who did work were widows or divorced. They used to work as maids in other people's houses, or they would learn how to sew and work as tailors from home," he said as he looked at Amani, hoping she would contribute to the discussion. Often, she would make helpful suggestions and inspire him to elaborate or delve deeper into the points he'd researched. Besides these key bits of information, he would find additional guidance from old history books.

"Papa, a woman is as much a person as a man. She has the full right to live her life to the maximum of her potential, without males treating her as a second-class citizen, or as part of the furniture. That's why men in the old days used to marry two, three and four women, and put all of them together in the same house with no care for their feelings or emotions."

"Zahra," his tone was sharp this time. "Allah in

the Holy Qur'an permits men to marry four women. There is no room to discuss what Allah allows or restricts us from doing unless the person bent on discussing it fully understands Allah's orders. For your information, the topic of marrying four women is a sensitive issue. While Allah granted males the right to marry four, it does not mean that they must marry four. It does not mean the purpose of it is physical only. Females often outnumber males. If a man may marry only one, what will the other women do without husbands?" He was wondering how he could simplify the idea to broaden Zahra's understanding. She was still at an age where emotions override the brain, which was apparent from the words spilling out of her mouth.

"That's why a woman must be independent and free from any need for a man," Zahra said.

"On the contrary, the husband will spend money on all his wives. He'll treat them like queens and keep them busy with the most important purposes that Allah created them for, including bringing up children properly. Thus, they are pivotal in building a prosperous nation," he said with a smile. He knew the topic would be sure to irritate his wife, but apparently, she was in control of her impulses at that moment and did not interrupt.

"How can a woman teach her children in a civilized manner if she doesn't go out to study and obtain degrees to keep up with the latest technological and scientific advancements?" Zahra asked.

"If a woman studies her religion well," he said, "that will be enough for her to bring her children up in a civilized manner and create a generation able to surmount all the obstacles in life. Plus, who says that women in the old days did not study and learn?"

"No," Amani snapped, irritation clear in her voice. "In the old days, they considered the girl who wanted to continue her studies a bad girl. I am one of those girls who was forced by my family to stop going to school after the sixth grade. My eldest brother said, 'No girl from this family will walk alone on the streets or study among men.' Even though it was a nun's school, and no males were ever allowed inside. All the staff were females, from the custodian to the principal."

He had long known how sad and dejected Amani had felt when her family forced her to stop going to school. She'd been frustrated by her lack of education until she married him and he, at last, helped her improve her reading and writing skills.

"The whole family considered my cousin Samya dishonorable because she continued her studies on into high school." Amani went on. "I will never forget the day her father slapped her, leaving a bruise on her cheek for a fortnight, all because she asked permission to continue her education at the university."

"You are the biggest proof that a girl doesn't need a school education to bring up a new civilized generation to be proud of. Look at Zahra. She is bright and intelligent, and we are very proud of her."

"Oh, give me a break," Amani said. "If what you are saying was true, you wouldn't let Zahra go to school."

"I didn't say your family was right to force you to stop going to school. For sure, a woman must study and learn in any place and time available to her. She can use what she learns to tutor her children, but not to compete with men. What we're seeing in the community is that every opportunity a woman takes is an opportunity lost to men. Moreover, a man is responsible for feeding a whole family and sometimes more than one family, depending on how many wives he has." He realized, too late, that his wife was getting irritated by this topic and wanted to change it.

"You men always think this way. How many women do you want to marry? While Allah, Most Exalted, demands that you be fair and impartial. Please show me a man these days, with more than one wife who is able to remain fair and impartial?"

He looked at Zahra and joked, "Look at the difference between women now and women in the old days. In the old days, women used to kiss their husband's hands and call him 'Master.' Nowadays women are scolding their husbands!" He and Zahra giggled.

Amani snapped back, "You men! That is what you are looking for, a woman to kiss your hands and call you 'Master.'" She rose and disappeared into the bedroom, putting an abrupt end to the discussion.

***

The opening ceremony was at a theater in Madinat Jumeirah on Thursday morning. Lectures were being held at a soccer stadium in Dubai's Sports City on Emirates Road. The stadium, which held thousands of attendees, was covered and fully air-conditioned, despite the mild March weather. The majority of attendees were females from all around the world. Not only Arabic Muslim women, but people from many races and religions as it was taking place on International Women's Day.

The lecturers were both male and female, and they each spoke in their mother languages. Thousands of machines translated the speeches into many languages. Thousands of women listened, as the speakers explained how women's suffering is similar everywhere, regardless of their culture or origin.

Mullah Abdullah's speech was scheduled in a huge auditorium for the third day of the conference. After that, he would move to a conference room in the Intercontinental Hotel in Dubai Festival City to answer attendees' questions on behalf of all the women in his territory.

On the eighth of March, a big celebration of International Women's Day took place. The ceremony was designed and performed by females only, from all the nationalities present.

CHAPTER 5

Monday, March 8, 2010

Salah glanced in the mirror at his reflection, clad only in his boxers. The slim body of a young man, with charcoal black hair and brown eyes beneath arched eyebrows. A sharp nose, dark red lips, and a newly born mustache contrasted with his fair skin. Finely chiseled shoulder and arm muscles, a broad chest and six-pack abs. There was a narrow line of fine hair running from under his boxers to the matted area between his pecs. He admired the perfection of his body.

His mobile phone vibrated. He walked to the table beside the bed and looked at the screen. It was 3 am, and the message on the screen was short. "Can you come to my apartment now? I need you."

"Of course. Is everything ok?" Salah texted back. Something must be wrong. He knew his mentor to be a confident person who asked no one for help.

"Yes, but please come as quick as you can," came the reply.

"Is everything ok?" he typed again.

-message failed, please try again later
-message failed, please try again later
-message failed, please try again later.

He put on jeans and a white cotton T-shirt with white sneakers. His parents wouldn't ask him why he was going out at this early hour, as they know he's in charge of opening and closing the mosque and keeping it clean and tidy. Especially this week because the Mullah was out of the country.

It's a 20-minute walk to Abu Badr's apartment in Sina'a street from where Salah lived. He wasn't afraid to walk there alone, as Damascus was one of the safest cities in the world. But he was surprised why Abu Badr asked him to come at such a time and place. Abu Badr preferred to meet with him during the day when there were plenty of people on the streets. No one would take any notice of two ordinary young men sitting in a coffee shop or restaurant.

He's quite proud of his achievements so far. He has always dreamed of having power and influence, and now he's in charge of a team of 45 males and 9 females who must obey him. What a triumph. And the most exciting thing is that he will be part of the newborn Islamic Caliphate and his power will extend to the sky.

Today was the memorial of the Syrian revolution, which took place in 1963. National flags, as well as those of the Arab Baath Socialist Party, hang in most parts of the city. Salah recalled when two years ago, also on the Memorial Day of the revolution, his mentor Abu Badr Ashami approached him and introduced him to this new, exciting path. Who could have imagined that Abu Badr Ashami was a member of the influential organization planning to revive the Islamic Caliphate?

That night, after Isha's prayers, Salah switched off the amplifiers, rearranged the Qur'ans on the shelves, and finished cleaning the carpets as usual.

An average size man, probably in his thirties, was still sitting over in the corner. Salah recognized him as a regular attendee in the mosque, but he'd never uttered more than a polite greeting to him. He smiled to let the man know it was time to go home. Instead, the man approached him and introduced himself as Abu Badr. Outside, as Salah was locking the door, Abu Badr asked him to accompany him on his way back to discuss an important matter. Salah smiled and answered in the affirmative, out of courtesy to the man, no more.

As they both walked with their hands deep in their jackets' pockets, Salah listened. Abu Badr's words, accompanied by clouds of steamy breath, had a motivational effect on Sallah, like the energy tablets he used to boost his energy at the gym. The words came out haltingly, but with confidence. He watched Abu Badr's face closely as the vapor of his breath rose and dispersed. *What is the secret of the positive energy that surrounds the man?* This was exactly the way he himself wished to be in the future.

Abu Badr told him there was to be a small gathering at his house to commemorate the memorial of the revolution and invited him to join them.

So, Salah went to the party and met the most interesting bunch of people he had ever encountered. The party went well, with pleasant conversations, excellent food and drink, and a friendly atmosphere. Nothing extraordinary happened, but Salah found out they held these gatherings every week. They invited him again, and he became one of the first to arrive and the last to leave every week.

The meetings were always held in the house of one of the permanent attendees. Some fresh faces joined, and some stopped coming. Every newcomer had to choose a new nickname, and everyone in attendance had to call him by that nickname. The nicknames all start with Abu. This is followed by the name of the first child, since men in this culture know what the name of their first child will be, sometimes years before the child is born. Finally, they add the name of the city or country of their birth. Salah's nickname was Abu Sami Ashami, which meant the father of Sami from Damascus. Because of the use of nicknames, very few ever know the real names of the other members.

The attendees were all Arabs from various countries. Despite none of them being past their thirties, all of them appeared to have plenty of money. They wore fancy clothes and designer watches, carried expensive smartphones, and drove luxurious cars. That was no doubt what every young man wants in this life, but not Salah.

He was from a wealthy family, but the seemingly perfect lives these people led kept him coming to the meetings. They seemed perfect in every aspect of their lives. They had everything they needed and got everything they wanted. They were all good-looking, well-educated, and seemed to have no complaints. Most importantly, they appeared not to have any fear in their hearts. They were ideal Muslims, and Salah felt like he belonged.

The only rule in these meetings was you don't ask questions about the members' private lives. Most of the time, discussions centered on Arab Spring and what was going on in Arabic countries like Tunisia, Egypt, and Libya. After a few weeks, he realized these meetings were not random. Hundreds of meetings were being held in three main cities: Dar'a, Homs, and Baniyas. The most important leaders of the organization lived and met outside the country. Everyone who brought a newcomer to a meeting took responsibility for them. Abu Badr Ashami soon became his closest friend. Salah received money, gifts, help, and support. Whatever it took to make him feel secure and happy.

Then one day his life changed completely when Abu Badr asked him, "Would you like to learn how you can make it so every human on earth can live a life like this?

"Yes indeed," he answered with a broad grin.

"It won't happen on its own. We must make it happen." Abu Badr said.

"Yes, but how?"

"Well, would you rather I tell you, show you, or let you experience how?"

"I want you to tell me, show me, and let me experience it," Salah said with a grin.

So, he was introduced to the grand plan, which would start from there and return the glory to Muslims around the world. He soon realized the meetings were only a means of observing the members to single out the trustworthy ones and invite them to join the organization. After joining, the member would no longer attend the meetings and would be connected to only one mentor. The mentors would then give the new members official missions to accomplish. Salah's mission was to recruit newcomers, and he was terrific at his mission. Abu Badr had become proud of him and was soon his closest friend. Not a day passed without their meeting.

Now, as Salah jogged toward Abu Badr's apartment, a kind of mania filled his heart. He was happy that his mentor had chosen only him for whatever urgent matter was.

Despite the chilly weather, Salah was sweating as he jogged. The sound of his own breath was audible in the silence of the night. He didn't hear the susurration of the engine of the shiny black van slowly following him at a distance.

On both sides of Sina'a street, each set of six buildings forms a U-shape. A square park with tall eucalyptus trees sits in the center of each U. Abu Badr lived in U5, building 3, on the first floor, in apartment 2.

Salah slowed to a walk, with the wide road on his right and the buildings on his left. Every few minutes, a car passed, its engine breaking the pervasive silence. In some of the U's, streetlights rose above the trees, but in U5, the lights were off, and the space between the buildings was shrouded in gloom. The crescent moon threw little light, and the black shadows beneath the trees reminded him of the horror novel he was currently reading. For a moment, he half expected to see a werewolf slinking out from between the trees.

Building 3 was on the corner of the block, its gate shrouded in blackness. He needed to touch both walls to prevent himself from tripping as he climbed the seven steps to the first floor. He pulled out his mobile phone and used it to light his way to door number 2. The fifteen seconds he waited after pressing the doorbell seemed like an eternity. He glanced around, imagining for a moment he saw something black moving outside the open gate. Just then, the door opened, and he turned back toward the door.

With one glance, his brain went blank, and he lost complete control over his limbs and his tongue.

CHAPTER 6

Tuesday, March 9, 2010

Mullah Abdullah had scheduled time on his last day in Dubai to visit Mazen Mis'ed at his workplace in Dubai Healthcare City. The driver looked at the address he provided, scribbled on a piece of paper by Zahra. She had Googled it and found the location quickly after he gave up trying to get it from Mazen's family.

"Dubai Healthcare City. Ok, sir." The driver opened the car's rear door, and Mullah Abdullah slid inside.

The driver watched him in the rear-view mirror as he talked, not waiting for any response. "Dubai Healthcare City is the world's largest healthcare free zone, dedicated to healthcare and medical education for all. It was built in 2002 to increase medical tourism in Dubai ..." The mullah just nodded in agreement.

The building was located after the first roundabout, in phase one of Dubai Healthcare City. The roundabout was topped with a large leaf of green cannabis, the city's logo. The building was one in a group of three-story buildings, all identical in design and color; maroon and white. They gave the peaceful appearance of a suburban European house, not like most of the fancy, mirror-covered buildings in the crowded areas of Dubai. A security guard accompanied Mullah Abdullah to the second floor, where he pointed to the door of the Silky Skin Company, and politely took his leave. To the right of the door was a light-blue logo with the name of the company.

Mullah Abdullah knocked on the door. He could hear voices coming from inside, so assuming they hadn't heard his knock, he knocked again. A female voice seemed to respond, saying something he couldn't understand. He knocked on the door yet again and waited. Finally, he heard the clicking of high heels approaching the door.

The door opened to reveal a young woman dressed in a white shirt, a short grey skirt, and, of course, high-heeled shoes. She was Asian and spoke in English, but he couldn't understand a word she was saying.

"Peace be upon you and the mercy of Allah," he said in a polite tone, trying not to stare at her face.

She answered with one inexplicable word, which he assumed was a response to his greeting of Salaam. He couldn't imagine that any person in the world wouldn't reply since it was universal and also an obligation.

"Mazen?" he asked as he stepped through the door. The reception area was a vast space with marble tiles polished to a mirror-like brilliance, reflecting the extra bright spotlights. At the end of the open space was the reception desk, also made of marble, slightly darker than the floor, and the name, Silky Skin, and the logo of the company on the front. The desk was wide enough for at least four people to work at, but there was only one office chair. Behind the counter, a floor-to-ceiling, opaque glass wall bore the same light-blue logo. He noticed there was a door at each end of the glass wall, presumably leading to whatever lay behind it. The secretary slipped back behind the reception desk, with a few angrier clicks on the tiles.

"Mazen?" he repeated two or three times, his cheeks becoming red. "My name is Abdullah, and they call me mullah. I have come from Syria to meet with Mazen. My daughter Zahra wrote the address on a piece of paper, and the driver brought me here." Even as he spoke, the girl was talking to him, her tone becoming sharper. Still, he couldn't understand her repeated mumblings, even though he was pretty sure she was speaking English.

A tall blond lady appeared from behind the opaque glass, her skirt noticeably short, and her jacket tight. The secretary stood up but still had to look up at her because of the significant difference in their heights. They exchanged a few words, then the blond lady turned and smiled at him. She said two words and waited for him to respond.

He froze, his face hot, as if she'd breathed fire on him, and not only spoken to him. Finally, she beckoned with her hands, signaling him to follow her behind the glass wall.

Behind the opaque glass was a large area with two oversized square desks, each desk divided into four sections, for a total of eight girls sitting in front of computer screens. There were several wooden doors around the room, some open and some closed. He imagined they probably led to other offices. The tall blond woman led him to one closed door and as she ushered him inside, he could see it was a large conference room.

The woman said something else he was unable to translate, then she left, closing the door behind her. He assumed she had asked him to wait there, so he took the opportunity to glance around. In the center of the room was a fancy, dark maroon conference table with 12 expensive-looking, leather covered seats surrounding it.

Mullah Abdullah collapsed onto one of the plush seats and tried to relax as he looked around. On his far right hung three colorful banners, emblazoned with near-naked girls standing beside some bizarre-looking machines. They looked like the machines in the dental clinic. He avoided looking at them. But then he asked himself, *why...? I am alone in this room, and no one will see what I do or where my eyes roam. I could just tilt my head and look at those naked bodies just to amuse my eyes for a few seconds. No ...* The word slammed into his mind. *I am not alone in this room; Allah is with me, seeing and hearing everything.* He said out loud, "I seek refuge in Allah from the accursed devil." He turned his chair, so the banners were behind him. Then he noticed a video screen playing on the wall in front of him showing a naked girl lying on a clinic bed, her upper body covered with a white towel. Another lady in a white doctor's coat was immersing her hands in a bowl full of something green that looked like mud, which she then rubbed on the naked lady's legs. He shivered and said aloud, "I beg Allah for forgiveness," and he turned his chair to face the window, not daring to look right or left.

The door opened, and a man darted into the room rather aggressively. It reminded him of how his school principal would enter the classroom looking for the student who used a slingshot to shoot tiny paper balls at the art teacher's back. But unlike his principal's tatty old clothes, this man was wearing a black suit, white shirt, and a grey silk necktie. He was clean-shaven, and his hair was black and shiny.

He stared at him for a moment before blurting out, "Oh, Mazen."

When Mazen had come with his son Khaled to the mosque in Syria to ask him to be Khaled's mentor, he had been wearing a white dish-dash, and his hair was gray, with a long gray beard. When he was at Hadiya's funeral, only a few months ago, Mazen's gray beard had been long, and his clothes were just average; a shirt, trousers, and he was even wearing slippers then.

"You have honored us by your visit," Mazen said as he approached. His expression and cold eyes did not quite match the geniality of his words.

"Peace be upon you, and the mercy of Allah," Mullah Abdullah said, and exchanged kisses on the cheeks with Mazen while embracing him gently.

"How could you be in Dubai without my knowing?" Mazen asked as he walked to the TV screen on the wall and clicked a switch at the back to shut it off. Then they both sat down.

"I wanted to keep it a surprise," said the Mullah. *It's easier to find the phone number of our prime minister than it is to get yours from your family.*

"It is a great surprise," Mazen said. "And what is the reason you are in Dubai? How long are you planning to stay?"

"I am here simply to take part in an Islamic convention, and tomorrow I'll be on a flight back to Damascus."

"Have you had lunch?"

"Not yet."

"Let's go have some lunch and talk," Mazen said as he got to his feet. "Please excuse me for a moment. I will just ask my assistant to cancel all my appointments for this afternoon."

"No, please," Mullah Abdullah darted forward, catching Mazen's arm. "Don't cancel any of your appointments. I came here only to say hello and to be sure that you are alright, as a duty toward my old school friend." His voice sounded strained.

Mazen smiled a fake smile and whispered, "Your visit is an honor to my company and to me. Please don't worry about my appointments and duties here. My partner will take over in the event I am busy." Then Mazen left the room and closed the door behind him. He had the feeling that Mazen was rebuking him because his voice had been unnecessarily loud.

He paced around the conference table, avoiding the pictures of naked women. Windows on one side gave him a view of a nearby building. Windows on the opposite side of the room were covered by venetian blinds. With two fingers, he made a gap in the shutters so he had a view of the clerks sitting and staring at their computer screens, all of them gorgeous ladies. In the far corner of the room, an office door stood ajar. He could see leather chairs and a small glass table in the middle, but he couldn't see who was sitting behind the desk except for an arm. He thought it was Mazen's arm. The tall blond woman's back was to him as she stood talking to the person behind the desk.

She moved as if floating past the desk as the same arm he'd seen encircled her waist and pulled her out of his line of sight. Mullah Abdullah lowered his hand, letting the shutters close, blocking out the view. He was frozen with disbelief. What had he just seen? Overcome by curiosity once more, he teased open the shutters to peer through again, but Mazen's office door was now closed. Why were there clouds of disappointment hovering over his head? Was it because he wanted to condemn Mazen? Or maybe he wanted to convince himself that he hadn't seen what he'd seen. Anyway, he was not sure if the arm was Mazen's. Oops. All the girls in the office were now watching his every move. He quickly closed the shutters, and like a guilty student, he sat motionless, awaiting Mazen's return.

Mazen finally opened the door and poked his head in, his broad smile exposing brilliant white teeth. "I apologize for keeping you waiting, Mullah. I've been waiting for confirmation of a booking at the restaurant. We can leave now." He opened the door wider, allowing the mullah to pass through.

He followed Mazen through the reception area, but just before they stepped out, the receptionist called, "Monsieur Dan." She approached Mazen with some quick questions regarding business matters. As she spoke with him, she pointed to the contents of a document. Mazen took his time explaining things to her in detail.

Mullah Abdullah did his best not to feel stupid as he stood awkwardly between the receptionist and the door. Should he put his hands in his pockets to look cool, or keep them out? No, no... crossing his arms on his chest would look cooler. *Come on, when are you finishing?* He struggled to hide his frustration.

Finally Mazen turned to go, embarrassment visible on his face, as he explained, "They call me Monsieur Dan here in the office because I don't want infidels to utter my Muslim name on their wicked tongues."

Mullah Abdullah withheld comment, given the delicacy of the moment. If Mazen hadn't explained why he had a different name in Dubai than he did in Syria, he wouldn't have even noticed.

The air inside Mazen's black car was chilly and smelled very fresh. The seats were leather, and the windows were tinted black. He felt as if he was inside a futuristic vehicle, not like any sort of car he'd ever ridden in before. Later, Mazen told him the car was a Bentley, and cost over a half million dirham.

When they arrived, it took him a few minutes to understand what was going on. It was the first time in his life, and likely the last time, he'd ever visited a restaurant in a submarine.

When all the guests had arrived, there was a long, loud whistle blast from outside. With a sudden jerk, they began to submerge. The thudding noise of the engine and the hissing of air being released from the ballast tanks drowned out the soft background music for a few minutes until the vessel finally leveled out. The trembling and shaking of the glasses and utensils ceased, and the music became audible once more.

When the waiter came to their table, Mazen

ordered for both of them in English.

Mullah Abdullah looked out the round window. With a hand on either side of the frame, he resembled a child with his nose pressed against the glass. The submarine ended up in a valley-like spot surrounded by a vast expanse of marine plants, coral, algae, seaweed, and many fish of a variety of sizes and colors. The submarine's powerful floodlights turned the surrounding area into a painting of moving colors.

Mazen said, "Usually, submarines don't have windows, but this one had them added by special request and equipped to operate as a restaurant. The windows allowed the diners to enjoy a view of live fish just outside their windows, as well as the cooked fish on the dishes in front of them."

Two waiters shifted the plates from a shiny, stainless steel trolly to their table. Grilled salmon, deep-fried shrimp with rice in a pineapple, grilled duck, and some type of salad the mullah didn't recognize.

As he looked across at the diners seated at the other tables around them, most were barely visible in the dim light. To him, they looked like aliens in their strange clothing. He had never seen an old man with white hair, wearing green pants, a golden jacket, and golden shoes without socks. Next to him sat a young man dressed in a tight t-shirt that showed off his muscular chest. *That must be the old man's grandson.* At the next table sat an old woman wearing a black dress and an elegant pearl necklace.

While not intending to look at her body, he noticed she was quite fat and wore long black gloves up to her elbows. She was fanning herself with a hand fan despite the air being nearly freezing. In front of her at the same table was an old man, most likely her husband, who spent most of his time looking out at the underwater world. Behind the fat lady's table was an old man who looked like the president of the United States. He couldn't remember his name at that moment, but he was fair-haired. And the woman next to him, who appeared to be his wife, looked exactly like the queen of England. At least, that's who he was reminded of as he studied them.

Lightheaded, Mullah Abdullah looked around at the luxurious lifestyle he had been exposed to so suddenly. He was like a newborn infant. Having expected life outside the womb to be five or ten times bigger, discovers the world multiplied by billions or even trillions.

Mazen ate with a fork and knife, his hands moving with precision, as if he was doing surgery. Very calm and efficient. *Is this really my friend Mazen, whose family still lives in poverty in Damascus?*

He didn't follow Mazen's example, using a fork and knife. Arabic food usually requires a spoon or can be eaten by hand with pita bread. Besides, Islam strongly discourages using the left hand for eating. He used his right hand to cut the fish and duck, then put down the knife and picked up his fork to eat.

"When do you intend to come back to Syria and live with your children now that their mother is gone?" he asked. Maybe because of the dim lighting, he could detect no signs of surprise on Mazen's face.

"The children are living with a golden spoon in their mouths. I am sending money enough to keep five families living well," Mazen said.

"Unfortunately, that golden spoon is invisible," Mullah Abdullah said.

"Their mother was taking the money and hiding it to give it to her own siblings. Now, their grandfather, Haj Adel, is taking care of them. Their present circumstances are far better than when their mother was alive." Mazen spoke in a voice so low it forced Mullah Abdullah to move his head closer.

"This is only an assumption on your part. You didn't live with them before she died, and you are not living with them now. Do you have any proof that she gave money to her siblings?" His voice was a little higher than normal. Mazen glanced around at the surrounding tables. The overweight lady and her husband had awakened from their stupor and were now staring at him.

"Their mother used to turn the children against me. She made them hate me and wouldn't allow them to talk to me over the phone when I called them every Friday at their grandmother's house. Before she died, she was nagging to come and live with me here in Dubai."

"Why to their grandmother's?" The mullah's fingers were shaking, so he put his hands between his knees.

"What?" Mazen raised his glass of water and drank, looking at him from over the glass.

"Why was there no telephone in your house? You could have called your family directly without the hassle of making them go to your mother's house to talk on the phone."

"I didn't know how to tame my wife. One day she would go to her sisters' homes, and they would incite hatred against me. Another day, she would go to her brother's house and give him some of the money I sent for the family. Imagine if she'd had a telephone in the house. What would have happened? Her siblings would have called continually, trying to manipulate my children and convince them I have another wife here in Dubai, and I had ditched their mother."

To Mullah Abdullah, such a strange answer showed a strained relationship between Mazen and his late wife, Hadiya. There was no doubt, the impact of all these factors would be harmful to the children.

He didn't want to hear more of these accusations, so he asked Mazen, "What about the money you owe Ahmad?"

"That was just a story Ahmad and his sister made up to justify taking the money I sent for the family. If Ahmad has proof that he actually lent me any money, then he must show it, and I will definitely pay him back." Mazen said.

"You sent the money to her directly?" Mullah Abdullah asked.

"Never. I send the money to my father. He buys what they need."

"That was so you could guarantee that no cash was reaching your wife, because you assumed she had been stealing the money and giving it to her siblings?"

"Yes," Mazen said.

And the grandfather kept most of the money and giving little to the family.

"We should wish nothing but mercy for the dead. Allah will hold them accountable on the Day of Resurrection," Mullah Abdullah said.

Mazen wrinkled his forehead, his eyes almost disappearing beneath his eyelids. His words came out like poison. "My last trip to Syria was to divorce her. If she were still alive, I definitely would have divorced her to ensure she would stay with the children and not leave them ever."

The desserts were no less exotic than his experience. A heavenly honey glazed brownie wrapped in pure gold foil, with a sweet saffron drink.

They finished eating their desserts as the submarine gradually resurfaced and returned to the dock. Back on land, Mazen ordered a taxi to drop Mullah Abdullah at his hotel.

* * *

As Mazen drove back to his grand villa in Barsha. he recalled the discussion with the mullah, evoking memories he'd kept buried in the remote recesses of his mind.

The last fight with his wife before she passed away was during a phone conversation to his mother's house, as usual, a few months earlier.

It was the first time Hadiya, rather than pleading with him, had made some rather bold demands of him, that rendered him speechless for a few seconds. What was going on? The wife, who had always done whatever he ordered and replied with respect, was now talking to him in this manner?

"I can't wait any longer. Either you come back from Dubai, and we live together as a family, or you take me to live with you in Dubai." There was a tremor in her voice.

"Are you crazy?" he yelled. "You want to leave four daughters alone and come to live with me?"

"So, come back here, and we will live together as a family. No matter how much you earn, we will happily live like poor people, but together."

"How many times do I need to repeat it? I have a lot of debt to pay because of you and your children. I am working here in Dubai, day and night, to repay the debt and provide you with enough money to keep you living in luxury."

"We don't need to live in luxury! We just need you to be with us, to take care of your children. It has been sixteen years since you left. I can't live like this anymore."

He smiled when he remembered how he'd answered her cruelly and heard her weeping over the phone.

***

Hani stood beside a white Peugeot parked on Ibn-Assaker Street, in Damascus. Taking out his notebook, he tore a page from it, wrote 7:30 on it, and put it under the windshield wiper of the Peugeot. He recalled what had happened between him and Asmar because of this car.

It was midnight during a cold September, three years ago. He had been standing by his Honda police bike on Ibn-Assaker Street, near the roundabout of Bab-Mussalla. That roundabout has four exits to important parts of the city center, and a police officer always needs to be there to direct traffic. That day the smooth asphalt was slick from the drizzle, and drivers were driving cautiously to avoid sliding off the road. A white Peugeot passed by at high speed, failing to stop at the red light before the roundabout. A quick glance at the car showed him the silhouettes of two people in the front seat. Jumping on his motorbike, he gunned the engine and took off after the car with a roar. He purposely didn't switch on the siren or the red and blue flashing lights, as he didn't want to alert the driver.

Despite the car leaving Hani's assigned turf, he didn't stop the chase or even slow down, since the driver had committed a traffic violation. He kept a safe distance so the driver wouldn't notice him until the car reached Mazzah Street and entered an alley, which was eerily quiet for the time of night. Reaching the entrance to the alley, Hani stopped briefly and then switched off the bike without stepping down. The trees on both sides of the street had thick trunks, their tangle of bare branches creating a tunnel.

The driver of the car was still in the process of parking between two vehicles in a long line of parked cars on one side of the street. He planned to wait until the car was parked, then ride up and stop right beside it to prevent it from leaving.

Seconds passed, and the car went silent and dark as the driver switched the engine off, but no one stepped out of the car, so he waited a little longer, still no one moved. *That's weird. There's only one reason to park in such a dark, isolated alley and not leave the car.* A sly smile played on his lips as he imagined a fellow and a girl begging him not to take them into custody on a charge of obscenity.

He stepped off the bike and crept behind the line of trees without making a sound. He froze when he spotted what was really going on inside the car; it was such an abnormal scene. Yanking out his mobile phone, he turned on the camera's flash setting. His hands were shaking, and his heart thundered in his chest.

Moving closer to the front of the car in a crouch, he raised the phone and snapped a photo. Two young men jerked their heads apart from each other and stared at Hani as if they had seen the devil outside the car. The one in the passenger seat opened the door and ran away without closing it, as if the devil himself was chasing him. Hani didn't follow, but stood staring at the man behind the wheel. He gestured for him to step out of the car.

The young man climbed out slowly but remained behind the open car door as if using it as a shield. Hani secured his mobile phone in his inner jacket pocket carefully, then approached the young man, and slapped his face with all his strength. The sound of the smack left a ringing in his ears, and the blow nearly knocked the young man off his feet. He couldn't help noticing how handsome the young man was, who was now staring at the ground without speaking.

"Give me the registration for the car and your driving license." Hani's throat was dry, and his voice came out rough.

The young man took his license out of his wallet and reached inside the car for the registration on the visor over the steering wheel, then handed them over. Hani took them without looking at the details and put them in his pocket. Stepping behind the young man, he cuffed him and pushed him to sit back down in the driver's seat. He snatched the car keys and said before closing the door, "You animal. You'll wait here until another car gets here and takes you to the police station for interrogation." The young man didn't speak or move, his gaze remaining fixed forward as if he was in a trance.

Hani returned to his motorbike and rode it back to the car. He was mulling over what was the best solution for this situation. He stopped beside the car, stepped down, and opened the car door to find the young man as he had left him, sitting like a statue. He called the station to request a car be sent, and while he waited, he looked at the young man's license. His name was Asmar. The motor vehicle was registered to a secret intelligence agency. Hani's eyes widened as if he was looking at a sparkling diamond. Turning his gaze to Asmar, he said with genuine astonishment, "A secret agent?"

***

The officer on duty looked at Hani angrily and said, "What the fuck do you think you're doing, bringing a secret intelligence agent to the station just because he crossed a red light? You should have just written him a ticket for a fine and let him go. Tomorrow morning, his agency will dump the city over our heads."

"He was very insolent when he talked to me," Hani said calmly.

The duty officer interrupted him, "For Allah's sake, Hani. Of course, he would be rude. Don't you know what even the most junior agent from secret intelligence is capable of?"

"I wanted to teach him a lesson in respect and discipline," Hani said in the same calm voice.

The duty officer exclaimed, "You alone will bear the consequences."

"No problem Sir. I will sign the report and take the consequences. Just let me handle the situation with no interference," Hani said.

"You got it. Now get lost."

Hani left the officer and went to the interview room where Asmar had been taken. The room was nearly empty except for a table and two chairs; one which was occupied by Asmar. Hani entered and sat in the other chair. He looked at Asmar, whose despondency was clear from his body language. The angry red marks from when he'd slapped him were still clear on Asmar's right cheek.

"Do you know what the punishment is for the average citizen who does what you were doing?" he asked. He avoided naming the act, in case anyone might overhear. "You are an intelligence agent. The security of this country depends on the honor and dignity of people in positions like yours, and you choose to betray your country in this shameless way?" He spat on the floor and banged his fist on the table, shouting, "Why aren't you talking?"

Asmar raised his face. Their eyes met, and he said in a weak voice, "What do you want me to say?"

Hani's words were laced with contempt. "True, insects like you don't have a right to speak, and your mouth should remain shut for the rest of your life. Someone like you has no place among humans. You should just die and free humanity from your filthy behavior." He felt a sense of victory when a single teardrop fell from Asmar's right eye.

He left the room, locking the door behind him. When he returned more than an hour later, Asmar was on the brink of collapse. Hani slammed his hand down on the table with all his strength, leaving a traffic ticket for running a red light. Asmar glanced at the paper and then up into Hani's eyes.

"Listen carefully. You are an intelligence agent, and if you have compromised the reputation of this great country, you will be brought to ruin. I swear that is the last thing I would allow to happen to my homeland. Moreover, don't think for a fraction of a second that I care about your reputation. Never. Someone like you should be erased from existence." He threw the paper in Asmar's face and continued, "This is the penalty for running a red light, just to justify my bringing you here." Then he lowered his voice and moved his face closer to Asmar's. "I will keep the photo on my mobile and I swear to Allah, if you go back to your queer behavior, I will ruin you. Am I understood?"

Thus, since that night, Asmar had become a source of abundant information. No matter how private or confidential, even information buried in the deepest holes, was all granted to Hani whenever he demanded it.

The piece of paper he'd put under the windshield wipers of Asmar's car was a message to tell him what time he must be online with his phony Skype account. The discussion would be brief without a preamble or chit-chat. Hani would spell out the information he needed, and Asmar would provide it within 24 hours.

***

Khaled opened the closet in his mother's bedroom. From under some folded towels, he took out the last photographs she'd taken prior to his father's last visit. She had wanted to apply for her passport in case his father agreed to take her to live with him in Dubai.

To him, his mother was Allah's finest creation on earth. She had always helped him. Washed his feet, cooked his favorite meals, cleaned his room, and never complained about the unpleasant smell or the mess he made. He couldn't imagine anyone else on earth could have such a tremendous love for their mom, as he did for his.

He hated everyone who didn't see the real value of his mom. Beginning with his father and his four sisters, the neighbors who were always gossiping about her, his relatives, who always bragged about how much they loved her, but had never come to visit her while she lived in this apartment. Even her friends, pitied her when they saw her old, worn-out clothes. Everyone else should suffer and live in pain. But not her. She wasn't just a mere human; she was an angel. He wiped his tears with his sleeve.

She was only 39 when she left. But she had wrinkles on her forehead and at the corners of her mouth from the long nights she stayed awake, taking care of him. Her hair had turned gray so early because her life was full of calamities and tragedies. Her hands were calloused because she never allowed her daughters to do any housework. To avoid disturbing their studies, she was the only one who cleaned the house, washed the clothes, ironed, and cooked. Her heels were like a cracked stone, because of the dozens of times she'd taken him to see the specialist, trips to the market to buy groceries, and also to his grandfather's shop to take the weekly payments.

She'd always kept a lovely smile on her face, her eyes full of affection for her children, and her mouth speaking only kind words. She'd always hugged him tight whenever he cried when he was a kid and continually questioned why Allah had him a cripple. She'd always told him that heaven was meant especially for people like him.

He got up, wiped his tears on his sleeve again, and hobbled to his sisters' room, where he opened the door, and looked inside without entering. Farah, Marwa, and Ro'wa raised their eyes from their books and glared at him. Zakiya was hugging her knees and weeping from the pain. He closed the door of his sisters' room, hobbled back to his room, and closed the door. He didn't want his mentor to hear Zakiya's wailing. She had been in pain since the accident, but pain was a cleansing of the soul.

He took out his laptop from a drawer and put it on the bed, then he pulled a plastic chair to the side of the bed and sat on it. He inserted the thumb drive into the laptop, which provided a protected connection by changing the IP address of the computer every few seconds.

He put in his earphones, gave the call order and listened to the ringtone, waiting to hear his mentor's voice without seeing his face. Only high-ranking people within the organization were allowed to see their mentor's faces. It was his dream to become one of them someday. It was, however, mandatory to turn on his webcam so his mentor could see his face. His recruiter and his mentor were the only ones who knew his identity, and the only ones he knew from the organization. The mentor was higher in rank than the recruiter, so Khaled could not share with his recruiter the things he discussed with his mentor.

A broad smile spread across his face when he heard his mentor's voice. Abu Gaith Atturkey. After his mother's death, his friend and recruiter Salah and his mentor were the only ones who seemed to care about him, unlike everyone else who looked at him with contempt.

"Salaam be upon you Abu Nar," Atturkey said. "Please turn the camera to face the closed door."

Khaled turned the laptop slightly to the left to face the door, then proceeded to answer the questions his mentor always asked at the beginning of each session to make sure his apprentice was still pure and hadn't shaken hands with the devil. Salah had explained to Khaled, asking such questions was necessary to be sure he was following the Islamic rules and doing everything he could to draw new people onto the true path.

"You can use any method you feel is useful to attract new believers. Advise them, give them gifts, give them money, and don't worry, whatever you need, just ask for it and it will be made available," Atturkey said.

Atturkey showed him the correct path to serve Allah and his religion. He was determined to do whatever Atturkey asked him to and not disappoint him.

"Tell me, what are you feeling right now?" Atturkey asked him.

"I am blessed to be a part of this group of believers trying to return the caliphate and realign the world under the umbrella of Islam."

"But it is not an easy job. It will take a lot of devotion and effort. It will require a lot of sacrifices."

"I don't think it will be more difficult than my usual life," Khaled said with a laugh.

Atturkey didn't laugh. Khaled swallowed.

"Your difficulties are nothing compared to the challenges we are facing to raise the new Caliphate," Atturkey said.

Khaled just nodded.

"Salah hasn't shown up or called me for a few days now," Khaled said.

"Who's Salah?" Atturkey asked.

"Sorry, I meant Abu Sami," Khaled said.

"Do not defile your tongue with his name," Atturkey snapped.

Khaled's heart skipped a beat. "Wha... what happened?"

"He has proven himself to be a traitor," Atturkey said.

Khaled stared at the screen, waiting for more details.

"If anyone asks you about Abu Sami, you must say you didn't know him," Atturkey said.

Isn't lying a grand sin in Islam?

"What ordinary people think of as sins are

not necessarily sins for those of us who serve the newborn caliphate."

How did he know what I was thinking? "Yes, of course," Khaled said.

At the end of the session, his mentor said, "You have to be extra careful. You need to make sure that any new prospects you try to recruit are genuine and not spies for our enemies."

Khaled looked at the closed door, then looked at the blank screen. "I am always extra careful."

"Good. Allah chose us for this noble mission, so we must tolerate all of Allah's tests along the way until we win."

Khaled nodded.

"You will receive your usual payment on Friday. After the prayer, someone will find you and hand you your money in an envelope along with an address where you will be given a gun."

Khaled wiped his wet hands on his trousers. "Okay."

The only person I know from the organization now is Atturkey. The only person I can trust in this life is Atturkey. I must do everything I can not to lose him as well.

CHAPTER 7

Wednesday, March 10, 2010

Wednesday morning, Mullah Abdullah lay back in his fully reclined first-class seat and smiled. He would be meeting his wife and daughter in just a few short hours. Although his visit to Dubai had only been for a week, he felt as if he had not seen them for months. He fell asleep and awoke to the flight attendant announcing their descent to the Damascus International Airport.

In the airport, Mullah Abdullah handed over his passport to an immigration officer, a clean-shaven young man in uniform, seated at a marble counter. He took longer than usual, examining his passport and checking the screen in front of him. The Mullah fidgeted. His wife and daughter were no doubt waiting for him outside. The immigration officer made a call, whispering a few words before putting down the receiver, then continuing to stare at the screen, ignoring the Mullah completely. Other people in the queue fidgeted too, some peering at him, with curious expressions as if wondering what might be causing the delay. Some failed to hide their contempt because he was making them late to reunite with their families and loved ones.

Four men approached the counter. Three were wearing the same uniform as the man behind the counter, while the one in civilian clothes with a gun tucked in his belt was obviously in charge. The sight of the gun alone was enough to spread terror like a virus. The guy in charge stepped behind the counter and stared at the screen while listening to the immigration officer's whispered explanation. He snatched up the mullah's passport and gestured to the other three, who were waiting for his orders.

The Mullah's hands were cold and clammy. He swallowed, trying to moisturize his throat, but it was as dry as sawdust.

One of them grabbed under one arm and snapped, "Come with us." When Mullah Abdullah tried to wrench his arm away, the man twisted his arm behind his back, forcing a scream of pain from his throat. That made everyone stop what they were doing and stare. They propelled him roughly down the corridor past gaping onlookers.

The Mullah was certain people around him could hear his heart hammering as he was hustled away. He fixed his gaze on the floor, fervently wishing the earth would swallow him up before people noticed a man in religious garb being led away like some kind of criminal.

They escorted him to a large office on the second floor, with a desk against the far wall and a conference table in the middle. Behind the desk sat another officer, perhaps in his fifties, clean-shaven, except for a thick mustache. He had gray hair on the sides of his head, but the hair on the rest of his head was black and shiny, slicked back with gel or oil. His skin was dark, indicating long years of service in the field before being assigned to this well-furnished office. A row of stars and a metal eagle adorned his chest. He couldn't tell the officer's rank, but from the luxurious office, it seemed he must hold a position of importance.

The guy with the gun tucked in his belt raised his heels and clicked them forcefully on the floor. It appeared to be the official salutation for this branch of the force.

The Mullah looked at the tile under his heavy shoes, surprised it was still intact.

Then, like a robot, the fellow stepped forward, handed over the passport, and whispered something in the officer's ear.

The officer glared at the Mullah with obvious suspicion and said, "What is your name?"

"My passport is in your hand," Mullah Abdullah answered matter-of-factly.

"Just answer the question. Do you

understand?" the officer yelled.

The mullah swallowed but didn't answer. The officer shouted again, "Do you understand?"

"Yes," he said, avoiding eye contact.

All four men jumped in surprise when the officer shouted, "Yes, SIR!"

Mullah Abdullah was taken aback. He had never said 'sir' to anyone in his life. After all, he was a well-respected cleric with influential friends in government circles. People called him sir when they talked to him. He swallowed and forced himself to say, "Yes, sir."

"What is your name?" the officer asked with contempt written all over his face.

"Abdullah."

"Your full name." the officer yelled again.

"Abdullah Al-Allab."

"What is your mother's name?"

"Salamiah Altahoon."

"Take everything out of your pockets and give it to him," he said, pointing to the police officer standing to the Mullah's left.

Instead of reaching into his pockets, he said, "What is going on? Why am I here?" Then he remembered, "Sir."

"You don't know why you are here?"

"No, I don't know," he said, his voice betraying his growing panic.

The officer ignored his denial and said, "Take everything out of your pockets. Now!"

The Mullah slipped both hands into his

pockets and started taking out his belongings, including his wallet from an inner pocket, and handed it all to the police officer without further hesitation, although he was clearly agitated. When he took out his mobile phone, he dropped it, and the screen broke. As he bent to pick it up and give it to the officer, he felt hotly embarrassed that all the men were looking at him in the most demeaning way, yet he regained control over his emotions, determined not to show these goons any more debility.

When his pockets were empty, the officer in charge asked one cop to search him thoroughly. As the man started searching him, the Mullah sighed dejectedly in his frustration.

The officer handled him roughly, targeting certain body parts. He felt as if hot steel was touching his body. With each touch, he shut his eyes and clenched his jaw harder. He could smell the officer's breath as he searched under his collar. Stale cigarette smoke. He moved his hands behind his back, trying to hide their shaking.

When the cop discovered the prayer beads in his pocket, he snatched them out. The Mullah protested, "Please leave them with me. I need them for my prayers." The cop glanced at the officer, waiting for permission to return the beads.

His boss snapped, "I said everything."

Mullah Abdullah shut his eyes and sighed.

The boss ordered, "Take him to the interrogation room."

His blood evaporated when he heard the officer's order. He wanted to protest, but his throat was as dry as a cactus in the Mojave Desert. Most of all, he wanted to ask why they were detaining him, why they were treating him in such a disrespectful way, and why they were not treating him as a religious devotee and respected leader.

"Please, sir, may I use the telephone? I need to call my wife and daughter. Surely they are already worried about me, as all the passengers from my flight have gone out, and I was not among them."

The officer ignored him and gestured for the cop to lead him away.

Grabbing him once again under each arm, they propelled him along between them. They passed many corridors and descended several flights of stairs until they came to a long corridor with multiple wooden doors on either side. They were all painted the same color as the ceiling and walls, a somewhat yellowish white.

Shoving him forcefully into the empty room, they locked the door behind him and left.

*****

Amani and her daughter Zahra were waiting in the arrival hall and growing increasingly worried when her husband didn't show up. She took out her phone and dialed his number. It rang several times before a voice announced, "The party you are calling is not available at the moment. Please leave a message at the beep."

Was it possible he could still be waiting for his

luggage? Amani didn't have the slightest clue what his reaction would be if he encountered problems in such a situation. After all, this was the first time he had made a journey of any significance since their wedding many years ago. Likewise, it was her first time coming to the airport on such an occasion. She tried calling him again, with the same result. She kept calling until Zahra snatched the phone from her hand and pocketed it. Guiding her to the information desk, Zahra explained the situation to the gum-chewing lady sitting at a computer screen.

The lady was eager to help, and asking for his full name, she dialed a number and inquired about the mullah. She listened to the person on the other end of the line. Then she put the telephone down, turned back to Amani, and said, "Maybe your husband missed his flight." Then she turned to deal with another customer.

Just then, the mobile phone in Zahra's pocket rang with its unique musical ringtone. Zahra handed her mother the phone as soon as she spotted the name on the screen.

Amani snatched the phone and glanced at the screen. Seeing it was her husband, she was overwhelmed with joy. She hit the green OK button, raised the phone to her ear, and said, "Thanks to Allah for your safety, my dear."

"May I know who this is?" It was not the Mullah's voice.

"Excuse me, brother, but you are the one who just called from my husband's phone," Amani said.

"I am calling from the security office at the airport. Your husband is now in our custody. In a few minutes, someone will come to bring you to our office. Please wait near Gate 2." The line went dead.

Amani dropped the phone and collapsed on Zahra's shoulder, her legs shaking. The large hall seemed tighter than a coffin at that moment. She struggled to get enough oxygen. Her daughter's eyes were full of fear.

Amani looked around anxiously for her husband as the guard led her into the security office. Mullah Abdullah was not there, but she spotted his cell phone and wallet on the desk in front of the officer. She felt weak in the knees again, but Zahra grasped her arm to steady her. She failed to hide her fright and weakness from her daughter.

The officer stood and walked from behind the desk to the conference table, motioning for Amani and Zahra to sit. He glanced first at Zahra and then directly into Amani's eyes. Amani said, "Zahra, please wait for me outside." Zahra grudgingly left the room at her mother's insistence.

"Your husband has been accused of being involved in a matter of national security, so we are detaining him."

Amani wanted to speak, but her throat wouldn't obey her. Not even the slightest sound came out of her mouth.

"First, no one will hear what we say in this room. Should you choose to tell anyone of our conversation, it will prove that you are also involved with your husband in this grave matter. You, as well as any person you tell, and your daughter will all be arrested. Am I understood?" He waited for her answer. When she didn't speak, he said, "Am I clear? I need to hear your answer."

"Yes," she said weakly.

"I interpret that as your pledge that our conversation is confidential, and you won't talk to anyone about it." He pushed a paper toward her, pointing to the bottom. "Please sign here."

She tried to read the details, but the words swam on the page because of the tears blurring her vision. She signed and pushed the paper back without understanding it or even reading it.

"I have a few questions about your husband, which I hope you will answer with complete honesty and frankness. What your husband needs most now is transparency as you answer these questions." The officer opened a notebook and spent the next 45 minutes questioning her and writing her answers. In the end, Amani begged, "For how long he will be detained, and what precisely are the accusations against him?"

"I am afraid I can't reveal more details than what I've already told you. At least not at present." He closed his notebook. "You are free to go, sister. When you reach home, you will find a team of experts from the national security agency waiting for you. Please cooperate fully with them while they search your house."

Amani had entered the airport infused with

happiness and now exited overcome by grief.

Zahra pressed her to tell her about what the officer had said, but Amani was deep in thought.

Back at the house, six men waited out front with their black bags. Amani unlocked the old wooden door and pushed it open. Once the men had entered, she shut the door firmly, causing its knocker to rattle. The courtyard was filled with the aroma of expensive Oud wood, smoking over the embers in the incense burner. Amani had put it out for the Mullah before she'd left the house. Amani and Zahra sat together on the sofa in the liwan. The fountain bubbled and splashed in the center of the courtyard.

The men remained silent while they worked, but the sounds of the search were painful for Amani and Zahra to hear. In the liwan, the pictures frames were taken down and torn from behind. In the courtyard, the dirt around the plants was dumped out to check if anything was buried underneath. One man went around knocking on each and every stone in the courtyard, including the stones in the walls. In the kitchen, the jars of pickles, olives, jam, and halloumi cheese were opened and searched. They searched the bags of rice, wheat, and flour. In the attic, they examined the water tank. In the living room, the seat cushions were ripped open, and with each one, Amani felt her heart being torn apart. In the bedrooms, the mattresses were slashed open. Everything that could be opened was methodically opened and inspected. For everything else, they snapped dozens of photos. Hours had passed before the men finally gathered by the door carrying Zahra's computer to take to the lab to have its hard drive scanned.

Zahra objected as she saw them leaving with it, but her mother shushed her and told her to let them take it because they had nothing to hide.

****

The mullah took off his cloak and spread it on the dirty floor, then lay down on his back on it and stared blindly at the ceiling. "Oh Allah, I have only you." The silence in the room annoyed him more than any noise would have. However, his racing heart was gradually slowing; his breathing becoming steadier. Verses he had memorized from the Qur'an helped to restore some tranquility to his soul and reminded him of the necessity to trust in Allah with complete and absolute surrender. He hadn't committed murder or any other crime. Surely this detention was all a big mistake, and soon they would discover their error. They would apologize and send him home to be reunited with his family.

The three uniformed men came and took him to another room on the same floor. A large room, empty except for a metal table and a single chair. A young man wearing a military uniform was seated on that chair, the buttons nearly popping off his jacket that was stretched so tightly over his huge stomach. They left him standing in the middle of the room and closed the door behind them. The man with the bulging jacket was holding the Mullah's passport, copying down details from it into a thick notebook, without looking at him.

A few minutes later, the man laid down his pen, raised his head and peered over his glasses at him. He motioned for him to come forward, and the Mullah approached.

"You will tell me your life story from the day you were born to this minute," he said, then looked at the passport and added, "Abdullah Al-Allab."

Mullah Abdullah was shocked by the request. He was beginning to think he was not only having a nightmare, but living it.

"Look, Abdullah, my assignment is to write a report about you," the man said. "As you can see, I am sitting in a chair, and you are standing. It is better if you get started immediately before your legs give out."

By now, the Mullah's legs felt like marshmallows already. "I will tell you my life story, but please tell me the reason for detaining me. Please, if you don't mind."

"I don't know what kind of shit you were involved in to cause the authorities to detain you. Now start talking."

He slowly told his life story, as the man wrote everything down, without once commenting or even looking at him. Minutes became hours, and he felt as if time was barely moving. His eyes filled with tears when he remembered his wife and daughter, and how frightened they must have been when he failed to meet them at the airport. Had they left the airport yet, or were they still waiting for him?

When he'd finished his story, he was told to sign the officer's notes, and he did so with trembling fingers. Thirteen full pages of the messiest handwriting he'd ever seen. How would anyone read it? The man abruptly got up and left without saying a single word, taking with him both the chair and the table. He closed the door and turned the key in the lock. His footsteps faded away with each step, leaving an eerie silence. Mullah Abdullah again spread his cloak on the floor and lay down on it.

There was no way to know how much time passed since the room didn't have any windows. The only thing in the room was a bare bulb in the center of the ceiling. The dazzling white light would burn the eyes of anyone who looked directly at it. Wispy spider webs hung in the corners.

The cold penetrated deep into his bones, and he realized he would freeze to death if he stayed on the floor any longer. Getting to his feet, he clasped his back as a sharp pain shot up his spine. He rubbed his palms together and blew on them in an effort to warm them up. Painfully, he began pacing slowly from one end of the room to the other, counting his steps. The length was 80 steps, and the width was 56. He slipped his hand into his pocket to take out his prayer beads before he remembered they had taken them.

The missing prayer beads didn't stop him from offering his customary praises. "Thanks be to Allah. There is no God but Allah. Allah is the greatest." He felt gratitude when he remembered the endless generosity of Allah. He believed that every time a person praises Allah, he or she will be granted a tree in heaven. He continued pacing from one end to the other and mumbling his words of praise, when suddenly the realization of his total solitude hit him, the pain squeezed his heart. Fresh tears streamed down his cheeks until his beard became wet. He compared his despair to what his sense of isolation would be in the grave after death, as the mourners were leaving the gravesite. After they buried him in a narrow hole in the ground, they would all return to their daily lives. His silent cry became a loud wailing as he, at last, raised his head and looked up beseechingly. "Oh Allah, I pray you will surround me with your mercy."

The sound of the key in the lock startled him. The door opened, and a man in civilian clothes and a gun under his belt came in. The Mullah wiped his tears on his sleeve, then looked again at the man who was carrying a notebook and pen, followed by two cops carrying the same metal chair and table the first man had taken out previously. They put them down and left. The newcomer spoke politely, "Peace be upon you, brother."

The Mullah replied to the greeting in a feeble voice, while hundreds of questions spun around in his head.

"Please have a seat," the man said, gesturing to the chair, as he dropped the notebook and the pen on the table.

Mullah Abdullah immediately sat down, put his hands on his knees, and sighed audibly.

The man leaned on the table to be as close to the Mullah's head as possible, saying, "I want you to write your life story from the day you were born until this minute?"

Appalled by the request, he said, "Please tell me why I am here. I am sure there has been a mistake." The man's breath smelled like he'd been eating onions.

The man looked into the Mullah's eyes for a while as if he was reading something written in them, before he proceeded, "So, you don't know why you are here?"

"I swear to Allah, I don't know."

"Me neither," the man said before he moved toward the door, where he turned and said, "You have one hour to write what I've asked of you. If you take longer, you will be here for another day, waiting for the next shift and another officer." He walked out and locked the door behind him.

Mullah Abdullah wrote his life story exactly as he had dictated it a few hours earlier. Or had it been longer than that? Time seemed to pass normally everywhere except in this room. His hand shook, making his writing almost illegible, as he was very much out of practice.

The door opened, and four police officers stepped inside, accompanied by the man in the civilian clothes who had taken him from the immigration counter. Apparently, police supervisors always wore civilian clothes and kept their guns tucked in their belts. The man took the notebook from the Mullah, opened it, and pointed his finger at the end of the last page, "Sign here."

The Mullah tried to pick up the pen, but it fell on the floor, his hands were shaking so badly. He picked it up as quickly as he could and signed. His lips were like dry wood, either because he was thirsty or because he was afraid. He wasn't sure which.

The man gestured to one of his team members, who took out a pair of handcuffs and snapped at the mullah, "Stand up."

Momentarily frozen in his seat, he pointed at the handcuffs. "Those won't be necessary."

Two more cops came forward and forced him to his feet. The third turned him around roughly and slapped the handcuffs on his wrists. The Mullah repeated to himself, "There is no power except Allah Almighty. Allah is sufficient for me, and the best guide."

One man slipped a black canvas bag over his head. He felt as if the blackness covered his heart as well as his eyes. The canvas bag was filthy and thick. He inhaled deeply in an attempt to get more air, but the canvas blocked his mouth and nose. Panic rose in him, and the lack of oxygen made his heart hammer violently.

A sudden, blinding pain pierced the back of his head. His legs buckled, and he was in a free-fall, but two cops caught him and dragged him out of the room.

***

The mullah's head teetered as if he was on the brink of losing consciousness. Unbearable noises swarmed inside his head. Were they human? Were they animals? Were they Ginn from under the ground? Or angels whispering? He wanted to scream, but his throat felt strangled, and his tongue wouldn't work. He wanted to flee, but the men were dragging him like a cow to the slaughterhouse. His legs wouldn't respond properly.

They shoved him in the back seat of a car, and one climbed in on each side of him, boxing him in. Having his hands behind him caused the weight of his body to compound the pressure. The cuffs pinched his wrists so tightly the blood was trapped in his hands, which seemed as if they might explode at any second. The noise of the city around him was intolerable.

When the car stopped, the two guards yanked him out of the vehicle. Gripping his arms roughly, they hustled him along, lurching and stumbling between them. His head was still covered, but from the sudden echo of their footsteps, he deduced they had entered a building. Walking was easier now, but he couldn't guess if they were in a corridor or an open area. They descended a few steps, and he would have fallen on his face, but they grabbed his arms with iron fists and jerked him back upright. They remained on the level for a few steps, then descended another set of stairs, much longer than the previous ones. A sudden left turn at the bottom of the steps, then walking straight again. Despite the thickness of the canvas over his head, a moldy acrid smell penetrated his nose, and he felt as if he would vomit.

Finally, they stopped. A padlock clanged, then the click of a key. Rusty hinges squealed. Someone pushed him forward, and he almost fell to his knees, but was somehow able to catch himself. Then the sound of the door closing and the click of the padlock.

They hadn't removed his handcuffs, and the canvas bag still covered his head. A cold horror like nothing he'd ever experienced descended over him, due to not knowing where he was or what might be in the room with him.

He called out anxiously, "Anybody here?" but there was no response. He continued to call out again and again, louder and louder. Still no reply. He inched forward slowly and carefully, dragging his feet. Through the soles of his shoes on the ground, he could tell it was a dirt floor, like a dungeon. After only seven steps, he bumped into something cold and hard. Slowly, he turned so he could feel with his hands cuffed behind his back. It was a wall. Maintaining contact with the wall, he walked a few short steps sideways, trying to estimate the dimensions of the place. He soon discovered it was a square room; wall to wall, only 50 steps.

Leaning his back against the wall, he squatted

until his rump and hands touched the ground. As he did so, his hands plunged into something cold and slimy. He gagged with the urge to throw up, but fortunately, his stomach was empty.

He coughed and gasped for air, but the black canvas over his head prevented him from getting enough to satisfy his lungs. Using only the little strength left in his legs, he managed to stand up again, but a sharp pain wracked his left knee. He bent his head forward, hoping the black canvas would fall off, but no such luck. His head was sweating profusely, soaking the canvas, which made his mission nearly impossible. He stood still for a few seconds to regain his strength. He shook his head right and left, but still the hood stayed stubbornly in place.

Feeling dizzy, he leaned against the wall until the dizziness subsided. He repeated the same technique again and again, but the result was still no relief. Finally, he leaned against the wall again, contemplating possible ways to remove the mask.

Squatting down, he lowered his backside, keeping his knees at the same level as his head, and tried to grip the mask between his knees. Unfortunately, it was nearly impossible for his head to reach to his knees, given his stomach size, yet he tried many times until his clothes were soaked in sweat. Finally, he sat still, trying to catch his breath, which was becoming more strained by the second. He sat crossed-legged wondering whether his head could ever reach his knees, with his hands locked behind his back, sitting in this position. Zahra used to sit like this when she did her yoga workout with its strange body movements. He leaned his upper body as far forward as he could, lodging his right heel against his left knee, feeling the suffocating thickness of the canvas bag in between his heel and knee. He pulled back abruptly, but the hood remained in place. So, he tried once more, and to his great relief, the canvas slid off. He was gasping like a drowning person who had just broken the surface. His hair and beard were drenched in sweat. Gradually, as his breathing slowed, he became aware of a weird odor, a mixture of dampness, mold, and the smell of rusty metal. The room was pitch black. He leaned against the wall and started repeating a verse from chapter two in the Qur'an out loud. "Who, when faced with a disaster, say, 'Surely to Allah we belong and to Him we will return.'"

CHAPTER 8

Monday, March 15, 2010

With shriveled lips, half-closed eyes, filthy clothes, and a growling stomach, Mullah Abdullah was dragged into the interrogation room by two guards. He had no idea how long he'd been in the damp, dark cell. The interrogator sat behind a massive metal table which split the windowless rectangular room in half. One side was for the interrogator and the other for the prisoner. With half-closed eyes, he could see a mahogany brown leather bag and next to it, his mobile phone and wallet lay on the table in front of the interrogator. On the table was a voice recording machine and a video camera stood on a tripod just to his right. On the opposite side of the room was a small bench for the prisoner to sit on.

The interrogator stopped writing in his notebook and pressed a switch. An intense bright light shone from behind him, aimed directly at the mullah's face.

So far, no one insulted him, addressed him, or even spoke to him, for that matter, which added to his stress even more. He wanted desperately to know what was going on, especially the reason for this unwarranted arrest? Why had they brought him to this scary place? Not knowing was harder on him than any physical pain.

The interrogator pressed a button on the tape recorder and started asking a series of personal questions, starting from his childhood up to the present day. All the questions were derived from the life story he had written out for them. Apparently, his captives had read it carefully and selected questions that only he would know the answers to. Questions like the names of his schoolteachers, where they were from, and if he still had a relationship with any of them?

Then the interrogator asked about the university's lecturers. Of course, he still kept in contact with many of them, especially since they are well known and work in the most important mosques in Damascus. Next, the interrogator asked about the smallest details of his three years living with Sheikh Afeef after his father passed away when Mullah Abdullah was only fifteen years old. What was the reason he'd gone to live with Sheikh Hasan after Sheikh Afeef? From there, the interrogator started combing through the most personal details of his family members, one by one.... his spouse, siblings, uncles, aunts, and cousins. Then the questions were about his friends, and his other contacts; names they'd gleaned from his mobile phone's directory.

He was exhausted from trying to remember every detail connected with each contact, but he wasn't given a choice. Next, the interrogator questioned him about the contents of his wallet. Finally, he was compelled to relate his entire life story in great detail all over again. The mullah found the effort grueling and tedious to the extreme. They fetched him some water, and he regained a bit of strength to focus on what he wanted to say.

The interrogation consumed long hours until suddenly the questioner ordered the guards to return him to his cell. Once more, he begged to be told the reason for his detention.

They grabbed him under his arms, but he wrenched himself free from their grasp and threw his weight against the table with a crash. "Why am I here?" he demanded.

The interrogator jumped back, sending his chair crashing to the floor. Snatching the gun from his belt, he pointed it at the mullah's head. The two guards tackled him from behind, knocking him to the floor. One of them put a knee in the middle of the mullah's back, pinning him down. The other guard pressed his head to the floor while they waited for the interrogator's orders.

"Either shoot me, or tell me why I'm here," the mullah spluttered out of desperation. His cheek was pressed to the dirty floor, giving him a close-up view of the cracks in the old tiles. The response again was complete silence. The guards manhandled him up off the floor and hustled him out of the room, returning him to his cell. Total exhaustion overtook him, and he fell asleep the minute his head touched the filthy floor.

He was jarred awake in confused terror by a horrific smash. His heart was racing wildly, thinking he was about to receive a violent beating. His eyes searched the gloom, trying to find the source of the loud bang as he struggled to comprehend what was going on. A tall, mustached guard was standing outside the open door of the cell, holding a thick metal rod. The mullah stood up, prepared to go out with him to the interrogation room for another session. The guard gestured for him to stay where he was, so he laid back down, hoping to go back to sleep, but the guard smashed the steel rod against the bars once again. Mullah Abdullah finally understood his intentions.

Hours passed, and he wasn't allowed to sleep even for five minutes. He no longer had the energy to plead with the guard for a few minutes of sleep.

After a while, a new, younger guard replaced the first one. The new one was full of energy, and without delay, he started banging the rod with all his strength against the metal door. Something inside Mullah Abdullah shattered. He was no longer the powerful person he'd always thought he was. He didn't know how many hours had passed, or even how many days. The inky darkness surrounding him seemed to penetrate his brain, and his view of the guards became blurry. Was it the same guard banging or another replacement? Were there two guards or more? Had the guards been replaced five times, ten times, or fifteen times?

For the next interrogation session, two guards had to drag him to the interrogation room, since he could no longer walk under his own power. As they entered the room, he caught sight of a glass water jug on the table, and his throat clenched in desperation. He dashed forward to grab it, but the guards were quicker, pulling him away and dumping him on the bench with no backrest. He was unable to remain upright. He was beyond physical exhaustion. He toppled forward, but the two guards were alert and caught him before he hit the floor. The interrogator, at last, asked one of them to fetch a regular chair to support the mullah's weakened body.

This session was with the same interrogator, but this time, the questions were about the answers he had given during the previous period. Of course, they'd already done some fact checking on the information he'd provided. He cursed himself when he realized that the length of this session would be because of the extensive list of names he'd given the last time. He should have pretended he couldn't remember his teachers' names or his university lecturers.

During the session, he fainted, and a guard doused him with water to force him awake.

***

The Ministry of Endowments assigned Sheikh Omar to stand in for the imam of Shagoor mosque, known as Mullah Abdullah. When Sheikh Omar arrived, the worshippers exchanged questioning looks, which Sheikh Omar found baffling. By the second week, they started to speak with him and asked him where Mullah Abdullah was and why he hadn't returned.

Sheikh Omar didn't have an answer. He even contacted the ministry and asked if the mullah had resigned without telling anyone. Their answer was the reason for the mullah's absence was unknown, but they did say he had not submitted his resignation. Sheikh Omar went with a group of people and knocked on the door of the mullah's house to ask his wife about him.

She gave her answer from behind the closed door. "He will attend to his duties in the mosque when he returns."

Sheikh Omar and his associates assumed the mullah had to stay in Dubai for personal reasons. But after Salah disappeared with no trace, new questions arose. As the questions circulated, they expanded to include other mysteries that had no answers. Thanks to typical community gossip and conjecture, many stories spread throughout the neighborhood about the disappearance of the mullah and Salah. Soon the women were visiting from house to house, spreading stories, most of which bore no resemblance to the truth.

***

Ahmad tried to call the mullah's cell phone, but no one answered. He called the mullah's house, and eventually, after many tries, the mullah's wife answered in an odd, lifeless voice. She informed him that the mullah was still away, and she didn't know when he would return.

He called Hani, who had sent him to the mullah in the first place, to ask if he had any explanation for the mullah's disappearance. Hani didn't know anything either, but he didn't seem bothered by it. He simply told Ahmad to wait until the mullah returned from Dubai and ask him the reason for his delay. Ahmad was convinced the mullah was still in Dubai, so he stopped asking questions.

***

The portions of drinking water they gave the mullah were barely enough to keep him alive, but not a bite of food was provided. In secret, one guard slipped him two or three dates, but his stomach now felt hollowed out. The hunger pangs had been unbearable for the first few days, but after that, he suffered most from thirst. His appetite for food died away, but his thirst became an obsession. His brain was shutting down now and then. His mind took naps every few minutes, and he soon lapsed into a stupor. He fainted every two or three hours as if he had a dying battery. Every time his battery would die, a guard would come to recharge it; splashing water on his face or even slapping him to wake him. Loud bangs were no longer enough to keep him awake.

The first two days in the filthy cell, he had performed ablutions with the little water the guard had brought in a dark aluminum bowl for him to drink. Also, he would recite a few short verses from the Qur'an for prayers. Soon, however, he no longer had the energy to perform ablutions or pray five times a day. His prayers were reduced to the tiniest of gestures. Without even moving his tongue to recite canonical verses.

He stopped trying to meet Allah at every prayer time to enjoy the spiritual benediction, as was his custom. Instead, it became merely a performance of duty. As despair settled in, his bones felt heavy. He recalled how he was the one who'd always told worshippers to be patient and not despair under any circumstances. Now, this... Was he being patient enough? Could he withstand all of this in the name of Allah?

The next interrogation session was in the same room, with the same table, same tape recorders, same tripod and video camera, same flashlight, same mahogany brown leather bag, but a different interrogator. This time, there were two men wearing army uniforms. Their questions were about the mosque on Shagoor Street where he served as imam. They wanted details of his lectures, his students, and everything related to his duties there.

His eyesight was no longer reliable. It was as if he was looking through a haze. The shapes around him blurred at times. Most sounds were incomprehensible. He was beyond hunger and thirst. He had abandoned any notion of somehow getting out of this situation. He stopped counting interrogation sessions. He stopped looking at the guards' faces when they came for him, hoping one of them would say, "You are free to go..." He was almost convinced of what they wanted him to believe; that he was a disgraced individual who deserved to stay in prison.

And now he only wanted to die.

At first, this death wish was a conflict within him, especially as he battled for truth against the lies the interrogators were spinning about him. In the beginning, he planned to fight for the truth until the end. He had believed his faith was unshakable, but he now realized he'd been wrong.

His faith had collapsed at the first test Allah put before him. He knew that because of the doubts assailing him from all sides. Those doubts made his life even more miserable than what he was going through physically.

He wondered why Allah would not intervene to end these unbearable circumstances. What was the purpose and impact of all his prayers? He couldn't imagine what he had done to deserve such treatment. He had spent his life serving Allah and fulfilling the needs of His worshippers. Never a day passed without performing his prayer or reciting from the Qur'an. Never a year passed without fasting during the month of Ramadan, or dutifully paying alms. He had even gone on a pilgrimage as soon as he'd started to earn his own salary.

He had taken the task of instructing people and educating them about their faith seriously. He had advised them not to succumb to the major sins and to treat everyone with respect and dignity.

He realized that his malignant side was stronger than his immaculate side. It had been hibernating within, waiting for a rock-hard situation to awaken him and crack the wall of his faith, which had turned out to be so fragile. He believed that all humans have a dark, lethal side, and a bright, immaculate side and their duty during life's journey is to tame the dangerous side; making it smaller, locking it in a cage, and not letting it escape. They must then nurture their pure bright side and allow it to take over.

He'd discovered that the malignant side was not inside the cage he'd imagined it to be in, but was roaming free, openly mocking the righteous side of existence; waiting for the slightest opportunity to destroy what he had built over decades of devotion.

The next interrogation session was held in the same room, with three young religious men. Their attire was the same as his had been before it got dragged around on the filthy floor of the cell. He still wore his trousers and T-shirt, which had once been white, but now were dirty and baggy since he'd lost a considerable amount of weight. The men wore white turbans. Their short black beards were not as long as his. They looked to him as if they were in their thirties.

Some hope returned to his heart when he saw them. Surely they were just like him, serving Allah, and, of course, they would help him. Especially since they were much younger than he was, they must have mercy on him and help him. His tears started dripping. He covered his face with both hands and cried freely until his beard was quite wet. The three young men didn't move or talk until he broke the silence, asking in a feeble voice, "Why am I here?"

They looked at each other, and the one in the middle said, "You don't know why you are here?"

"I swear by Allah that I don't know," he said in a faint voice without the energy to even open his eyelids.

"We are from the Unit for Combating Religious Extremism in the Ministry of Endowments. The issues we are tasked with investigating are related to religious extremism and terrorism," the same man said.

"But I am not ..." He couldn't gather enough energy to complete it.

"We work in cooperation with the anti-terrorism department of the Ministry of Defense. Usually, they do not tell us the nature of the charges against the person being interrogated. If we had any details, we would not hesitate to disclose them to you," the man on the left said.

"What we can assure you is, our role in these investigations always comes in the final stage. After our meeting today, your case will be pushed forward significantly," the man in the middle said.

They started with their questions about religion that ordinary people would avoid asking, or even thinking about. Topics that people only whispered about, and even then, would look around to see if anyone was listening.

"Do you agree with the multiplicity of sects? Do you believe in the elite sect? Are you ready to change your doctrines? Why not fight for those misguided teachings? What do you think is the best method to fight? Who are the infidels? Is it mandatory to fight them? Is it permissible for Muslims to fight another group of Muslims? Do you accept the existence of Christians among Muslims? Do you consider Christians to be infidels? Should we fight them and force them to become Muslims? What do you think about Al-Qaeda in Afghanistan? Do you believe they are Muslims or infidels? Do you agree with their actions around the world? Do you believe it is our duty to fight them? Do you know if they are present in Syria? In Damascus? In Shagoor alley? If you believed them to be present, would you report them? Would you denounce any member of your family in the event he or she was involved with Al-Qaeda? Do you know anyone involved in Al-Qaeda?

After the mullah's answers were put on paper by the interrogators, the guards dragged him back to his cell.

He slumped to the floor and even before the door slammed shut, sleep came at last, a merciful void.

CHAPTER 9

Sunday, March 28, 2010

Those days of waiting and dark despair were the hardest Amani had ever lived. Sleep abandoned her at night, and worry overran her thoughts during the day. She watched the front door all day long, expecting the mullah to throw it open and walk through at any moment wearing a smile. The smallest sound startled her. She remained at home, staying away from her usual ladies' meetings. She realized the path to patience was a rocky one. Nineteen days had passed since that gloomy day at the airport, and she felt as if she'd descended into a dark pit. She didn't dare confide her sorrows to anyone. The worst part was she couldn't even explain to Zahra the reason for her father's disappearance, and Zahra, despite her anxieties and worries for her father, didn't dare ask.

On Sunday morning, the phone in the bedroom rang. Her heart nearly hammered out of her chest, as it did every time the phone rang or there was a knock at the door. She answered, and a deep demonstrative voice told her to come and take her husband home and to bring along some clean clothes, not his religious attire. Then he hung up abruptly.

Still holding the receiver, Amani started sobbing, afraid she was dreaming and would wake up to realize no one called. She looked around for Zahra to tell her the news, but realized her daughter was still at school.

The caller had only given her the name of the place. The State Security Administration. He didn't need to mention the address. When she heard the name, she shivered. The building in Fairooziah, Damascus, much like the Lubyanka in Moscow, was the backbone of security for the country. In its basements, secrets were revealed, and conspiracies were suppressed.

She took a taxi, arriving within an hour of the phone call. From the moment she gave him her destination, the taxi driver kept glancing at her in the rear-view mirror every few minutes. Upon arrival at Fairooziah Street, he didn't even wait for her to close the door properly, just sped off with a screech of tires. She didn't blame him, not many liked to be on this street.

Fairooziah Street was long and bare, with no place for anyone to hide. No trees, no advertisement signs, and no light poles. On both sides were the many buildings housing some of the highest-ranking administrators in the country. All the buildings were surrounded by high, thick concrete walls, and watched over by security guards and surveillance cameras.

She looked at the vast wall in front of her. There was no sign indicating what the building was, but she doubted if there was a citizen of the country that didn't know. Outside was a small concrete cube with a single window opening, without glass, where the guards sat. Behind the room was a black steel door for pedestrians. On the left was a massive steel gate for cars, painted black, white, and red, the colors of the Syrian Flag.

Several people were lined up in front of the window. The wrinkled clothes of some of them hinted they may have come from long distances in answer to calls just like the one she'd received, or maybe to ask about a family member who had come here but had not come out yet.

She stood in the queue, waiting her turn to register with the guard. Ahead of her was an old guy, wearing the traditional clothes of the people of Dar'a, a city to the south, most of whom were farm workers. Behind him was an old lady in full Islamic attire. Black dress, black socks, black shoes, black gloves, and a black scarf, with only her face showing. Behind her was a young woman wearing clothes like those of most of Damascus' suburban inhabitants.

The old guy had gone inside and the woman-in-black was now talking to the guards. Behind Amani was a long queue of people awaiting their turn. Why were they here? Was it because of a phone call asking them to come and retrieve their loved ones? Was it because they were looking for someone who had vanished? Was it because they were called to be interrogated themselves?

Finally, it was her turn; the guard at the desk with a large notebook, its pages newspaper-sized, demanded with an authoritative voice, "Your ID."

After he'd recorded her details in the enormous book, he pointed to a guard standing nearby and said, "Follow him."

She stared at her ID still in the guard's hands.

"You will get your ID back on your way out," the guard told her.

She followed the guard through the visitor's door, carrying the bag with the mullah's clothes. A loud voice yelled, "Stop!"

She froze, and turned her head slowly until she saw who was shouting. One guard with a Kalashnikov on his shoulder pointed at the bag she carried. She exhaled, walked the few steps back, and opened the bag. The guard searched the contents of the bag and then waved her on.

In front of her was the legendary building of the State Security Administration. It comprised three blocks of eight floors above the ground, and of course, a few floors were underground. The guard led her to a room on the first floor of block A1.

The room was empty except for two chairs and a table. On the wall hung a life-size portrait of the president. The door opened, and two men in military uniform entered, supporting a ghost-like figure between them. They lowered it onto a chair. She stepped back as if the body was contagious. He was almost naked, wearing only dirty underwear, his bones almost popping out of his filthy skin. His eyes were swollen shut, and his hair matted with dirt. She stared at the near skeleton before her, then dropped limply on a chair out of shock when she realized this was her husband.

Tears streamed down her face as she helped the corpse-like mullah into clean clothes. It was a struggle because he barely had enough strength to hold up his head. She had to stop at one point because she was choking on her sobs. When she finished, the guard ordered a taxi, and the men manhandled the mullah out to the car and shoved him in the back seat.

* * *

After his return home, the mullah appeared to be spiritless to Amani. He jumped at every little noise, and woke up shaking in the night, covered in sweat. The once overconfident, always full of joy man who had kissed her forehead and his daughter's cheek before he left for Dubai, had come back as a ghost. His smile had vanished, and he rarely spoke with her or Zahra. If he was not sleeping, he was sobbing or staring at the wall opposite the bed.

Amani took care of him as if he was a newborn. Fed him daily with lentil soup, mashed spinach, and beetroot juice, until his stomach would accept solid food again.

Although she believed he was innocent of the accusations, she too was now haunted and perplexed by his daily tragic sobbing. Was it possible he had been involved in the alleged activities? But if he was guilty, he would never have been released from prison. But why? What was the reason behind all of this misery and suffering?

If only he would confide in her as he'd always done over the years.

From the moment he'd returned to his house, dragging himself into the courtyard with Amani's support, the mullah remained in complete seclusion with her. He could not leave home because of his frailty and exhaustion, and she didn't leave the house knowing he needed her every moment, night and day.

They remained in the house like two birds confined to their nest.

***

"Your students are outside asking about you," Amani said. "Should I let them in?"

"Yes, please," the mullah said, and Amani's eyes widened in surprise. She hesitated before leaving the bedroom.

He limped his way out to the liwan, sat and watched as the four students approached. Saeed, Salem, Moneer, and Fathi. Their eyes widened in shock when they saw him.

"Welcome, my dearest ones," he said, a genuine smile on his lips. He had always been fond of his students and felt happy whenever he saw them.

They sat in the liwan after kissing him on his forehead.

"Praise Allah Almighty for bringing you back safely," Saeed said.

"I beg Allah to grant you all long and healthy lives to always serve Him on each and every religious occasion," the mullah said with a sincere hope that his beloved students could carry out their religious duties with diligence in the future.

"What happened to you, mullah? You've lost so much weight?" Fathi asked, looking puzzled.

Salem shot Fathi a warning look before the mullah had a chance to answer, and said, "You honor our alley by your very existence, mullah."

"You honor me by your visit," the mullah said, pleased by Salem's reaction. He turned and slowly adjusted the pillow behind his back as he spoke so they wouldn't see his smile.

"We felt something was missing, as you were not among us in the mosque all of this time," Moneer said.

"Soon you will see me amongst you again," the mullah said.

"Wonderful, that's great," they all said.

"Who's been leading prayers at the mosque while I'm away?" the mullah asked.

"Sheikh Omar - he is praying as imam, and conducting the Friday prayer as well," Salem said.

"We pray to Allah to grant you enough strength to come back to us and mentor us as usual. Don't get me wrong, mullah, I'm not saying Sheikh Omar is boring, or his Friday's sermon topics are shallow," Fathi said with a sly smile.

The mullah chuckled, "Allah knows how much I have missed you and missed teaching you; you are all very gifted and talented students."

"You are a talented mentor," Salem said.

Amani knocked on the kitchen door to attract their attention, and the mullah asked Fathi to fetch the tea from her. Saeed placed a small tea table in the midst of them, and Fathi put the tray on it. The tray held a teakettle, a plate of homemade cakes, and several tea glasses. Salem filled the glasses as they all looked on, watching the steam rising from them. Moneer passed out the cups, starting with the mullah himself, and everyone sipped hot tea and ate cakes.

The liwan was soon filled with laughter and excited young voices as they talked about things that had happened at the mosque during his absence. The mullah smiled, nodded, and commented from time to time. But someone was missing from this lovely gathering. A student remarkably close to his heart and soul, whose presence would have allowed him to feel fully happy.

"Why didn't Salah come with you?"

They all looked at each other but remained

silent.

"What is it? Is there a problem?" Still no response, as they avoided looking at his eyes and stared at their empty tea glasses instead. When he realized they weren't going to answer, he asked Saeed directly; the student who couldn't deny him an answer, since he believed not obeying the mullah was a sin.

"Saeed, what has happened?"

"After you left for Dubai, Salah disappeared, and no one has heard from him since," Saeed said.

Salem jumped in, "Within two days of your absence, Salah stopped coming to the mosque. We thought he was sick at first, but when he was absent for more than two days, we called his father. He told us Salah hadn't slept in the house for two nights and he was very anxious about him. When he didn't show up for four days, we went to his father's shop, and he informed us there was still no trace of Salah."

The mullah stared at the four students, hoping for more details, but received only silence.

The mullah's eyes filled with tears, his hands were trembling, and he shouted, "Amani!"

The four students looked at each other.

Amani left her room and entered the liwan covered from head to toe.

"Take me to my bedroom, please," the mullah said with a shaky voice.

Amani helped him stand up and slowly helped him into the bedroom.

As he lay on the bed, staring at the ceiling,

Mullah Abdullah knew he wasn't entirely healed yet, but he realized the time had come to leave his bed and face the world. It was time to find some answers about his arrest and Salah's disappearance.

CHAPTER 10

Thursday, April 15, 2010

"Brother Mahmoud, please be patient," Mullah Abdullah said, laying a consoling hand on Salah's father's shoulder. They were in the inner office of Mahmoud's dessert shop, named Crazy Sugar. The shop was in the traditional Hamidiyah Souq, within the walls of the old city of Damascus. The office was in the middle, with a showroom on one side and the factory on the other. The sweet aroma of traditional Arabic ghee, which is the most important ingredient to ensure the authentic flavor of Arabic dessert, assaulted the mullah's nose the minute he stepped inside the shop.

The showroom had a huge glass window, which allowed people outside to view the glistening golden trays mounded with Arabic desserts in an array of colors and trimmings. Fried vermicelli added an orange tint to the outer layer, and ground pistachios added a pale green color to the filling. The factory inside was full of skilled staff who were busily crafting the traditional delicacies.

"He just disappeared with no warning, like a pinch of salt in a glass of water. His mother and I are worried that something bad has happened to him." A fresh wave of tears caused Mahmoud to stop talking. He paused and wiped his eyes. "We've called all the police stations and all the hospitals, but no one has seen him. We put an advertisement in the local newspaper with his photo, but no one has called back with information."

Mahmoud blew his nose before continuing. "Although Salah doesn't have a passport, my cousin Fawaz, in immigration, checked the system, and there is nothing to show that he has traveled outside the country or crossed any border."

"There is no power but from Allah," the mullah said, as he searched for words to express his concern and console his friend. "Did you try asking his friends if they have heard anything or have any idea where he could be? These days, the younger generation prefer to tell their friends their secrets rather than to say anything that might upset their parents."

"As far as I know, all of Salah's friends are your students. I talked to them, but they don't have a clue. They even helped me call all the hospitals."

"Has Salah ever stayed out late, or slept over elsewhere before?"

The phone rang, and Mahmoud answered it after excusing himself. It was a client wanting to place a large order, so while he waited, the mullah cast his gaze out through the showroom door. Tourists and locals thronged the market, walking up and down along both sides. Hamidiyah Souq is one of the most ancient shopping streets in the world, within the old walled city, next to the Citadel of Damascus. The two parallel rows of shops are less than 500 meters long. The distance between the two rows of shops is less than ten meters wide. Hundreds of stores, from fabric and clothing shops to perfume and spice shops, added to the market's unique aroma.

The market is covered by a curved metal ceiling, supported by hundreds of ornate iron arches, beginning at Thowra Street and ending just before the Umayyad Mosque. The ornate iron has turned black from the elements after all this time. The curved ceiling has hundreds of scattered holes from bullets fired during the revolution at the time of the French occupation. In the daytime, beams of sunlight trace the ground with random spotlights from the holes.

Mahmoud finished speaking and put down the receiver. "Mullah, I'm so sorry I haven't served you any drinks." He rose without waiting for a response and disappeared into the factory. Soon he was back with a plate of freshly made desserts, gleaming with syrup, in one hand, and a fancy box bearing his shop's colorful logo in the other. He handed the box to the mullah. "This is for your family." He put the plate on the desk in front of the mullah.

"Thank you, brother. You don't need to burden yourself at such a difficult time." The mullah was embarrassed by Mahmoud's generosity.

"On the contrary, mullah. You have honored my shop by your visit. Every time I look at Salah and see how well-mannered he is, and so well-tutored in the Qur'an, I remember you, his great mentor. I am grateful to Allah for the man he is becoming," Mahmoud said.

The mullah's cheeks were hot. "He is the most enthusiastic and active among my students." He couldn't keep himself from smiling every time he thought of Salah. "He has a bright future waiting for him in the faith and service to humanity. His colleagues love him without reservation. Almost all the worshippers who attend prayers know him. He is the first to open the mosque doors and summon everyone to prayer. His voice combines his seriousness with warm sympathy. His litanies on the loudspeaker before prayers are so touching that neighbors have mentioned shedding tears upon hearing him."

Mahmoud's eyes glistened with fresh tears.

"You have brought Salah up with excellent manners and the noblest of ethics. I will beg Allah to return him to you safely, and that he will regain the honor of serving you and his mother."

Mahmoud picked up a napkin, blew his nose, then picked up the phone and informed his wife that the mullah would be his guest at dinner.

The mullah tried to object, "No please, I have to perform the Isha prayer at the mosque."

"No problem. I'll go with you to the mosque, then after the prayer, we'll go together to my house. My wife prepares irresistible foods. You will lick your fingers or maybe even eat your fingers afterward," Mahmoud said with a grin.

"No, please, I need my fingers," the mullah said. Both laughed and reached for a delicate piece of baklava at the same time.

***

By the time they left the shop, Hamidiyah Souq was aglow with light from dozens of electric lanterns hanging from each stone pillar separating one store from another. The Souq was packed, so it was slow going amid the throngs of pedestrians. The two men were continually forced to stop and wait for others ahead of them to move forward.

The ground was paved with ancient stones, worn smooth by millions of feet over the centuries. The chattering of the crowd was deafening, echoing beneath the curved metal ceiling. Now and then, loud shouts when a vendor hawking his wares would add his voice to the din, only to run away if the police arrived. Selling on the street was not permitted because of the crowds and unfair competition with the shops. After the quietness while recovering in his home, Mullah Abdullah felt as if the continual din was piercing his skull.

When they finally reached the end of Hamidiyah Souq, the vast area beneath the sky dome facing the main gate of the Grand Umayyad Mosque was less crowded and much quieter. The massive stone wall had always fascinated him. He loved to walk beside this giant wall as if he could derive spiritual energy from it.

Old Damascus was like a poem, and every narrow alley a line from its stanzas. When they reached the beginning of Shagoor Street, the melodic sound of the call to prayer erupted in the air. The mullah tucked his hand under his friend's elbow, and the two walked a little faster. He didn't like keeping people waiting for him at the mosque. Upon reaching the mosque, he went straight ahead to perform his ablution, then entered the prayer area, and the entire congregation stood to show their respect as he greeted them. He immediately focused his attention on the mihrab (niche) and led the prayer session.

***

It was not the first time Mullah Abdullah had visited Mahmoud's home, so he was not surprised that the air was redolent with the smells of bread and sweets wafting through the house. It was a typical old house among the famous houses of old Damascus, just a ten-minute walk from the mullah's home through a web of narrow alleys. Despite the house's age, it was in excellent condition. The walls and floor were covered with expensive Italian marble; the artistic tinted window-glass seemed more appropriate to a museum. The chairs were luxurious, made of exotic woods, decorated with shells, and covered with silk cushions.

The liwan was three times bigger than the liwan at the mullah's house. On the wall hung black-and-white portraits of Mahmoud's ancestors. In the middle, an enormous round table was covered with steaming plates. Intestines stuffed with spiced rice and beef, grape leaves filled with rice and lamb, plus Koba, hummus, beef soup, green salad, tabbouleh, and fresh-squeezed orange juice. The aroma of the food alone was enough to classify it as a work of art. The unmistakable smell of goat's intestines filled with rice and roasted almonds, the fresh scent of cucumber, the rich aroma of beef, and the fruity fragrance of expensive olive oil made Mullah Abdullah's mouth water.

After dinner, Mahmoud's wife brought out a sumptuous baklava, hot tea, and a couple of hookahs. Both inhaled the smoke and exhaled, filling the air above their heads with apple-scented smoke as it ascended slowly into the dark sky.

"Mullah, please forgive me, but I have been so preoccupied with Salah's disappearance and I neglected to ask you about your trip. What caused you to become so thin?"

Mullah Abdullah was quiet momentarily, searching for an answer that wouldn't reveal what had happened without lying. He believed one of the biggest sins in this life was to lie. "My dear brother, only Allah knows the unknown future. Every one of us goes to sleep each night and doesn't know if he will ..."

His new mobile phone started ringing. Embarrassed by the interruption at this late hour, he excused himself, and holding his phone out to the full length of his arm, he squinted at the screen, trying to see who was calling. A broad smile spread across his face as he recognized his home phone number.

It was his wife telling him she was going to bed and would leave his dinner in the kitchen. He quickly told her he'd had his dinner already, and there was no need to save any for him. He calmly switched off the mobile phone and put it back in his inner pocket.

"Have you tried searching Salah's room? Maybe he left a message or a sign that would give us something to go on?" the mullah said, changing the topic.

"His mother cleaned his room but didn't find anything," Mahmoud said. Then he added with an air of intrigue, "Would you like to take a look? Maybe you would notice something we didn't."

"Sure. Why not?"

As they rose, Mahmoud pointed to the stairway. "Salah's room is upstairs on the right."

As they arrived at the closed door to Salah's room, the mullah looked down at the open liwan. He glanced at the black-and-white photo of one of

Mahmoud's ancestors and felt as if the steely gaze had been piercing his back during dinner, and even now, was staring directly at him. He turned and followed Mahmoud into the room.

The room was dark and smelled of detergent. Mahmoud brushed his palm against the wall beside the door like a blind person searching for the light switch. He pressed all the buttons he could find, and a light flickered a few times before staying lit. The ceiling fan began to spin, and a red bulb lit up the doorway. He switched off the fan and the lamp.

A single bed pushed against the right wall was covered with a white sheet. A small table beside the bed held several books. The gold lettering on the covers evidence they were religious books. To the left of the table was a cupboard covered with posters of soccer players. Against the left wall was a chair and a small reading table with several books on it and a reading light. To the left of the door was a mirror over an ornate bureau. A Persian carpet covered the floor.

The well-furnished room gave a feeling of familiar comfort. It reminded him of his own room when he had been a single student. He'd spent all his time studying religion in the room his mentor, Sheikh Hasan, had rented to him. Unlike his friend Mahmoud, Mullah Abdullah knew exactly where to start. He began by opening each of the books on the reading table, searching for letters or notes between the pages. Mahmoud started right in following his example. Several minutes passed, with nothing but the sound of pages flipping.

They heard a feminine voice calling Mahmoud's name, so he immediately placed the book he was holding on the table and went to find out why his wife was calling him. The mullah didn't listen in on the ensuing discussion, but he assumed Mahmoud's wife needed him for something because he went all the way down the stairs. After the mullah finished with the books on the table, he moved to the pile of books beside the bed, opening one after another. He noticed the books were not the books he taught his students from at the mosque. He read the title of one and was taken aback; Almisbar Fi Jihad Alkuffar.

He had always taught his students that the biggest jihad is the jihad inside each person to prevent oneself from committing sins. He had never taught students about the lesser jihad, which refers to physical warfare. Confused, he put the book down and picked up another and another, scanning the names of the authors and the titles.

'AL-Jihad Dictionary'

'AL-Jihad Fi Sabeel Allah' (AL Jihad in the Path of Allah)

'A'edo Ma Istata'tum Min Quah' (Prepare as Much as You Can in Terms of Strength)

'Al-Jihad Hu Altareek Alaqrab Ela Allah' (Jihad is the Shortest Path to Allah)

'Alradd Al-Amthal Le Monker AL-Jihad Alahwal' (The Proper Reply to the Blind People Who Reject Physical Jihad)

'Al-Asha'o Alakheer M'a Rasool Alazeez Alqadeer' (The Last Dinner With the Prophet of Allah Almighty)

'Jihad Almustakbreen' (The Jihad of Arrogance)

He put down the last book and went back to the regular reading table to check the titles, which all turned out to be ordinary religious books. He continued his search, trying to avoid thinking about the weird titles he'd seen. He didn't want to jump to the one conclusion he feared the most. A few minutes passed while he searched the rest of the room, but he could barely concentrate.

He went back to the books beside the bed and picked up the first one again and opened the back cover to read the index. He did the same with all the books. He noticed some books had particular topics underlined. He was still perusing the books when Mahmoud appeared in the doorway.

The mullah looked at his watch and gasped when he realized it was past midnight.

"Anything useful?" Mahmoud asked.

"Not really," the mullah answered without looking at Mahmoud's eyes, "I really must go home. It's getting late."

They descended the stairs together, and when they reached the front door, he asked, "Except for Salah, has anyone else been in his room besides you and your wife?"

"I am not sure I'm the best one to answer that question since I am out of the house most of the time. As far as I know, whenever Salah's friends came over, they sat in the liwan. Why do you ask?"

"Nothing significant, I hope. I found a few books which we don't teach at the mosque, and I wondered what sort of friends would bring him such books. Anyway, a warm goodnight and please convey my regards to your wife and thank her on my behalf for the fabulous dinner."

***

After midnight, the narrow alleys of old Damascus were deserted except for stray cats wandering and digging through the rubbish looking for food. His footfalls echoed between the walls of the empty alleys. He tried to walk quietly, but it was difficult because of the varying sizes of the cobblestones. If the people who had walked on these ancient stones over the centuries were still alive, some of them would be over a thousand years old now. *A person should feel guilty when stepping on such ground.* He enjoyed walking in the alleys of old Damascus. He loved the look of the walls, covered in white limestone and black basalt. The jasmine trees behind the walls filled the air with their heavenly scent.

A bicycle whizzed past, the rider calling out a greeting. He turned to see who had just greeted him, but the bike had already disappeared around the corner. It could have been one of the men who usually attends the mosque, or it might have been one of his students. He turned to continue walking, but then he froze in his tracks. He turned again to look back, but no one was there. He thought he saw a silhouette of someone standing at the end of the street looking at him. He started walking again, whispering to himself, "I seek refuge with Allah from the accursed Satan." The hair on the back of his neck stood up as if invisible eyes were drilling into his back. He stopped suddenly, snapping his head around quickly, but no one was there. He waited, heart thumping, peering down the street, scarcely daring to breathe.

An inner voice screamed at him, nagging him to 'get out of there, now!', but he ignored it and continued trudging slowly, carefully, making as little sound as possible. Ahead, a room built over the alley connected two houses on opposite sides, forming a short tunnel. The tunnel was shrouded in darkness because someone had blown out the light. His heart raced as he walked under the arches, almost tripping in the small, dark space.

He walked on, trying to resist the urge to look back. Alert for any voice or sound. He still expected to hear someone following him, but there was nothing. Once again, he turned quickly, hoping to catch someone trying to hide or throw themselves on the ground, but still nothing. He quickened his pace without looking back anymore, but after twenty meters, he heard someone running. He spun around, staring wildly. There was no one in the light, but he thought he could see something or someone skulking back in the dark tunnel. He shielded his eyes from the bright light over his head with his hand and focused his gaze into that dark space.

He was tempted to walk back towards the tunnel for a closer look, but stopped himself. What if his pursuer had a weapon? He turned and continued toward home. When he reached the T-junction where he would normally turn right to go to his house, he had a quick thought that he should go left instead. Then, at the last second, he changed his mind and turned right.

He walked briskly for a few steps, then pulled up in a patch of shadows, waiting for his pursuer to appear. A chill went through his body from the enormity of the silence. What's the point of waiting? He didn't want to fight with anyone. What if the guy was stronger than him and decided to kill him? His wife would be a widow, and his daughter an orphan.

He sprinted toward home. Reaching his front door, he inserted his key and gave the door a shove, causing it to slam into the wall with a loud bang. He entered and slammed the door shut behind him, causing a bang much louder than the first. For sure, his neighbors would be awake now and peering at him from behind their curtains. He leaned back against the door, resting his head on it, and let out a huge breath of relief.

CHAPTER 11

Monday, April 19, 2010

Ahmad gasped when he saw the mullah. It was as if the man had aged ten years in less than two months and he was shockingly skinny. He decided not to pry into the mullah's private life, so he wouldn't ask him what happened or why he had been detained in Dubai, if he really was in Dubai. Now he sat in the mosque waiting for the mullah to finish his prayers.

Ahmed stood up as the mullah slipped his prayer beads back in his pocket and placed his fez on his head in preparation to leave. He hurried forward to greet the mullah.

"Hi, brother, you came at the right time," the mullah said.

Ahmed avoided looking directly at the mullah, fearing he would recognize the pity in his eyes. "I'm hoping you have good news for me."

The mullah glanced around before he spoke. "I met Mazen in Dubai. He says he doesn't remember any debt between the two of you. If you have any documents of proof, he will be more than happy to help you."

Ahmed was annoyed, but he suppressed his emotions and said, "As I expected, but as I told you the first time we met, I have only a handwritten paper with no witnesses."

"Can you give me a copy of that paper?" asked the mullah. "I will also go to Haj Adel's shop to talk with him regarding the matter. Maybe he can help his son remember his debt."

"Ok, I will give you a copy, but I am not here regarding that matter. I'm here because Zakiya is in the hospital."

"Zakiya?"

"Zakiya, my niece, Mazen's daughter," Ahmad said.

The mullah gasped. "What happened to her?"

"Their neighbor, Um-Saleem, calls my wife from time to time to keep her up to date with news of the girls, especially since Hadiya passed away. This morning, she called my wife and informed her that the girls went to the hospital because one of them was sick."

"Let us go outside." The mullah adjusted his fez, pulled on his cloak, and walked out, with

Ahmad following closely behind him.

Ahmad watched the mullah's hand shaking while trying to insert the key to lock the door of the mosque. He resisted the urge to ask the mullah what happened to him while he was away.

The mullah grabbed Ahmad by the arm and yanked him out of the path of a speeding bicycle being pedaled furiously by a teenager. He yelled at the retreating bike, "May Allah guide you," but the teenager was already too far away to hear him.

Ahmad thanked the mullah and resumed the conversation. "They took her to the City Hospital. I went as quickly as I could to catch them there, but when I reached the hospital, the girls had already left. A nurse told me Zakiya had been admitted. I met with the doctor who had examined her and told him I was her uncle.

"The doctor told me there were marks of physical torture on her body and that he had already called the police to investigate."

"My great Lord! Torture! Are you sure?" The mullah stopped walking.

"At first I doubted the doctor." They proceeded walking again. "I wondered whether he was telling the truth or perhaps exaggerating. I insisted on seeing her with my own eyes. He took me to the ward where she was lying and uncovered her back. There were a lot of marks. Both old scars and new wounds." Ahmad choked back his tears and proceeded, "But that was not the reason they took her to the hospital."

"Allah is the greatest. What was the reason then?! What could have landed her in the hospital that's more serious than physical abuse?"

"She has an infection in one ear and possibly internal bleeding," Ahmad said. "There is a yellow discharge coming out of her ear. After examining her, the doctor says the infection was not new, and they should have brought her to the hospital much sooner. The doctor informed me there is a high probability she won't be able to hear with that ear anymore." Choking back more tears, he bent his head and stood in silence for a moment.

With the mullah's encouragement, Ahmed continued. "I asked the doctor if Zakiya told him how she got those terrible marks and the ear injury. He said the only answer she gave him was, 'Either you stop the pain or kill me right now!"

"Were you able to speak with her and ask the reasons for all of this?" the mullah asked.

"She was sedated. The doctor turned her over to uncover her back, but she didn't wake up the whole time I was there."

"My heart aches for Hadiya's children. But what can I do to help? Do you think we have to wait for the police report?" The mullah asked.

"I would like you to go with me to the hospital."

"When?"

"Right now, if possible."

The mullah checked his watch and said, "Okay, let me call my wife to let her know where I'll be."

***

The mullah admired Ahmed's BMW, but he couldn't help comparing it to Mazen's much newer Bentley in Dubai. They reached the hospital in twenty minutes, but it took Ahmed thirty minutes just to find a spot to park.

The City Hospital is on a busy road which connects two vital areas of Damascus city: Bab-Mussalla and Kafarsousah. Even though the noise and air pollution are at the highest levels, in an overpopulated city like Damascus, there was no choice but to keep the hospital where it was. Thousands of patients, relatives, hospital staff and visitors come in and out of this large public hospital daily. The emergency room's eight beds are constantly busy. The place hums like a beehive throughout the day. People can enter the hospital either through the emergency room or through an external gate.

The pair stopped at the external gate in front of a security guard, who was taking the details of each visitor. When their turn came, they handed over their IDs.

"What are you here for?" the guard asked.

"To visit my niece," Ahmad said.

"Where was she admitted?"

"I am not sure which department. I was here this morning. I met with a Dr. Raed."

"Ok, you will find him in the ENT department. You take the corridor to the right of the reception area and the ENT will be the second turn on the left."

Their nasal passages were assaulted by the strong odor of disinfectant, sweat, blood, and urine. They arrived at the ENT department, which was only a room with a desk for the doctor and a bed. Ahmad pointed to the doctor inside the room and said, "Dr. Raed."

The bald doctor in a white coat was looking through an otoscope into the ear of a young boy lying on the bed. Around them, four younger doctors carrying notebooks were obviously observing. The mullah assumed they were students in their final year at the university.

Dr. Raed noticed their presence and nodded for them to wait until he'd finished what he was doing.

When he had completed his exam, he stepped out into the hallway to talk. "She is doing well."

"That is great to hear, but do you know how she got the infection in her ear?" Ahmad asked.

"It could have been caused by a severe blow to the side of the head," Dr. Raed said.

"Allah is the greatest," the mullah said. "So, you think someone hit her?"

"I can't be entirely sure. Maybe someone hit her, or maybe she fell very hard on that ear."

"What exactly is the extent of her problem?" the mullah asked.

"She initially had a middle ear infection, which was left untreated for several days. Then, the infection spread from the middle ear to the brain. Unfortunately, she has developed bacterial meningitis. She was brought to the hospital by her sisters because she had a high fever, which led to a seizure and subsequent loss of consciousness."

"Almighty Allah," the mullah said.

"We did a CT brain scan, took blood samples and a lumbar puncture, gave her IV drips, and started her on a course of antibiotics. She is responding well, and we thank Allah they didn't wait one more day to bring her to the hospital. She is critically ill, but it could have been far worse."

"Have the police been here yet?" Ahmad asked.

"Yes, two police officers from the Fifth Territory Police Station came and wrote a report. They asked if there was anyone from the patient's family to sign it. When they didn't find anyone, they left." He turned to go back into the room. "I am sorry. I am busy. I can't spend any more time with you today. I will have my nurse, Areej, show you the way to Zakiya's ward." He looked around just as a nurse arrived wearing very heavy makeup. "Areej, please show these gentlemen to the female ward." Then he went into the room, closing the door behind him.

Areej's green nurse's uniform struggled valiantly to contain her generous proportions. Her gleaming white rubber-soled shoes squeaked on the floor tiles. They followed her along a depressing green corridor with peeling paint. The cheap white floor tiles were worn thin because of thousands of feet pounding on them daily. Long fluorescent light fixtures dangled from the ceiling.

The corridors were crowded with patients, doctors, nurses, and visitors. Hospital beds were scattered here and there in the corridors, some with patients sleeping on them, some empty.

Thousands of patients walked through these halls with a diverse range of aches and pains. Almost as many aches and pains as the multiplicity of germs and bacteria. The hallways seemed to hold within them the sorrow of all the patients and their families over the years.

Mullah Abdullah's palms were clammy, and his heart racing. As they followed the nurse, he wanted to go faster, assuming he would feel better once they reached Zakiya's ward, but that soon proved to be wrong.

They entered the ward after Areej warned the women within that were male visitors coming on the floor. The open ward held eight beds with nothing separating them. Zakiya's condition was not too bad compared to some of the other female patients who were hooked to ventilator machines and cardiac monitors with their accompanying beeping sounds. Beside each bed sat a woman, who might be the patient's mother, their faces pale from staying awake all night looking after their daughters. Their lives were filled with endless waiting and anticipation, not knowing whether their patient would wake in the morning or remain asleep forever.

They passed by the occupied beds to get to Zakiya's bed. It was the first time the mullah had set eyes on any of Hadiya's daughters. Zakiya's face was as pale as ivory, unlike his own daughter Zahra, whose cheeks were always pink. She wore a white headscarf over her bandaged ear and appeared to be exhausted. Even though her tiny body was covered by a white cotton sheet, she seemed to be only half the size of Zahra, even though they were almost the same age.

Zakiya pulled herself into a sitting position as she saw them approaching. Her hospital gown hung down in front, exposing a dark red line on one side of her neck. There were no chairs available, so they remained standing. They both greeted her warmly, and she replied in a weak voice.

Then an awkward silence fell. Everyone in the ward was watching them covertly, of course, listening carefully for anything that might be said. The mullah glanced at Ahmad with a 'what-are-you-waiting-for' look.

Ahmad sat on the end of the bed, placing a hand on Zakiya's covered foot. "The doctor says you've had an ear infection for some time. Why did you wait so long to come to the hospital? You could have called me. I would have gladly brought you to the hospital. You should not have been in such pain all this time."

Zakiya didn't answer, only stared at him.

Ahmad stood up, moved closer, and spoke a

little louder, "The doctor said your ear--"

Zakiya interrupted him, "I heard you the first time."

"Whenever there is an emergency like this, call me from your neighbor, Um-Saleem's telephone. She won't mind helping you."

Finally, Zakiya spoke. "Where were you when my sister Ro'wa fainted before my mom died? Where were you when my mom was so desperate for someone to help her?"

"My dear Zakiya, your uncle is ready to take your parents' place in their absence. He is ready to sacrifice his life for you and your sisters. If I had an uncle like him, I would thank Allah day and night," the mullah told her.

Zakiya looked at him with disdain. "Where was Allah when I needed Him?"

Everyone in the ward gasped, and murmuring arose, "We seek the forgiveness of the mighty Allah," the mullah said.

He leaned against the wall and closed his eyes. Zakiya's words were extremely dangerous. It was the first time he had ever heard anyone dare to utter such blasphemy. He was speechless. What to do and what to say at such a moment? It was an extremely awkward situation. He wouldn't have been surprised if fire erupted from the sky and burned this room with everything and everyone in it at any moment. Was there really a person alive who didn't believe in the existence of Allah? He shook his head, dismissing any such idea. Even thinking about it felt like a big sin.

"If Allah existed, how could he allow us to live such a life?" Zakiya said, sobbing.

"What's wrong with your life? You have food to eat while people are dying of starvation. You have a house to live in while some people don't have a roof to sleep under. You have clothes, while others have only rags to cover their bodies. Why do we look at what we don't have and neglect to appreciate what Allah has granted us?" the mullah asked.

Zakiya was provoked. "I will show you what is wrong with my life." she turned sideways and pulled her shirt up to expose her back, now sobbing miserably.

The mullah turned his face away so as not to see her back, since it is forbidden for men to look at a naked female body except for one's wife. But he was not quick enough, and the horrible image of her wounds and scars became imprinted in his mind.

Crisscross lines beginning across her shoulders and stretching down across her back; dark red welts, and dark blue bruises. The variety of colors seemed to represent the various times she'd been tortured. At the end of each red line was an open wound, probably caused by a belt buckle. More recent injuries were covered with bandages and gauze pads, which shifted a little as she moved, exposing the rawness of the wounds beneath. No part of her back remained the natural ivory color of her skin.

"I seek forgiveness from the Almighty Allah. I beg Allah to forgive you and guide you, daughter Zakiya," the mullah said.

"If Allah exists, I beg him to take my life and give me relief from my suffering." She raised her voice. "Now leave me alone!" She pulled the cotton bed sheet up to cover her head, but her wailing could be heard throughout the ward.

"There is no power but from Almighty Allah. There is no power but from Almighty Allah." The mullah was mumbling to himself, as if to regain his composure.

"My dear Zakiya ..." Ahmad started.

"Leave me alone!!" she screamed from under the cover.

One mother stood up then and shouted at the men, "Please, just leave." She, too, was crying.

They both left the ward, shaken and speechless.

***

The traffic at that time of day was unbearable. The students had been dismissed from school and the government workers left their offices around 2 pm. The air conditioner in Ahmad's BMW worked well to keep them both cool for many long minutes in stop-and-go traffic.

"What was the story of Ro'wa?" the mullah asked.

The blood in Ahmad's veins was boiling, as he remembered the incident clearly. "Ro'wa had been diagnosed with a blood disorder. Thrombocytopenia. She had been bleeding intermittently until she'd lost so much blood, she resembled a ghost. After many days of suffering, she fainted, and her mother thought she was near death and needed to go to the hospital. The trouble was, they didn't have a telephone. Hadiya and her three daughters went out, running from house to house like crazy people, trying to find someone with a car to take Ro'wa to the hospital. At the same time, Khaled was hobbling around without his crutches. He went in terror to his uncle's house, a brother of Mazen. His uncle kicked him out saying he was too busy, so Khaled went back crying. The rejections by so many people hurt Hadiya more than Ro'wa's medical condition."

"There is no power but from Allah," the mullah repeated.

"What Zakiya didn't understand was that Mazen treated everyone in Hadiya's family deplorably. That's why all of us were keeping clear of her, so as not to cause her additional problems. Mazen's brother and father were continually avoiding their responsibilities. As a result, Hadiya was compelled to face all the obstacles on her own, without a man to stand up for her and protect her."

"What a lady," the mullah said. "She will surely be rewarded in the hereafter."

Ahmad dropped the mullah as close to his home as he could get with the car, promising to return for him in two hours after he'd had lunch with his family.

By 4 o'clock, he was back, and they headed to the police station. It took only fifteen minutes to drive from the mullah's house to the Fifth Territory Police Station. The two-story building, surrounded by a high fence, was in a residential area where all the surrounding buildings were five stories high. There was a slogan over the main entrance: 'The police are in the service of the people'.

A set of stairs at the end of a hallway led to the second floor. A door on the right opened into a room with several police officers sitting behind worn desks, drinking tea and chatting. Their weapons were either handguns holstered at their waists or dangerous-looking Kalashnikovs laying on tables or hanging on the wall. To the left, another door led to a corridor.

"How can I help you today?" a burly, middle-aged officer asked them.

"Someone in this department wrote a report about my niece Zakiya in the City hospital," Ahmad said.

The police officer gestured silently to the door to the corridor and went back to his conversation.

Ahmad glanced at the mullah as they walked up the corridor towards another room they could see at the end. Something seemed wrong with the mullah. His face had gone pale as if he'd entered a graveyard, rather than a police station. *Is it possible he has a phobia, or does he have a secret of his own?*

What is he hiding? Does he feel guilty about being in a place like this?

They entered a small room at the end of the corridor. Old, worn leather sofas lined the walls. A police officer sat at a desk busily writing in an enormous book. On the wall behind him was a large, framed photo of the president, Bashar Assad. A small plaque on the table had the name Lieutenant Hamad Alwasat engraved on it. Without getting up or even looking up at them, the man asked, "What can I do for you?"

"We are here regarding a report for …" Ahmad said.

The lieutenant interrupted him. "Under whose name?"

"Zakiya Mis'ed. Her mother was Hadiya Kishat," Ahmad said.

The lieutenant stopped his scribbling, examined him for a moment, and asked, "Are you her father?"

"No, I am her uncle."

"Aren't we all her uncles?" the lieutenant declared in a sarcastic tone.

He was irritated, but he hid it well. "I am her maternal uncle, her mother's brother. I am Ahmad Kishat."

"I am honored to meet you," the lieutenant said evenly. "The report has been signed off on, the case is closed, and it has already been sent to be archived."

"With no investigation?" Ahmad asked.

"Investigation of what? A young girl is in the hospital. What is there to investigate?" the lieutenant asked.

His face was heating up, yet he controlled his temper and said in a calm voice, "Did you see or examine the girl with your own eyes?"

"Can't you see I'm busy? There is nothing I can do for you. As I said, the report has been signed off on. Please be on your way."

"Did you see the girl with your own eyes?" Ahmad demanded.

The lieutenant leaped to his feet despite his bulk, causing his chair to crash to the floor. "You will not raise your voice to me. Get out, now."

"I won't leave this place until I see the report," Ahmad barked.

The lieutenant stepped from behind the desk, walked to the open door, and shouted, "Guys, come in here!"

The mullah whispered in Ahmad's ear, "Let's get out of here."

He ignored the mullah's suggestion and roared, "I will not leave until I see the report."

Moments later, the room was swarming with police officers. The lieutenant stood by his desk, pointing at Ahmad, and demanded, "Throw this animal out."

Blind with rage, Ahmad yelled, "You're the real animal here!" He darted forward, intending to attack the lieutenant. Another policeman grabbed him by the shoulder, spinning him around. He resisted and tried to push the police officer off him, but the officer kept a tight grip, tearing Ahmad's shirt. He raised a fist to punch the policeman in the face, but the mullah quickly leaped in and blocked Ahmad's blow before it found its mark.

In one continuous motion, the policeman shoved the mullah aside and punched Ahmad in the mouth.

Ahmad's upper lip spurted blood. He saw stars in front of his eyes. The room was spinning, and like a comical superhero, he swung his fist and struck the policeman with all his might. The policeman screamed in pain. Another policeman grabbed Ahmad from behind and yet another kicked him in the gut, throwing him to the floor. The policeman sat on his chest, punching him with all his strength.

Ahmad landed another blow, causing the policeman to yell, "Come and hold this pig's hands!" Two of his colleagues knelt on Ahmad's hands, pinning them to the floor. The policeman started slapping his face again.

"Please stop," the mullah shouted, but his voice was lost in the commotion.

Ahmad was barely maintaining consciousness on the floor when a voice in the doorway screamed, "Atteeeeention!"

Ahmad looked up, and all the police officers jumped to attention, even the lieutenant. A senior officer wearing an elegant uniform festooned with rows of stars and birds stood in the doorway, demanding, "What in hell is going on here?"

"Sir, he raised his voice at me." The lieutenant stood stiffly at attention with his eyes fixed straight ahead, pointing at Ahmad on the floor.

The senior officer looked at Ahmad. "What is it you want, my son?" he asked, his voice calm.

A police officer interjected, "Sir, he wants to ... "

The officer quickly snapped, "I didn't ask you. I asked him." He glared at all the police officers, still standing at attention. "All of you, return to your duties immediately." Then he pointed at Ahmad and the mullah. "Bring them to my office."

***

The senior officer's office was a large one, with an immense window overlooking the neighboring buildings. It contained a grand mahogany desk and four matching chairs, with a small glass tea table in the middle. The far wall featured enormous portraits of the president, Bashar Assad.

"Please come in," the officer said when Ahmad and the mullah appeared in the doorway.

"I am Abdullah Al-Allab. People call me mullah in our alley, and this is Mr. Ahmad Kishat."

"I know who you are. You are well-known, mullah. I am general Zafer Abyad."

"May Allah bless you," the mullah said.

Ahmad was not entirely comfortable with what he saw as the general's feigned kindness and questionable hospitality.

He looked to be in his seventies. His hair was

all white. His movements showed he was athletic. His proud demeanor implied he was probably pretty full of himself. He exuded overconfidence, which was probably a sign that he had sacrificed a lot in his life to become a general.

Beneath the clean sheet of glass covering the general's desk were many photographs of varied sizes and different ages. Some were in color while some were in black and white. It was apparent that the photos summarized the general's accomplishments.

A gold nameplate on the desk was engraved with General Zafer Abyad. On one side of the nameplate stood a tiny Syrian flag, and on the other side, the Arab Socialist Ba'ath party flag.

The office boy came in with hot tea, serving the general first, then Ahmad and the mullah.

The general regarded them thoughtfully as he sipped his tea, then he placed the cup back on the saucer. "I apologize for the behavior of my officers. They are always very enthusiastic in their law enforcement efforts. Unfortunately, they can't always curb their tempers when someone raises their voice at them." He chuckled to himself before proceeding, "Why exactly are you here?"

"My niece is in the hospital and the doctor who examined her told me she has unmistakable marks of torture on her back. Upon discovering that, he called the police to investigate and find out what exactly was going on with her. The doctor asked us to come here to sign the report."

"It is indeed a necessary procedure," the general said.

"And that's why we are here," Ahmad said.

"So, what is the problem?" the general asked.

"They told me someone else has already signed the report," Ahmad said.

"Still, I don't see any problem with that," the general said, peering more closely at him. "Maybe one of her parents signed the report."

The mullah jumped in then, "The girl's mother is dead, and her father lives outside the country."

The general called his assistant and asked him to fetch the report, then he looked seriously at Ahmad, "So all the commotion was because you were not the one who signed the report?"

Again, the mullah answered on his behalf, "He asked the gentleman downstairs to show him the report, but he refused to do so."

The assistant entered the room and handed the report to the general. The general grabbed it, but before reading it, looked at the mullah. "Our precious country has a lot of enemies. We must keep our eyes wide open day and night, and not give them any chance to destroy it. There is nothing more precious than our land, and we must sacrifice our souls, our blood, our bodies, our families, and our money to keep it safe. Don't you agree?"

"Yes, of course." The mullah swallowed.

The general peered at the report and said,

"The one who signed this report was ... a member of her family." He handed the report to Ahmad.

"Who is this member of the family?" he said aloud, but more to himself than the others in the room. He snatched the paper from the general's hand, looking immediately at the bottom of the page.

"Haj Adel," Ahmad said and looked at the mullah, then read the report, his eyes scanning the script as if he was solving a puzzle. Finally, he raised his head, muttering to himself. "How weird is this? Doctor Raed told us he called the police, and that he would never have called them without a valid reason."

Passing the report to the mullah, he said, "In this report, the doctor says the girl suffered from a minor infection of her middle ear, and the injuries found on her back were prenatal or from birth." The mullah's left leg was trembling while he scanned the paper.

"Sometimes doctors make mistakes," the general said.

"General, you wouldn't need to be a doctor to conclude the girl had been tortured if you saw her back," Ahmad said.

"As you know, in our line of work, we rely on the opinion of experts; we don't act according to our emotions or our personal beliefs," the general said, his voice firm.

Ahmad heard the general's words as no more than blah blah blah. He was not convinced in the least, but he was also sure there was little point in arguing. He gave the mullah a look, as if to say, 'let's leave'.

The mullah didn't waste a second getting to his feet, ready to go.

They both said goodbye to the general and moved towards the door. Before they stepped out, the general said, "Mullah, everything we hold precious and dear is worthless without our homeland's security."

The mullah's knuckles went white, and beads of sweat popped out on his forehead as he stepped in front of Ahmad out of the room.

CHAPTER 12

Tuesday, April 20, 2010

"Peace be upon you and the mercy of Allah," Mullah Abdullah said.

"Oh mullah, you've lost a lot of weight. What happened? You look tired," Haj Adel said, dismay written on his face, as he rose from behind his desk. It was an old desk whose top was overlaid with a sticky, black substance, not easily loosened or wiped away with the wave of a rag. It was like gum a kid had thrown, then stepped on until it became black, dry, and immovable. To hide the dirt, Haj Adel had tacked layers of sheets of cardboard on top, which had decomposed from many fingers touching it over the years. He'd fixed it in place with thumbtacks.

Haj Adel was in his seventies, with a full head

of white hair and a well-trimmed beard. His teeth were still intact, in contrast to so many men his age who had lost all their teeth and needed an artificial set. He had a long, curved nose, like an eagle's beak, and charcoal-black eyes. As an independent businessperson who in his struggle to build a small financial empire, he had earned the title Sheikh Altujjar, Godfather of merchants, in the Bozooriyah market in Damascus. He wore a gray three-piece suit over a white linen shirt, now faded from hundreds of washings. He never wears a necktie because he believes only infidels wear them, and he often brags about that fact in social gatherings.

Haj Adel kissed the mullah's forehead after they shook hands. Then, inviting the mullah to take a seat beside him, Haj Adel lowered himself behind his desk. "You bless my shop with your visit mullah, it is indeed an honor."

"The shop is honored by your existence. How's business?"

"I swear by Allah, never has there been such a terrible year as this one. Thirty years I've been in the market and this year is the worst," said Haj Adel.

He had expected this very answer since he heard the same one every year, or at least every time he asked him this question.

"We ask Allah's support and help for you and all people around the globe," he said.

"Amen," Haj Adel said, glancing over at a customer who had entered the shop and asked for a specific brand of rice. As Haj Adel looked after the customer, the mullah looked around at his surroundings. For ten years or more now, nothing had changed in this shop; the same wooden shelves lined the walls. Every year they become gradually darker and darker from grime. They were stocked with a wide variety of products, from biscuits to chocolate to soap to shampoo. The large cans full of candies in the middle of the shop were dull and dented from age. The wall behind Haj Adel was covered with multiple posters, all faded. Some of them had been there for twenty years or could be much older.

He smiled when he noticed one poster of an advertisement for a type of cheese from Germany, which he had used to watch on TV in the 80s before the sanctions started and it was banned. A dust-covered clock on the wall had stopped at nine o'clock. Only Allah knew how many years it had not worked. Old newspapers, brown from years of hanging over the glass door to block the sunlight. One headline congratulated the victors for winning the war against Israel in 1973. He could not prevent a smile as he realized this place should be an antique shop.

Haj Adel returned and plopped behind his desk again. "You are most welcome here. I respect you, mullah, because you are unlike other religious leaders. They wouldn't visit a wealthy man unless they were begging for money."

The mullah rolled his eyes. "Oh, no. I am here for a very different reason."

He told Haj Adel what happened the previous day at the hospital and the police station, without mentioning he'd seen Zakiya's back injuries. He was worried about Haj Adel's reaction. He was afraid he'd view it as interference and meddling in his family's private affairs.

"Our respected mullah, you have always had a big heart and love to help people. Since I am standing in for my son Mazen in his absence, I am the one who signed it. Allah be blessed, Khaled is the man of the house and takes care of his sisters. He called me and informed me. I called the police, and the report was brought to me right here, since I am so busy and don't have time to go to the station."

"Did Khaled mention anything about Zakiya's back?"

"I don't believe Ahmad was telling the truth about the marks on the girl's back. If it was true, it should have been mentioned in the report, and Khaled would have told me about it immediately."

"But why would Ahmad make up such a story?"

"It's not the first time. He's always trying to prove that Mazen is not taking care of his family properly. Especially after Hadiya's death. My grandchildren have a hardworking father in Dubai who sends them money and to allow them to live in the best of circumstances. Even though their mother died and left them, their grandmother and I wouldn't let them fall short. We are always available to serve them. Whatever they desire, from fruits to vegetables to meat, I will buy it for them. Two days ago, I purchased a goat's liver and sent it to them. Every time I go to the farm, I pick out green peppers, zucchini, and eggplant. I drop by their house and one girl will come down and pick up the vegetables. Please tell me what more than this they could wish for?"

"Of course; no one can doubt you are doing your best. However, I believe they should not keep living in isolation. For my part, I will do my best to arrange marriages for them. They won't be arguing endlessly with each other if they get married."

"To serve those four girls is sweeter than honey in my heart," Haj Adel said. "I don't feel in any way that they are a liability. If they somehow didn't get married for any reason, they would continue to live in their home like princesses."

The mullah didn't like the bluntness in Haj Adel's voice. "Please don't get me wrong; I have no ill-will toward anyone. And as I said before, it is my duty to convey my concerns."

"Allah bless you for your concern."

"Is there any possibility that Mazen will come back to Syria to live with them? Especially now that their mother has passed away?" he asked it anyway, even though he'd heard the answer from Mazen himself.

Haj Adel sighed. "Their father has had massive debt since the day he left Syria, and this large family liability is on his neck. With five children and their mother spending money like a sieve, he continues to work tirelessly day and night in an effort to fill their extraordinary demands. May Allah forgive the noble Hadiya. She could not manage their expenses, despite her best efforts; and that's why Mazen used to send the money to me. I would give them a thousand Syrian pounds weekly, besides sending them groceries and other consumable products from my shop."

"Allah blesses you, brother Haj Adel," he said while contemplating how little a thousand Syrian pounds is for a family of five, which is equal to about twenty American dollars.

"But what if Ahmad was telling the truth?"

"In that case, we should find out the reason for it," Haj Adel said.

"My religious duties require me not to remain quiet whenever I hear such details, and since I am not related to the girl, the most I could do was come and inform you. I beg you to find out if Ahmad was telling the truth or not, and if he was, you must investigate what happened to Zakiya."

"It is highly unlikely that it's possible, but I promise you I will investigate the issue," Haj Adel said.

"In the law, the punishment for hitting someone and causing permanent marks on the body is a prison sentence of six months to three years. If someone really laid hands on Zakiya, that person must receive the proper punishment," the mullah said.

"Did you study law?" Haj Adel asked.

"Oh, no, but since our law is Islamic, they taught it to us," the mullah said.

"Ok, I promise to find out if Ahmad was telling the truth," Haj Adel said.

The mullah stared at a small hole in the ground, which connected to an underground store. He couldn't see very far into the murky blackness. It made him think of the darkness of a grave, and how lonely every dead person will be in that grave. He shivered at the horror of it. Meanwhile, Haj Adel made himself busy calculating numbers on a remaining invoice in front of him, using an old calculator encrusted with dirt.

"Brother Haj Adel, by any chance, do you know anything about a debt owed to Ahmad?"

Haj Adel stopped what he was doing and looked at him. "Forgive me, I don't understand. Do you mean Hadiya's brother, Ahmad?"

"Yes exactly, he says his sister owed him a significant amount of money." He took out the copy of the letter, which Ahmad had given him, written in Hadiya's hand.

Haj Adel read the letter, then looked up. "I don't know anything about this matter."

"Earlier you mentioned Mazen had a massive debt. That's why he went to Dubai. Ahmad says that Hadiya borrowed money from him to enable her husband to go to Dubai."

"Mazen had an import and export business which lost all its liquidity because of the sanctions. The money he owed, he borrowed from several people, which, of course, he is obligated to return."

"But they must be partners in both ways, profit and loss. The divine and civil laws don't force him to pay back that loss."

"He was not a partner; he was an investor only."

"Still, there isn't much difference."

"He still should insist on taking complete liability."

"Allah never let a soul carry a burden beyond what he can endure."

"This is the first time I heard about this matter with Ahmad. Anyway, when Mazen calls me, I will ask him about it."

"That's alright. I talked about this matter with him when I was in Dubai. He just said he wants a document to prove the debt. I'm assuming that when he sees this letter, he will agree to pay Ahmad back."

"You went to Dubai?" Haj Adel asked.

"Yes, I was asked to give a lecture at an Islamic conference."

"May Allah give you long life and strength to serve Islam well."

"Amen." Then the mullah rose, indicating his intention to leave.

Haj Adel also stood and said out of politeness, "Please, it is still early. You didn't drink anything."

The mullah thanked him and made his departure.

CHAPTER 13

Saturday, April 24, 2010

Mullah Abdullah was seated on a couch, white towels covering his body, and a towel on his head, wrapped artistically in a way only experts in the traditions of the hammam (public steam bath) were capable of.

He had first relaxed for an hour in the steam room, lying on the hot ancient stones, their smooth surfaces drawing all the stress and tiredness from his body.

He never ceased to be impressed by the creative architecture of the bath. Built hundreds of years ago by skilled stonemasons, it seemed as if the builders had injected parts of their souls into the stones. The touch of the stones against his bare body carried him into a state of reverie, far away from life's overwhelming obstacles. Of course, he would return to the real world with all of its troubles the minute he left the hammam, but he would do so with renewed vigor.

The mullah came to this public bath every week, just to relax and enjoy the simplicity of its atmosphere and the humbleness of its surroundings. The steam was created using traditional methods. A coal-fired furnace beneath a massive stone storage chamber heated the water. The steam rose from the boiling water to glide into the rooms through channels carved in the walls. In each room, there was a stone water bowl with a copper cup so patrons could pour water over the head and body, plus a volcano stone to scrub callused skin, an organic sponge, and soap made from olive oil mixed with natural herbs. After his stress was dissolved by the hot stones, he got up and moved into the shower room next to the steam room.

He spent 30 minutes scrubbing, rubbing, and washing until he felt his skin couldn't be cleaner. He dried himself with a white towel, then wrapped a dry one around his middle and a second one around his chest, then went out into the courtyard. The fountain in the middle was surrounded by comfortable couches. Men who had already finished their baths lounged on the couches smoking hookahs and drinking various beverages.

The mullah sat holding the hookah, smoking

the Persian tobacco. In front of him was a cup of boiled herbs. He watched the amber glow each time he inhaled through the mouthpiece. A thick cloud of smoke floated up around his head before dissipating into the air above the courtyard each time he exhaled.

Ahmad came out and sat beside him and a boy hurried over to wrap his head in a white towel, then brought him a cup of tea and a hookah.

"I hope you enjoyed your bath," the mullah said, to be sure Ahmad was happy with the experience since he was the one who had asked him to meet there.

"It has been a while since I last came, but it is important to come here at least once a month to relax and forget the stresses of life."

"I am glad you enjoyed it."

"Yes, it was incredible."

The mullah told Ahmad about his visit with Haj Adel.

"Did you mention the signs that she'd been tortured?" Ahmad asked.

"Yes. He was surprised to hear it. According to him, the report didn't say anything about torture."

"Well, I'm not surprised he didn't believe it then."

The mullah took another drag from the hookah, then continued to talk as he exhaled, the smoke billowing out between the words. "It doesn't matter if he believed it or not. The purpose of my visit was to address the issue, out of personal duty, nothing more. I'm satisfied that he was the one who signed the report and had full knowledge of what was going on in Khaled's house." He reached out and rearranged the charcoal on the top of his hookah.

"On Thursday, I went to the hospital to meet Dr. Raed again. I convinced him to tell me the truth after I gave him a generous sum of money as a gift," Ahmad said.

The mullah jerked his head back, stopped inhaling, and gaped at Ahmad, who continued, "He assured me that the police wrote a report at the hospital that mentioned their suspicions that my niece had been tortured. He told me to wait for him to get a copy of the report from the archives, since they keep a copy of each report on file. He came back with panic visible on his face and informed me he couldn't find the copy of the report. I asked him to go with me to the police station and back me up when I argued the police report was not authentic. The doctor refused to help. He asked me to leave, and not come back. He warned me that if I mentioned his name to the authorities, he would deny any knowledge of the matter."

"But what about the report we read at the police station?" the mullah asked.

Ahmad rearranged the towel over his head. "It is not the same report that was written at the hospital."

"Why would someone hide the fact that the girl was tortured and not work day and night to find out who the abuser was?" the mullah asked.

"Well, there is a long history of Haj Adel's family manipulating such official reports and hiding their dirty activities."

What was going on in that house? Who would want to change the report and why? Someone was trying to hide something. Was it possible that Haj Adel was abusing his grandchildren? Could he be taking advantage of the parents' absence and doing things to the girls?

He leaned in and said, "Brother Ahmad, I will find out what is going on, I promise."

The boy approached and changed the embers on top of the hookahs. He wore the traditional pants worn by the ancestors during the Ottoman occupation. Wide loose pants with an extended sack between the legs. From a distance, it looked like he had three legs instead of two. He also wore a white shirt under a vest embroidered with golden thread. The rest of the costume comprised a wide belt made of red wool. A fez similar to the mullah's, but without a turban. Traditional attire for all workers in the hammams in Damascus.

"I am planning to call Mazen in Dubai and ask him for my money," Ahmad said.

"I wish you good luck, but my sense is he won't pay you back unless you provide official proof or some kind of evidence," the mullah said.

"If I can reach him, he won't dare to deny he owes the money," Ahmad said.

The mullah remembered how difficult it had been to get Mazen's contact details from his family before his trip to Dubai.

"What if Mazen refuses to give the money back?"

Ahmad sighed and sipped his drink. "I know how to force him to give it back."

"But that piece of paper you gave me didn't prove anything."

"No matter how many contracts a person signs, if he intends to steal and run away, nothing can stop him. The honest person does not need a signed paper to acknowledge his debts. His word should be stronger than any contract."

The mullah cleared his throat purposely. "In the Holy Qur'an, Allah orders us to keep a record under the eyes of witnesses in the case of any debt."

"But you believe me, don't you?"

He avoided eye contact when he answered, "Of course, I believe you."

Ahmad lowered his head and said no more.

***

After the hammam, Ahmad called Hani to arrange a meeting to talk about a critical issue. Even though it wasn't time for their weekly meeting, Hani welcomed him warmly.

Hani Farawati has been a traffic officer and Ahmad's close friend for many years. His coarse appearance commands the attention of pedestrians. His trumpet voice forces anyone that hears it to turn his head to see who is talking. He lives alone without a wife or children, because of his treatment of the women who were unlucky enough to marry him in the past. His third wife left him recently, and rumors are that he treated his wives brutally until they begged him for a divorce.

His apartment on the twentieth floor of a tall modern building overlooks the roundabout at the beginning of the airport highway, between Ibn-Assaker Street in the west and Bab-Sharqi in the east. Those tall buildings were the beginnings of modern-day Damascus, located beyond the older parts of the city.

Ahmad entered a broad hall furnished with luxurious mahogany chairs. The floor was covered with an elegant, thick Persian carpet. Two bohemian crystal chandeliers hung from the ceiling, each one costing 10 times Hani's salary. A huge abstract painting dominated one wall. He doubted if Hani understood the meaning of the colors mixed in a spiral and meeting in the center with something that looked like a moon. Every time he entered this house, he was tempted to call Hani 'your highness'.

They sat in a room with wide rear windows looking out into the heart of Damascus. The view was priceless. It was like looking at an antique oil painting painted by history itself. Spread out before them were hundreds of traditional Damascene houses interspersed by the minarets of mosques and church steeples until they reached the high walls of the Great Umayyad Mosque.

Hani prepared Turkish coffee, pouring the hot aromatic black liquid into tiny blue ceramic cups from a ceramic pot. He wondered whether Hani had traveled to China to buy these expensive pieces.

"I need a favor from you," Ahmad said. He knew Hani would never do a favor without something in return, even though they have been close friends since school days.

Without delay, Hani said, "Place your request. I wouldn't be doing you a favor. I would be doing my duty."

Ahmad tried to decide the best way to say what he needed to say, as Hani observed him attentively.

"My niece, Zakiya, was taken to the hospital this past week, and when the doctor examined her, he discovered she had been tortured." He shut his eyes and pressed the bridge of his nose with two fingers. He didn't want Hani to see his tears. "The doctor called the police to investigate. The police came and compiled a report. The doctor told me at the hospital that someone needed to sign off on the report since her parents weren't available. When I went to the police station to sign it, to my surprise, the report was already signed by Haj Adel, her grandfather."

"So, what's wrong with that?" Hani asked, rubbing his chin.

"The report at the police station differed from the report which was written at the hospital."

"How do you know that?" Hani asked.

Ahmad patiently explained everything that had happened when they visited the police station, and how on the second visit, the doctor couldn't find the copy of the report. When asked to accompany him to the police station, the doctor was horrified and asked not to mention his name at the police station and refused to testify.

"Is the girl still in the hospital?" Hani asked.

"No."

"Then it is now a dead end. It is not possible to open the report again and push for an investigation."

"No one is asking to open a new report or change the old one," Ahmad said.

"Then what is on your mind?" Hani refilled Ahmad's cup from the Chinese ceramic pot.

Ahmad raised the cup to his lips and sipped before continuing, "I want to know who changed the report from its original content?

"You mean, who paid the bribe?" Hani smiled.

"Exactly."

"Isn't it obvious? You said the grandfather was the one who signed the report. So, he must be the one who paid to change it."

"The grandfather denies Zakiya was exposed to any kind of torture. Let's just assume that he's the one who paid to change the report. I want to know the reason for his actions. I cannot imagine anyone. knowing their daughter or granddaughter has been tortured, would try to hide it. Unless ..." He didn't say it out loud and didn't elaborate further.

"The easiest way to expose a bribe is to offer a bribe," Hani said, as if he was lecturing Ahmad. "The one who accepted a bribe to write a fake report didn't do it because he loved the person who asked him to do it. He did it because of the bribe only. He will probably be willing to do anything for money, not only write false reports. That is what's known as a corrupt person. Such is the beauty of our country."

Ahmed thought Hani was talking about himself since he never did a thing without money in advance. He said, "It doesn't seem logical to bribe someone to admit that he has taken a bribe."

Hani laughed. "We won't tell him we know he took a bribe to write a fake report. He would only deny it and not cooperate. Also, he would certainly warn his colleagues not to supply any further information to us. If we make loud noises, he will claim that someone forced him or extorted him to draft the report. We don't need all of that. We just want to pay money to learn who had an interest in writing a report in that way."

"Is there any other way?" Ahmad asked.

Hani laughed, "Look who's afraid to pay a bribe."

"No man, I'm not afraid. I'm still not convinced this is the right technique."

"This is the only way I can help you. If there is another way, I am not aware of it," Hani concluded.

Ahmad shuffled his feet in the softness of the Persian carpet, admiring its perfect colors and the amazing embroidery. He wondered how old it was, and how much it had cost. Of course, there was no way Hani could afford such expensive furnishings from his meager salary.

He looked up, sighed, and said, "I saw Zakiya's

back with my own eyes, and I will never forget the horrible sight. I believe the one who did that to her is the one who bribed someone to change the report."

"Well, if you saw her back, you don't need me to prove anything, do you? As you said, the one who did that must be the same person who bribed to keep it quiet."

"I only saw the false report, not the real one," Ahmad said. "I want to know what was in the original report. I want to know if that report reached Haj Adel, and if he asked someone to change it or if the report had been altered before he saw it. I don't want to accuse anyone based on pure speculation."

"Ok, I will try my best to find out," Hani said.

"I don't want you to try your best. I want you to do your best," Ahmad said.

"Tomorrow, I will text you how much we need to pay for the right people to get the information we want."

Ahmad wondered if Hani would really pay someone, or would he keep the money for himself?

Before he left, Hani asked, "What do you plan to do when you find out who did that to Zakiya?"

He raised both hands and stared at them as if they were covered with blood. "I will kill him with my bare hands."

***

Monday afternoon, Ahmad was waiting in his BMW on Almazzah Street, opposite the gate of Damascus University. He watched the young students carrying their books, walking through the gate, chatting, and laughing. It hadn't been difficult for him to find his niece Farah's schedule on the university's website. He knew she would be out at 2 pm.

He remembered the days when he had studied mechanical engineering. Those days were full of stress and anxiety. He had been fearful for his unknown future.

He was proud to be a graduate of the oldest and largest university in Syria. He looked at the stone gate, where the university motto was carved in stone. It was from the Holy Qur'an: 'My Lord, increase me in knowledge' (20:114), established in 1923.

It was the largest institution in the world, specializing in the Arabic language, and it attracted students from all over the globe.

Farah appeared with three other girls, all of them wearing conservative attire, long navy coats and white scarves. He waved to her. She looked around anxiously to see if anyone had noticed. She said something to her friends before leaving them and then approached the BMW.

"That was fast. Did you bring it?" she asked.

"Yes, of course."

"Ok great," she said. "Can I have it now, please?"

"Please get in the car."

"People won't know that you are my uncle and might gossip," she said.

"They can go to hell. Please, just let me drop you at your home."

She slid into the car and slammed the door. If she hadn't been wearing a scarf, he was sure he'd see her ears red with heat.

He stopped two streets away from her apartment, and she got out of the BMW with a tiny box hidden carefully amongst her books.

CHAPTER 14

Tuesday, April 27, 2010

After the noon prayer was over, the mullah took off his cloak, revealing huge sweat stains under his arms. He folded it neatly and laid it on the carpet beside him as he sat down to recite from the Qur'an. The mosque was quiet except for the hum of the ceiling fans stirring the air overhead. He loved being alone here, engulfed in the spiritual tranquility of such a holy place.

He frowned and pressed his lips when Hani entered the mosque with Ahmad. He'd explicitly instructed Hani not to let people see them together and, most importantly, not in the mosque.

The pair approached and sat beside him as he continued reciting. They waited for him to finish and when he greeted them; they returned his greeting.

"What is so important that you had to come and meet me here in the mosque?" he asked Hani.

Hani plunged right in. "Ahmad explained to me his concerns about his niece, and after doing a little digging, I uncovered the reason the report was rewritten with no investigation." He flashed a winning smile and continued, "There was indeed a bribe paid to rewrite the report about Zakiya."

"What difference will it make knowing who paid the bribe?" the mullah asked.

"The one who paid the bribe is the one who abused Zakiya," Ahmad said.

"And who would that be?" the mullah asked.

"Well, isn't it obvious?" Hani said, "The one who signed the report would be the one who paid to have it changed."

Mullah Abdullah jammed his hands into his armpits and discovered the dampness there. "You think that's likely?" *Is it possible the grandfather spent money to hide something he did himself, or maybe hide something else suspicious that took place in the apartment?*

He came back to the present when Hani tossed a bomb into the conversation, "Yes, and it was not the first report bought and paid for, to hide suspicious activities in that household." Ahmad puffed out his chest as Hani continued, "Hadiya was murdered there, and the police report didn't even mention it."

"What are you saying?" The mullah thought he'd heard incorrectly.

"His sister was murdered," Hani said, pointing at Ahmad.

He stared at Ahmad and Hani while he waited for further explanation. He hadn't heard anything about a murder in this normally peaceful neighborhood.

"Did you know about this? Is that possible?" he asked Ahmad.

"I didn't know about the report," Ahmad said. "But I've had my suspicions since the day she passed away."

He wiped his forehead, causing a wet spot on his sleeve. "Please elaborate."

"My sister died suddenly. She was as healthy as a horse. I doubt Mazen killed her just to avoid paying back my money."

"Allah is the greatest," the mullah said. "Please, brother Ahmad, don't speak like this. It is a serious allegation. The punishment in the hereafter for such an accusation will be huge if you are not right."

"I am working hard to find conclusive evidence," Ahmad said, and the mullah clenched his teeth at his words.

Glancing over at Hani, he said, "How could you get such information?"

"The same way I got the information about Zakiya's report," Hani said.

"But Zakiya's report was about injuries to her back. Now we are talking about a deadly serious crime. For God's sake, if you are not 100% sure, you must not spread such allegations," he said.

Hani didn't seem bothered. "I am sure about the report. Don't worry, I would never have mentioned it otherwise." Then he said proudly, "I can get any kind of information I want."

The mullah strongly doubted that. Then a thought struck him. Looking Hani in the eyes, he challenged him, "I need information, but I am not convinced you can get it for me."

Hani looked offended. "You should know me by now, mullah. What information do you need?"

"It's about one of my students who has disappeared, and I'm very concerned about him. Can you find out what happened to him?"

Hani laughed, to the mullah's and Ahmad's surprise. "I can get you this information, but under one condition. In return, I need you to support me on a critical issue. No one can help me except you."

"Please go on."

"As you know, Allah doesn't like men to remain single, and the Prophet encouraged us to marry to avoid falling into sin."

"Peace be upon the Prophet," the three of them intoned in unison.

"I am planning to marry the daughter of Abu-Ahmad, the bean vendor in the neighborhood. I need you to recommend me to him, so he will accept me as his son-in-law."

"Have you approached the family yet?" the mullah asked.

"Not yet."

Despite already knowing the answer, the mullah asked, "Why do you need me for this? Why can't you just ask her father yourself? Are you in doubt that your proposal will be accepted?"

"You know how much nonsense people talk. Unfortunately, our community is filled with backbiting and gossip. Especially since I have been divorced three times."

The mullah frowned accusingly, "Is it possible your ex-wives were wrong all three times? There can be no smoke without fire."

"I am only human, and humans make mistakes. Everyone has unlimited opportunities for repentance," Hani said.

"No doubt about that. But…"

Hani interrupted. "Please mullah. Give it some thought, and I promise I'll find out where your student is if you decide to help me."

"I'll get back to you. And if I need any further details, I'll let you know." The mullah clenched his jaw when he remembered where they were. Discussing earthly matters in a mosque was not acceptable. He asked Allah for forgiveness and rose to leave.

***

Later that afternoon, as the mullah entered his home, the irresistible smell of food made him giddy with hunger. Amani and Zahra were waiting for him. He went for a quick wash, changed his clothes, then came and sat down at the dinner table.

As usual, they had their dinner in the liwan. The dinner included three types of Koba, fried, oven-baked, and one soaked in cooked yogurt. The side dish was a green salad with olive oil. The three of them devoured the food ravenously without talking.

After dinner, Zahra prepared tea for them. He was deep in thought as Zahra poured hot tea into his cup. After the gurgling from the kettle stopped, the only sound was the water splashing in the fountain. Steam rose lazily from the cups.

"Papa, is there any news about my computer?" Zahra asked.

"Oh Allah, I totally forgot. I promise tomorrow I will try to find out when we can get it back." His forehead wrinkled as his lips touched the hot rim of the cup.

"Thank you, Papa. I'll need it for my final exams next month."

He returned the cup to the table. "My dear Zahra, please come closer." Zahra approached obediently and sat beside him.

"Don't you worry about it. If I can't get it soon, I will buy you a new one."

"Thank you, Papa," she said and kissed him on his forehead.

The mullah looked across at Amani and said, "Ahmad came to see me today."

Amani listened as he told her what had happened with Ahmad at the hospital, and their visit with Zakiya, and then about the reports and the bribes. He concluded, "What do you think would be the best way to help Ahmad?" He already knew what he wanted to do, but he hoped his wife would suggest it.

A look of genuine concern crossed Amani's face. "Who could have laid hands on the girl? We have only the sisters to ask."

"But how best to approach the sisters?" he said.

Zahra said enthusiastically, "I could go visit them."

"No," he said firmly.

Amani shot him a warning look, so he turned to Zahra and said, "The problem is not who will go, but how to address the issue."

Turning back to Amani, he suggested, "Maybe you could invite them to the public bath."

Amani said sarcastically, "You won't allow Zahra to accompany me to the bath. Why would you allow the daughters of others to do so?"

He was embarrassed because in Islam, we are not permitted to be a double standard. "True, I seek forgiveness from Almighty Allah."

"Mom, why don't you visit them and take some clothes as gifts? You could ask them to try them on for you," Zahra suggested.

"That is a good idea," Amani said.

"You could take several sizes and let them choose the right size," the mullah said.

"Ok, perhaps I'll buy some low-cut dresses that expose their backs. The sort they like to wear around when they have friends over. We'll see what comes of that."

"That will be a great help," he said.

"Is this what has been bothering you?" Amani asked.

He sighed and told her about Hani's request.

"I seek refuge with Allah from the accursed devil!" Amani exclaimed.

"Why, what's wrong with Hani?" He wiped his forehead.

"Seriously? You're asking what's wrong with that monster?" Amani's face was as red as if he had slapped her. "If you want to destroy Samah's future, go ahead and recommend Hani to her father."

"You must ask for forgiveness from Almighty Allah," he said, as he struggled to keep his composure. "Why are you talking like this? This is backbiting, and it is a major sin." He regretted now that he had opened the topic with her, noting that nothing would stop her from voicing her opinions now, even if a bomb dropped in the middle of the courtyard.

"My dear, be careful of recommending that man." Amani was visibly trying to control herself. "You must see with your own eyes what he did to his last wife. She went back to her parents. Her face was disfigured by a cut that took nine stitches. That animal treated his wives most savagely. You must open your ears to all the talk in the neighborhood about him." Her voice was still rising and left him no chance to interrupt.

"He punched his second wife Monirah in the

face and broke her jaw. Her face was ruined, and her father didn't have the money to pay for plastic surgery. The first wife's story would cause rocks to cry tears of blood. He punched her in the face and took out one of her eyes. She became half-blind with only one eye."

"Almighty Allah," he said, terrified by the news of Hani's brutality.

"Of course, no one could ever do anything to him, because he has important contacts in the government. No one dares to face him or speak against him," Amani said.

"Allah is on the lookout for men like him if what you say is the truth," he snapped.

"And you want to help him marry Samah? If you want Samah to return to her parents' home handicapped, just recommend Hani to her father and convince him," Amani said.

"Did you see the three ladies with your own eyes and all the damage to their faces?" he asked, trying to remove the last traces of doubt from his head.

"I saw them with my own eyes," Amani affirmed.

***

Asmar spent a lot of time working out, taking care of his body. Besides his unusual charm, his eyes could steal a woman's soul. As a result, his presence in a public place would bring looks of admiration from the females and envy from the males.

He stared at the front window of his Peugeot

and spotted a piece of paper wedged under the wiper. He darted forward and snatched up the paper. Only the '7:00 pm' was written on it. He clenched his fists, causing his knuckles to turn white, as he crumpled the piece of paper and tossed it away before sliding into his car.

His vision clouded from tears, he punched the steering wheel and screamed in frustration. When his fists were covered with blood, he grabbed the steering wheel and shook it violently, while sobbing uncontrollably.

Asmar felt indescribable gratitude toward Hani, as if the barrel of a gun had been aimed at his head, and Hani had saved his life by removing it. When Hani had let him go that night with only a traffic light fine, he hadn't known he would fall prey to such a nasty blackmail scheme.

He was extremely unhappy with what was happening and how it happened. The information he had leaked to Hani was indeed priceless, and now, day after day, he believed more strongly than ever that Hani was totally corrupt and self-serving. At first, he'd thought Hani was helping him, but now he knew that was far from the case, and he had taken the bait. Hani would continue to extort him forever now because he had proof of his homosexuality.

He hadn't admitted to himself, his family, or the community that he was a homosexual, and he never would. He planned to marry his fiancé, Areej, and start a family to bury his long years of aberrant practices. Now this ruffian police officer was robbing him of his tranquil life.

He thought about the consequences of exposing his homosexuality, in the event if he refused to leak any more information to Hani. Some of the information affected homeland security. However, he did not consider the safety of the country more important than keeping his parents from the shock of finding out about his homosexuality. They would renounce him as a son, kick him out of the house and tell him never to come back. His relatives would avoid him, and so would his friends. They wouldn't want to be tarnished by his shame. His fiancé would leave him, and no girl would ever marry him. He would be laid off from his job, and most probably, he would face a trial and be thrown in jail for years. Asmar shivered in fear, while he thought of the list of calamities that would occur one after another. He reflected on it every night before he fell asleep. And now he hated Hani more than he hated the devil.

CHAPTER 15

Wednesday, April 28, 2010

Amani stood at the door to Hadiya's apartment and knocked for the second time. Noise poured in from the crowds of people and vehicles at street level. Someone was frying cauliflower or eggplant with rancid cooking oil, causing her to want to plug her nose. She breathed through her mouth instead. Finally, she heard a key turn in the lock, and the door opened a tiny crack. It was the first time she'd seen Khaled so close. A gasp escaped her lips. The pain from seeing her reaction was obvious in the boy's eyes. She lowered her gaze.

"Yes?" Khaled said in a barely audible voice.

She said, "I'm Amani, your mother's friend. I'm here to visit your sisters."

"Please come in Madam." He hobbled out of her way to let her pass through to the living room.

There was an odor in the apartment she couldn't identify, but she thought it smelled like a medical product used to clean wounds. The living room was sparsely furnished, with only a straw mat and two sofas. Khaled asked her to sit as he went to call his sisters. She sat down, placing her shopping bag beside her, and waited for the girls to appear. It had been a long time since she'd seen them last.

The kitchen was in full view from where she sat. If one could call such a tiny room with no door, a kitchen. Some of the cabinet doors had been left open, revealing numerous glass jars filled with olives, pickles, and Makdous. Many of the ceramic tiles were missing on the walls and ceiling. There was an old three-burner stove on the counter with a pipe connecting it to a gas cylinder in the corner. The faucet over the sink dripped with annoying consecutive clicks into a water filled pot.

The previous year, Hadiya had invited her here during the month of Ramadan to break her fast. Although the food was simple, boiled groats with lentils called Mujaddara accompanied by yogurt, the love with which it had been prepared made it one of the best dishes Amani had tasted in her life. Hadiya did all the cooking and cleaning, as she didn't want to take her daughters from their studies. She was like a protective tent over the heads of her five children. At one time, this house had been full of vibrant, positive energy. Unlike now.

Amani stood up with delight when Farah, Marwa, Ro'wa, and Zakiya came out. She kissed each of them on the cheek, then sat down. They sat huddled together on the other sofa. Farah, the eldest, was in her last year at the university. Marwa was two years younger, Ro'wa was three years younger than Farah, and Zakiya was the youngest. Amani couldn't keep from smiling. Four gorgeous girls, so slim and delicate, reminded her of her own girlhood before she met the mullah and married him.

Khaled came back, clumping along on his crutches and sat on the same sofa as the girls. Amani noticed the girls pulling away from him and moving closer to each other. Khaled noticed her looking, so he moved to the sofa where she was sitting.

Amani said casually, "Girls, why don't we make some tea, and we can chat about what you have been doing? I've truly missed all of you and can't wait to hear what you have been up to lately."

Ro'wa jumped up excitedly. "I will prepare the tea." Her sisters didn't even have time to blink before she was in the kitchen, grabbing the tea kettle and filling it at the tap.

Amani looked at Farah and said, "How are things at the university?" It was a great relief to many people that higher education in public universities around the country was free.

Farah wore a flowing yellow dress with light green flowers, her black hair cascaded down over her shoulders. She answered with a sweet smile, "I am doing fine."

"God Bless, isn't it your summer break already?" Amani asked.

"Not yet. We have a few days off to prepare for our exams," Farah said.

"Oh, I apologize for disturbing your study time. Please, don't mind me if you want to go inside and study," Amani said.

"No, not at all. I need a break from studying all night, and it's so nice to see you again," Farah said.

"What about you, beautiful flower? Have you started your summer vacation?" Amani asked Marwa.

Marwa wore a plain white cotton dress, her hair falling to her shoulders like a stream of honey. Her white skin and pink cheeks framed olive-green eyes. She said, "Ro'wa and I are also still preparing for our final exams."

Amani said, "Really, I am sorry to come. I forgot that university exams are often held later." Both Marwa and Farah exclaimed, "No, not at all Aunty, you are the only one of our mom's friends who has visited us. We are really excited to see you."

Ro'wa joined in the conversation from the kitchen. "We are happy to have you, Aunty. We needed a break from studying." The three girls burst into laughter.

"Farah, you are studying journalism, aren't you?" Amani asked.

Farah said proudly with a smile on her face, "Yes, I'm in my final year and I will graduate soon. I really can't wait!"

Marwa said sarcastically, "One year and she will be a journalist jumping like a kangaroo to cover the war in Iraq."

Amani smiled at her. "And you Marwa. You're studying dentistry, I believe?"

"Yes," Marwa said.

Then Ro'wa chimed in from the kitchen, "And what am I studying, Aunty?"

Amani smiled and said, "If I remember correctly, you were taking Arabic literature. Am I right?"

Ro'wa came in, carrying a tray of teacups filled with hot tea. She served her and said, "Yes, you are right." When everyone had their tea, she placed the empty tray on the floor.

She looked at Zakiya and asked, "And what about you, my dear?"

Unlike her sisters, Zakiya wore a black shirt with long sleeves and collar and a pair of black pants. A white scarf covered her head, exposing only her face and hands. She smiled and said in a muffled voice, without looking directly at Amani, "I am still in the eleventh grade."

"I hope you are studying hard, my dear."

Farah, Marwa, and Ro'wa looked at Zakiya. The smiles disappeared from their faces.

Zakiya said in a muffled voice, "I am doing well. Thank you."

Then Farah asked, "Zahra is in high school now, isn't she?"

"Yes, she is. Hopefully, she will also do well." Amani was not sure if Zahra would pass all of her exams successfully this year. The incident of the mullah going to prison and the emotional crisis thereafter affected Zahra a lot.

Khaled had been silent the whole time, observing his sisters. When Amani asked him about his studies, he answered without looking at her, "I am doing well too, Aunty."

Farah, Marwa, and Ro'wa did most of the talking, laughing, and enjoying her visit. They talked about many things, from romance to who the president of the United States was these days. Khaled and Zakiya remained silent the whole time.

Amani was happy to see the girls happy. She opened her shopping bag and took out the dresses. "Girls, these are for you." She stood up, holding them out. The girls squealed and chattered excitedly while checking out the dresses. The joy on their faces was gratifying. "Girls, do you know what would make me even happier?"

"What's that?" Farah asked.

"If I could see them on you before I leave," Amani said.

"Of course," they exclaimed and scurried off into their room, leaving her alone with Khaled. She could hear their endless giggling and chatter. It seemed odd, sitting there with Khaled without talking.

Farah, Marwa, and Ro'wa reappeared and were parading the dresses. She smiled, standing up, and getting each one of them to turn around so she could admire them. Farah had chosen the light green, which complimented her skin color. Marwa had on the dark blue, and Ro'wa was wearing a rich brown dress. Amani praised the girls, "You look brilliant girls, but where's Zakiya, isn't she coming out to show me her dress?"

The room fell silent. The three girls just stood there, awkwardly exchanging glances. Farah said, "Zakiya and Ro'wa are the same size. She has chosen the red dress without trying it on."

Khaled propelled himself off the couch with his crutches. As he hobbled toward the bedroom, he called back, "I will convince her to try it on."

Farah, Marwa, and Ro'wa watched as he approached the closed door. The only sound was the thumping of his crutches and his foot dragging on the floor. Amani studied the girls' faces. Were their odd expressions aimed at Khaled or were they looks of terror from knowing what was inside that room? Khaled went into the room and closed the door behind him.

***

The mullah paced back and forth in the courtyard. Every time he faced the hallway to the outside door, he stopped and stared at it. Amani knew he often took on cases as a private detective to earn extra money. She had even helped him sometimes, but he had never been anxious like this before. Maybe it was because previously the disputes were no more than arguments and he had never been involved in actual crime. This time, If Hani's allegations were correct, there was a crime that needed to be revealed, and a criminal to be arrested.

He'd promised his father-in-law before he died to keep Amani safe and happy. He would never forget how challenging it had been to convince her father to let her marry him. Her father had put him through a test that consumed six months of his life. She was seventeen, and he was twenty-three. Her father told him that his daughter was precious to him, so he wanted to be sure the man who married her was worthy of his daughter. The test was to author a book. To impress her father, he'd written a book about the women in the Qur'an. Not only did the book impress her father, but it also turned out to be an enormous success. Readers were impressed by how the Qur'an evaluated the woman and mentioned many women from ancient history - the Virgin Mary, Eva, the good wife of Pharaoh, and the mother of Moses.

The mullah's attention was drawn back to the door as he heard a key being inserted into the lock. The door opened and Amani entered, coming closer to kiss him on the cheek. He took her by surprise when he hugged her tightly. She was beyond happy.

"Thank Allah for your safety," he said many times.

She went to the bedroom to change her clothes. He followed her like a child waiting for his mother's milk. There were two windows in the bedroom, one overlooking the liwan and one that looked out over the courtyard. Sky-blue and banana-yellow curtains covered the windows. Fading sunlight shone between the curtains onto the hand-woven, blue and red Persian carpet, transforming the atmosphere in the modern room to that of a chamber from the Arabian Nights. He looked lovingly at Amani's skin in the feeble sunlight. She was like Scheherazade. He supposed he was the Shahryar, listening to her stories. He smiled.

While Amani was changing, he gazed at her face without speaking. She smiled at him and said, "The girls were overjoyed to see me. It was great to be with them, and the dresses fit them perfectly. They were very kind and polite, just as they were when I used to visit their mom."

"May Allah reward you for this great deed."

Amani sat on the edge of the bed, so he sat on the chair beside it. She continued, "When Khaled sat on the same sofa as the girls, they drew closer to each other and away from him. It was like the girls were afraid of him or disgusted by him. I felt sorry for him."

The mullah didn't comment.

She continued, "Khaled is the youngest in the family. Now both mother and father have abandoned him, by fate, if not by design. Not only that, he is too physically and mentally frail to take on such a position of responsibility. Why haven't any of the nearby relatives reached out to him under these extraordinary circumstances?"

The mullah was thinking what it would

be like being under similar circumstances. He murmured half to himself, "Power and strength have only Allah as their source and origin. Thank Allah for protecting me from the severe test He has imposed on Khaled." Then he said to Amani, "Allah will always be with those who are patient. So, did anything unusual happen?"

"Farah, Marwa, and Ro'wa tried the dresses on, but Zakiya didn't," she said.

"What can we conclude from that?"

"Not much, except Zakiya was not acting normal like her sisters." The bedroom was getting dimmer, and Amani rose to switch on the light, but he asked her not to. He wanted to keep imagining her as Scheherazade. She sat again at the end of the bed and continued, "Her three sisters were all wearing dresses like any typical girl at home, but she was wearing shirt and trousers. Her body and head were completely covered. When they went into the room to change, the three sisters came back out wearing the new dresses, but Zakiya stayed inside."

"What are you trying to say?" he asked.

"Well, let's see what we have here. We have a girl who didn't go to the hospital immediately with an ear infection. We have a niece who didn't show up to greet her uncle when he visited them. We have an uncle who witnessed his niece's terrible injuries from possible torture. We have sisters who treat their brother with contempt. We have a sad girl who wears clothes that cover her from head to toe, in the privacy of her own home. We have a girl who wouldn't try on a dress in order to keep her body hidden. Those things don't make much sense separately, but together they would make anyone suspect there is something fishy going on in that apartment," Amani said.

"I am not sure I can agree with you on that. As a man of faith, I can't judge or presume anything without hard evidence. I have to analyze all the details you have mentioned from a positive point of view.

"Being late to visit a doctor for an infection in our community is very common. You know how people here won't go to a doctor until they are in a desperate situation. Not showing up to greet her uncle could be because she was not feeling well. The sisters treating their brother with contempt may have nothing to do with Zakiya. Her outfit might reflect her personality, or maybe she is shy of her brother Khaled. She could have been exhausted from studying and didn't want to try the dress on, just wanting to go to sleep instead." Of course, the back injuries were the real mystery, and he would never forget the horror of that image.

"You could be right, but my gut instinct is telling me otherwise. I won't be able to leave it alone now that I've visited them. I wish there was something I could do to make Zakiya feel happy, like her sisters," Amani said.

"So, what are you going to do?" he asked.

"I need to talk to her, but not in front of her sisters," Amani said.

He sighed. "But how will you do that?"

"I will invite the four girls to our prayer circle," Amani said.

"But how will you be able to talk to her alone with all the women and her sisters there?"

"Don't you worry about it. Just leave it to me."

CHAPTER 16

Saturday, May 1, 2010

Um-Waseem, the neighbor who had informed Ahmad's wife that the girls had taken Zakiya to the hospital, was one of five women sitting in a circle on a red Persian carpet that Amani had laid out in the liwan.

They were veiled in white from head to toe, with only their faces visible, and each of them clasping their wooden prayer beads. Every Saturday morning, they gathered at a member's house and recited four verses from chapter 112 of the Qur'an, 1000 times. In the end, they prayed for all their families and relatives, men and women alike.

This Saturday was Amani's turn to host the prayers. Besides the regular attendees, Farah,

Marwa, Ro'wa, Zakiya, and, of course, her own daughter Zahra were present as well. The younger ones were veiled in pale blue.

The meetings usually lasted three to four hours, although reading the verses took only one hour. The rest of their time was spent chatting about things that had happened during the previous week and things they were planning for the week ahead.

When they finished their recitations, they removed their veils and moved to sit on the sofas.

Lamees, Etihad, and Um-Waseem wore the typical attire of any conservative woman in Damascus at the time; a dark blue coat, a white scarf covering the head with only their faces showing, black gloves and black stockings. Um-Tamer, the eldest, still wore traditional clothing: a black coat, black head cover, black face cover, and, of course, black gloves and stockings. Um-Tamer only uncovered her face while she sat chatting with them. She was the only woman in black among the five housewives. The rest took off their dark blue coats and exposed what they were wearing underneath.

Amani couldn't help noticing that all four girls looked happy, especially Zakiya. When she had stopped by their apartment to invite them, at first, they had declined, but when she told them the recitations would benefit their mother's soul, they agreed.

While Amani and Zahra were fetching the desserts and drinks, the older women started chatting with the girls. Zakiya and Um-Tamer weren't talking, only observing. From the kitchen, Amani watched Zakiya while Zahra was busy preparing the Turkish coffee.

Amani carried the fruit bowl in one hand and the dessert plate in the other to the liwan. Zahra followed behind, with a tray of tiny ceramic Turkish coffee cups and the coffeepot. The women were busy chatting and laughing. Amani was peeling and cutting up apples as she listened to the conversations.

Zahra poured the aromatic Turkish coffee in the cups and gave one to each woman, starting with Um-Tamer, the eldest.

Lamees, in an attractive maroon dress, asked Farah what she hoped to do once she finished journalism school. Um-Waseem, wearing a creamy blouse and a long black skirt, was telling Marwa, who was studying dentistry, about her husband's crummy tooth story and how the doctor had pulled it out instead of fixing it.

From the corner of one eye, Amani glimpsed Zakiya whispering to Zahra.

She got up and started passing out the fruit plates, beginning with Um-Tamer, the eldest. When she gave Etihad her plate, the story she was telling Ro'wa made her halt and raise an eyebrow. When the others noticed, they stopped chatting as well and listened in. Ever since the operation to remove her left breast because of cancer, Etihad always wore a shirt over jeans or trousers.

Etihad was saying, "... I tried to get up, but I was wrapped tightly in the blanket. I yelled for my husband, even though I knew he was already at work. He was the first one that came to my mind. I couldn't loosen the blanket or free my hands, and then I realized I was naked under the blanket. Whoever had wrapped me that way took my clothes off first."

Lamees gasped. Um-Tamer put the plate of fruit on the small tea table and leaned forward. Um-Waseem crossed her arms.

"I was staring at a scary creature with red eyes and dirty, straggly hair. My heart almost stopped. When the thing opened its mouth, a smell worse than a rotten grave filled the room. My eyes filled with tears. I don't know if it was from horror or the nasty smell. Then the dreadful creature started moving toward me. I screamed until my throat was dry and my lungs were empty." Etihad paused.

All eyes were focused on her, eager to hear the rest of the story.

Lamees, sitting right next to her, slapped her on the shoulder and demanded, "What happened next?"

Etihad said with a sly smile, "I woke up."

All the women burst into laughter. Lamees placed both of her hands around Etihad's neck, pretending to strangle her.

As the laughter died down, Amani said, "Zahra and Zakiya, would you like to join me in the kitchen to help prepare lunch?"

"Would you like me to help Aunty?" Farah asked. "I know how to cook better than Zakiya."

Zakiya rolled her eyes.

"No, Zakiya and Zahra will be more than enough for this time, but thank you," Amani said, and headed for the kitchen, with Zahra and Zakiya close behind.

Amani peeked out at the ladies from the kitchen, as they flipped their Turkish coffee cups to dry and had Um-Tamer read their fortune. Occultism was prohibited in Islam and Amani had warned them many times, but they always told her they didn't take it seriously; it was just for fun.

Amani took out a cut of beef she had already removed from the freezer that morning and put it on the wooden cutting board.

She took out a bag of frozen green peas, gave it to Zakiya and said, "Please put the peas in the pot and rinse them with warm water."

While Zakiya began that task, Zahra measured out the rice and dumped it into a pot of salted water. Amani was still thinking about Zakiya while she was busy cutting the beef into tiny cubes. Zakiya was a puzzle to her, a reticent pale-skinned girl with small eyes and ears and a little pug nose. She wouldn't have been surprised if Zakiya started to cry while preparing the peas, just from the tremendous amount of sadness that seemed to hang over her. Amani finished with the beef, then put the pot of rice on the burner. She put the tiny beef cubes in a pan and put it on another burner, enjoying the sizzle and the rich aroma. When the water in the rice pot boiled, she lowered the flame to its lowest and covered the pot.

Zakiya and Zahra were cutting tomatoes and lettuce for the salad. Zahra was talking the whole time, while Zakiya only nodded.

Amani was busy peeling garlic. She said, "I hope you liked the dress I bought for you on my last visit."

Zakiya looked at Amani for a couple of seconds and then said, "Oh yes, Aunty, thank you very much."

"I would love to have seen it on you, like your sisters."

"I was tired," Zakiya said, then she tilted her head and continued to pluck fresh mint leaves.

Amani peeked at the rice then turned the flame off under the pot and said, "The rice is ready." She put some peeled almonds in a pan to fry, then said, without turning her head, "Are you happy Zakiya?" No answer. She turned to look at Zakiya and said with a smile, "Yes, I am asking you."

Amani realized the girl was confused. She decided not to push anymore. Instead, she said, "When was the last time you cried, Zakiya?" Zakiya's eyes widened at the question. Amani laughed and said, "We have to cut some onions now." Zakiya sighed and smiled weakly.

Amani approached her, placing her hands on her shoulders. Zakiya was now forced to look into her eyes. "You are like a daughter to me. When I was your age, my biggest wish was for someone to listen to me. I want you to always consider me as the aunt who listens. You must feel you can come and talk to me anytime. You'd be surprised how good I am at listening." They stood looking into each other's eyes for a few seconds. Zakiya's eyes held many secrets, but her mouth remained closed.

Amani fetched the onions, and the three of them were soon laughing and crying while they peeled and cut them up. After that, Amani was busy putting the finishing touches on the main course, though still absorbed deeply in her thoughts. *How can I possibly get Zakiya to open up more? She seems so closed off. What will I tell the mullah? I wasn't even able to talk to the girl properly.* She sent Zahra out with Zakiya to arrange the table.

A few minutes later, the girls returned to help carry the food to the table, and the group was soon devouring it with a hearty appetite. All were pleased with the delicious food, and Amani gave most of the credit to Zakiya and Zahra.

After lunch, the five girls cleared the table and washed the dishes. Before they all sat down to enjoy some hot tea, they prayed the afternoon prayer.

Later, when they were all relaxing and chatting in the liwan, Zahra invited Zakiya up to her room.

They were absorbed in their conversation and didn't notice the time, so when Ro'wa looked at her watch, she panicked and exclaimed to Farah and Marwa, "It's four o'clock already." The women wanted to know why the time was cause for any concern. Ro'wa's cheeks flushed, and Farah said, "We have to be at home when Khaled returns. He has a medical condition, and we can't leave him by himself."

"Well, it was awesome to have you all in our home. I hope you can all come back for another afternoon together," Amani said.

"Now that we know how delicious your cooking is, we'll be at your door every day," Marwa said with a grin. Everyone laughed, and Amani called for Zahra and Zakiya to come down.

Amani and Zahra bid the girls farewell at the front door, then rejoined the women in the liwan.

Zahra prepared fresh coffee in the kitchen, then brought it out, along with a bowl of local citrus fruit, as well as peaches and apricots, and a plate of baklava.

Lamees brushed off a bit of dust from the bottom of her maroon dress, then asked no one in particular, "I wonder what Farah meant when she said her brother has a medical condition?"

Um-Waseem, looked at Lamees and asked, "You haven't seen him, have you?"

"I have never seen him," Lamees said.

"I don't like to say this, but he resembles Satan," Um-Waseem said.

Everyone mumbled, "I seek refuge with Allah from the accursed Satan."

Amani scolded Um-Waseem, "You must beg for Allah's forgiveness."

Um-Waseem ignored Amani's and continued, "He's a dwarf."

Lamees gasped and gave Amani an 'is-this-true' look?

"He was born with a deformity," Amani said, looking at Zahra, expecting her to add more details.

"His disease is known as osteogenesis imperfecta," Zahra said. "It's a kind of congenital dislocation."

Amani smiled proudly at her daughter's knowledge, thinking she could be a doctor one day. She quickly returned to reality as she heard Etihad say, "Is it true that his mother tried to commit suicide while she was pregnant, and this is the result?"

"I heard that if a man has sex with his wife during her period, the child could be born like that," Um-Waseem said. Amani shot her a warning look.

"No, I heard it differently," Lamees said. "I think it was like this. If a man has sex with his wife while thinking of a different woman, the child will be born like that."

Etihad crossed her arms across her flat chest and said, "No, no, no, the father was not a real man, and you know what I mean. They had four girls in a row with no gap between them, so the boy was born sickly."

"I heard that is why he abandoned his family," Um-Waseem said. "Because of the shame he went abroad. I guess he had always longed for a son and then, after four daughters, he couldn't deal with a son like that."

Amani could not hold back any longer. "From where have you heard these distorted thoughts? Daughters are indeed a gift and a mercy from Allah, and whosoever has four girls will enter heaven for their sake."

Etihad rolled her eyes and said, "Do you think the men in our society believe that? When I was pregnant with my daughter, Nana, my husband found out it was a girl, and asked me to abort the child. When I refused, he was furious and stopped talking to me. Then he started sleeping away from home, thinking he was punishing me. I went to his father and complained to him about his son. He admonished my husband, telling him if he would not return and reconcile with me, the curse of Allah would be upon him. Eventually, my man repented and came back to me."

"But Khaled was not their first son. They had a boy before him," Um-Tamer said suddenly. She'd been silent for so long; this announcement grabbed all the women's attention. The liwan fell silent as she blurted out, "I was the midwife for that child."

"You were a midwife?" Lamees asked.

Um-Tamer smiled broadly and said, "Yes, I used to work as a midwife. I must have delivered almost half of the children in this alley. One of them was Jamal, Hadiya, and Mazen's first son. She became pregnant with him after the birth of their first daughter, and I was the midwife for them both. They called her Farah, which means happiness, because they were overjoyed when she was born. Hadiya was living with her mother-in-law then.

"Her apartment was on the third floor in a four-story building on Ibn-Assaker Street. It had only four bedrooms. One for the mother and the father-in-law, one for their first daughter-in-law, Hadiya and her husband, one for the second daughter-in-law and her husband. The fourth room was for the old disabled mother of the father-in-law. She was 95 years old and counting her days remaining on earth. I used to be close friends with the mother-in-law.

"She would complain to me about her two daughters-in-law, saying they never helped with the household the way she would have liked. Of course, I didn't take her complaints seriously because of their unfortunate circumstances. The men used to work for their father, Haj Adel, in his shop in the spice market. They were always busy working, and the wives were always busy with the mother-in-law. She kept them on their toes all the time. It was always something. Cooking, cleaning, dusting, polishing, and sometimes they didn't even have time to take care of their own children. It was especially bad when the mother-in-law's own three daughters came to visit with their children. You should have seen how the apartment looked then. It was like a kindergarten." Um-Tamer paused, as if trying to remember something, and the ladies waited.

"What happened?" Lamees asked finally.

"Anyway, not to make the story longer. Hadiya

and her husband's lives were intolerable. They lived in that one small room with three children. Mazen, because of his expanding family, was constantly borrowing money from his father. And despite all their hardships, Hadiya was always smiling and maintained a positive, cheerful attitude until that grey day.

"That day, her son, Jamal, was playing with his cousins on the balcony and fell from the third floor and landed on the pavement."

The women gasped as Um-Tamer continued, "He died instantly. He had been the pride and joy of that family. He was only three when he died."

The women were silent. All of them were mothers and had known the fear when a child disappeared from their sight for even a few minutes. The impact on the parents' hearts would be huge from such an incident.

Amani was sure that, like her, the ladies had many questions. How did Hadiya feel when she heard the screaming of the kids on the balcony? Did she go out to the balcony and look down to see her young son lying on the pavement, with blood splattered on the ground around his head? Maybe she didn't dare to go near the door of the balcony and see the horrible scene. Had she had the courage to tell her husband? Did she console him, or was it the other way around? So many disturbing questions and many grey thoughts came to Amani's mind. She felt a sense of gratitude and praised Allah that she had not had to go through such a painful moment.

Zahra remained silent throughout the conversation. Usually, she contributed to any discussion in their home.

After the women left, Zahra went up to her room without a word and without even cleaning the liwan. Amani was worried. She cleaned the liwan by herself, then went up to Zahra's room.

Zahra's room was the one she herself had longed for when she was a kid. She wanted Zahra to spend time in her own space, not like she'd grown up sleeping with her three sisters in the same room. Not to mention the four of them sharing the same skirts, shirts, and even bras. She'd sworn an oath when she gave birth to Zahra to provide everything for her, she had gone without as a girl.

Zahra's room was more like a scientist's study than a girl's bedroom. One entire wall was lined with books on a wide variety of topics. She had the best desktop computer the mullah could afford, which was missing at the moment because it was still with the police. The only concession to femininity was that the closet, desk, and bed were painted in pale pink. Zahra sat on her bed, hugging her legs, and resting her chin on her knees. Her eyes were open, but she was staring at nothing. Amani sat on the end of the bed and gazed at her. Zahra moved her head just enough to look at her.

Tears flooded Zahra's eyes. "We have to help Zakiya."

The smile disappeared from Amani's face, but she chose not to interrupt her daughter's choked words. "I think something horrible is going on with Zakiya."

Amani's heart pounded in her chest.

Zahra continued, "She liked my blue dress. The one you and Papa bought me for my last birthday. I insisted she take it, but asked her to try it on first, just to be sure it fit. I didn't plan to look at her bare body, but when I saw her back, something stuck in my throat that prevented me from asking what had happened to her. Maybe I was just afraid to hear the answer."

Amani moved closer and hugged her tightly, never having felt more grateful for her than she did at that moment.

***

When the mullah and Amani were alone in their room that night after supper, she told him what had happened and Zahra's reaction at seeing Zakiya's injuries. He narrowed his eyes and clenched his jaw until it hurt. The last thing he had wanted Zahra to see was Zakiya's back injuries. He was much older than she and had seen so much in this life, yet the girl's wounds and scars had disturbed him for many days. What could such a sight do to someone as delicate as Zahra?

They lay down to sleep, and a few minutes later, he could hear Amani's quiet, even breathing. He gazed at her lips, her soft cheeks, her tiny, pointed nose. He watched her eyes moving randomly beneath her eyelids. What dreams was she having? Were they flowery and enchanting, or were they dark and scary? He kissed her on the forehead and saw a hint of a smile on her lips, then turned onto his back and closed his eyes.

Hadiya came back into his thoughts. He shivered at the possibility that she had been murdered. What if Ahmad's suspicions were correct? It meant a murderer was walking around free and would most likely commit another crime, eventually.

Mixed emotions flooded his mind. Mostly the fear of finding out Ahmad's suspicions were true, and Hadiya had been murdered. But he was also secretly excited by the prospect of solving an actual crime, just like a real detective.

CHAPTER 17

Sunday, May 2, 2010

He was hanging upside down, naked. Wires wrapped around his ankles cut deep into his flesh. Blood ran down his leg in rivulets. The rivulets reached his waist and spread out over his stomach. Soon they were creeping through his chest hairs and dripping off the ends. Little red dots crawled over his neck like his wife's fingers when she played with him at night, and finally, everything was red as the blood ran into his eyes.

    He tried to scream, but his lips had been stitched together with wires. The only sound he could utter was a moan from deep inside as the blows continued to rain down upon his naked body. The pain was unbearable. He couldn't see who was hitting him or what they were hitting him with. Finally, the beating ceased, and he moaned in relief. The person stalked around him with slow, deliberate steps, as if taking time to admire his handiwork. Then his torturer let out a loud, cruel laugh.

The mullah jerked awake, soaked in sweat, gasping for breath. His heart hammered in his chest as his panicked wife beside him kept repeating, "I seek refuge with Allah from the cursed devil." She got up and poured a glass of water from the jug on the bedside table. He poured it down his throat as if he had gone without water for a week. When he'd calmed down somewhat, Amani said, "You were screaming, stop it, stop it!" He looked at her with wide eyes and felt his mouth dry, although he'd had a drink only seconds ago.

He glanced at the clock. 4 am, time to get up for the late-night prayer, *Tahajjud*, before going to the mosque to perform the dawn prayer.

After the dawn prayer, he strolled down the street towards Khaled's home. A row of cars was parked on each side of the street. He studied them one by one. Not a single new model amongst them. The newest one was over 30 years old. If a photographer had snapped a black-and-white photo of the street, then asked anyone, in which year it was taken, the answer would be in the 80s. Most passersby greeted him respectfully.

He knocked on the door and Khaled opened it, seemingly happy to see him. He was wearing a light green, oversized shirt that almost reached his knees, and pants the color of ground cumin. The pants were wrinkled, either because they were too long, or Khaled's legs were too short. His shoes were covered with dust, but they had once been black.

"Do you mind if I come in for a few minutes?" the mullah asked.

Khaled hesitated. "I would love for you to come in, but I was just leaving."

"I want to discuss a crucial matter. Can you come to the mosque this afternoon?" He really wanted to ask Khaled where he was going at such an early hour, but he restrained his curiosity.

"Let's take a walk. Despite the crutches, I must keep moving my legs as much as I can."

"Are you sure? Won't you be late for your appointment?"

"I'm fine. Please, let's just take a walk," Khaled said as he pulled the apartment door shut.

The mullah was used to the rhythm of Khaled's movements because of his left leg being shorter than his right. He didn't mind strolling side by side with him at a slower pace. The bigger problem was Khaled's crutches didn't have rubber tips, so they made a loud clacking noise that echoed in the morning's quiet. A few people were sitting out on their balconies as they passed. Maybe they had nothing better to do than observe passersby at such an early hour.

"I remember when your father brought you to the mosque for the very first time," he said. "You were so shy. When I asked you your name, you hid behind your father's back, pulling on his dish-dash."

Khaled's face reddened.

"Do you remember that?"

"Yes, I remember what a moron I was," Khaled said.

The mullah chided him softly, "You were not a moron. On the contrary. You were full of love and generosity. Everyone who saw you praised you. They praised your mother too, because she was the one who brought you up with those principles. I remember during the month of Ramadan, you would carry packets of dates to hand out to the people outside the mosque when the time of fasting was over. At dawn, you would take a jug of water and ask all the guys in the mosque if they were thirsty before fasting began."

They came to the end of the street and passed through a market full of vegetable vendors and passing cars. The vendors shouted from time to time to attract buyers as people gathered around each booth to buy fresh vegetables. The road was full of energy and movement. It was nearly impossible for Khaled to cross, and for this reason, they walked along the side with cars passing very close to them.

"My son, your colleagues miss you during our Monday and Wednesday classes. Won't you come back to the mosque?"

Khaled was paying close attention to where he needed to set his crutches. "I must take care of my sisters. They need a man around to make them feel secure, especially after my mom went to heaven to rest."

"By the way, how are your sisters? I suppose they are happy and satisfied with you for sure, as it seems you are the only man they can rely on."

"My sisters have forgotten that I am the man of the house in my parents' absence. They are not considerate of the fact that I am a special case and I need exceptional care."

"What have they done to make you feel this way?"

"I only want the best for the people around me, so I ask them to obey the laws of Allah. You taught us we should spread virtuous deeds and prevent bad ones, either by actions or words, and if not, then by heart."

"Do you feel the need to hit them sometimes?"

"Of course not," Khaled snapped.

"You've always been one of my best students, and I always remember you as nothing but honest. Please, if you need any help, you must speak up."

"I don't understand. What makes you think I am hiding something?"

"Yesterday, your sisters were in my house, and my daughter saw Zakiya's back." He stopped and looked down in order to meet Khaled's gaze. "Khaled, what is going on? Did you know about this?"

Khaled looked at the mullah and asked, "What is wrong with her back?"

"It's covered in scars. She's been horribly abused." He couldn't read Khaled's expression at that moment. Was he angry? Scared? Upset? Sad maybe? But why were his knuckles so white?

Finally, Khaled turned and started moving again. His voice broke as he said, "I have never lied to you, and how do you expect me to know about my sister's back, mullah? You know it is forbidden to look at my sisters' naked bodies. But of course, I would speak up if anyone harmed a hair on my sister's head." He fidgeted as he spoke.

The mullah put a hand on Khaled's back, urging him to turn and exit the market on the road to the right. They were now on a street similar to the one where Khaled lived. The same ugly, grey, four-story buildings. Many of the balconies had laundry hanging on them.

"Is it possible that your sisters are fighting and hurting each other?"

"I don't think so. They are very polite and well-educated girls."

"Are any of your relatives coming to your apartment? What do you think happened to her?"

The tension was apparent on Khaled's face. "I don't really know."

"Tell Zakiya not to be afraid. We will punish whoever has hurt her. Just encourage her to speak up and give you a name or names," the mullah said.

Khaled said nothing. The only sound was his crutches clacking on the pavement.

Mullah Abdullah hesitated, wondering if the time was right to address the other issue. In a soft voice, he said, "Are you still mourning your mother's death, Khaled?"

Khaled swallowed. Beads of sweat glistened on his

forehead. His voice wavered. "My mom didn't die."

The mullah frowned as he waited for him to continue.

"She just moved out of this horrible life into her heaven." Khaled said, "So there is no reason for mourning."

"Yes, you are right."

"I know, I'm always right," Khaled said boldly.

The mullah ignored Khaled's impudent reply and said, "Why do you say, 'this horrible life'? Wasn't she happy? Did she have health problems? Did she have a heart condition or some other serious disease?"

"No, she was ok. But why all the questions?"

"I think your mother was murdered," he blurted out. The second he said it, he regretted it. It was a serious allegation, and he had no proof. "I mean 'we' think she was murdered. Your uncle Ahmad and I."

He wanted to slap his own face. *Why did I mention Ahmad's name? What if Khaled's mother had not been murdered?* With a clenched jaw and shaky left hand, he lifted his fez from his head and ran his fingers through his hair before setting it back down. Again, he couldn't interpret Khaled's expression, so he just waited for Khaled to speak.

"I really don't know what to say. What made Uncle Ahmad think such a thing?"

It was getting worse and worse for the mullah. He realized he couldn't avoid answering the question. His answer would accuse Khaled's father directly, and there was no proof beyond Ahmad's allegations. "Ahmad thinks your father killed your mother, so he wouldn't have to return the money he owed Ahmad." A heavy sigh escaped his lips.

Khaled responded with a rasp in his throat, "That is ridiculous. How could he accuse my father of such a thing? Just because he didn't get his so-called loan paid back?"

"That's why I need you to tell me what happened when your father was here. Maybe Ahmad is wrong." The pain in his jaw was getting worse, and he wished he could crush something. His words were only making the situation worse.

Khaled said, with a trembling chin, "What do you mean, maybe? Even you doubt my father. How could you think of him as a murderer? Do you really think he would kill for money?" They were standing across from Khaled's building by this time.

Khaled clacked off on his crutches without another word. The mullah sighed and muttered to himself, "Yes, you're right. How could I?"

Students were showing up on the street with tired eyes and sleepy faces. It was the first day of the week. He returned home thinking he must improve his skills as a detective.

***

When the mullah reached his house at ten past eight, he found Zahra had already left for school and Amani was holding breakfast for him. When they'd finished eating, he sat in the liwan to work on the notes for his meeting at the Ministry of Endowments at 11 am. By the time he was finished, it was five to ten.

He went to his room to change and get ready. As he adjusted his fez in the mirror, his mobile phone rang. It was Ahmad. He smiled, thinking that was good timing.

Ahmad's voice was nearly drowned out by the background noise of the looms operating on the factory floor. He updated Ahmad on his progress regarding Zakiya and Khaled's reaction to the idea that his mother had been murdered.

Ahmad said, "I need you to go with me to meet someone who can provide evidence that Mazen killed his wife."

"Sorry, I'm not hearing you clearly."

Ahmad yelled, "I want to take you to meet a person who will testify that Mazen killed Hadiya."

A chill ran down the mullah's spine. He wondered why he felt scared.

The certainty in Ahmad's voice led him to believe there really had been a crime, and a murderer was on the loose. "What time?"

"This afternoon," Ahmad said.

"I have my quarterly meeting at the Ministry in one hour. I am not sure the meeting will be over soon enough. Can we do it this evening, or perhaps tomorrow?"

"Wait just a second, let me check," Ahmad said.

He heard papers rustling.

"Tomorrow morning at 10:30, we will meet at Bab Tomah square," Ahmad said, "And you will hear the evidence with your own ears."

"Ok, see you tomorrow."

"Ok, take care," Ahmad said, and the line went dead.

***

When the mullah entered his house that evening after the last Isha prayer, he found Amani sitting in the liwan, her face pale and forehead furrowed. She was holding a piece of paper. As he sat down next to her, she handed him the letter without speaking.

It was a court order that outlined how he was prohibited from going near Mazen's house. On top of that he and his family were not allowed to communicate with any of Mazen's immediate family. As in the case of any breach of this court order, he and his family would bear severe consequences.

It surprised him how Mazen, while living in Dubai, could get such an order in such a brief time. Of course, he had used his power and money to get it handled so quickly, but what did it mean? Why was he trying to keep them away from his family? Of course, Khaled must have told his father what they had discussed earlier that morning. But if Mazen was innocent, what was he so afraid of? He wondered if he should call Ahmad and update him now or let it wait till tomorrow. Mazen was tightening the noose around his own neck.

CHAPTER 18

Monday, May 3, 2010

The mullah was waiting at Bab Tomah Square by 10:30 morning. He had always enjoyed the historical structure, especially the remains of the massive gate in the center of the square. Bab Tomah, or Thomas' Gate, is one of seven historical gates in the Old Damascus Wall in Syria and an early Christian landmark. Thomas was one of the twelve apostles of Jesus Christ. There is a symbol of Venus in the arch over the gate, while the other six gates bear the symbols of other planets. Millions of people have passed through this gate over hundreds of years.

At this time of day, all the students are in school, and the clerks are in their offices, causing the streets to be less crowded. A few taxis parked nearby, trying to catch their next customers. As usual, the scene was spoiled by the incessant honking of car horns. It was as if the cars wouldn't move if the drivers didn't honk.

He looked at his watch. He'd been here 30 minutes already, and Ahmad had not shown up yet. Although the sun had not yet reached its zenith, its heat insisted on evaporating all the liquids from his body. He called Ahmad's mobile phone, but there was no answer. Taking out his prayer beads, he started his daily praise. He responded to the people who greeted him from time to time in acknowledgment of his religious attire. Ten more minutes passed, and Ahmad still did not show up.

Behind him, on the pavement under an enormous umbrella, a lottery salesman was screaming Ashra million (ten million) to attract buyers. When the vendor noticed the mullah standing there with large sweat stains under his arms, he offered him a small plastic chair next to him in the shade of his umbrella. Suddenly feeling as if he had been standing for ten hours, the mullah accepted the offer with many thanks. He continued to try Ahmad's number, but still no answer. He tried calling Ahmad's landline, also no answer. It was already 11:30 and no word from Ahmad. He thanked the lottery salesman for the seat and walked back home.

***

That evening, after he returned from the last prayer in the mosque, he sat in the liwan with Amani. She was engrossed in reading a book, and he was still puzzling over the reason Ahmad hadn't shown up or even answered his calls. *Why doesn't he call and apologize for not showing up?* He decided if he didn't hear from him by tomorrow, he must either go to his factory or his house.

Zahra came out to join them wearing a pink sleeveless dress. She kissed his forehead and her mother's hand before sitting down.

"Papa, do you know when we can get my computer back?" Zahra asked while she rubbed the back of her neck and avoided looking at him.

"I've been trying to track it down. I have learned that your computer isn't considered forensic evidence, but they still haven't located it."

Zahra frowned.

"But don't worry my dear," he said. "Yesterday, one of my friends after our meeting in the ministry told me he knows someone in the criminal evidence department. Even if they don't have it there, they will find out where it is."

"Ok, Papa, thank …" The doorbell rang, interrupting her.

When the mullah opened the door, Hani stood there accompanied by another man with fair skin, brown hair, and a perfectly trimmed beard and mustache. The stranger, carrying a mahogany brown leather bag, was dwarfed next to Hani in his police uniform. The blank stare in Hani's eyes froze the blood in the mullah's veins.

"Mullah Abdullah Al-Allab?" a rough voice

came out of the stranger's mouth.

"Peace be upon you, brothers. Yes, I am Mullah Abdullah. And you are?" he coughed slightly to hide his nervousness.

"I am Detective Mansoor Chait from the Criminal Security Administration."

The mullah's heart raced. "Yes, how can I help you?"

"Can we have a chat with you?" Hani asked.

He shot them both glances, then shouted, "Ya Allah, Ya Allah," to warn his wife and daughter that male guests were coming in and they should make themselves scarce.

Inviting the two men to come in, he closed the door behind them, glancing at Mansoor's leather bag from behind. He remembered his interrogators at the prison had carried identical bags, and his legs felt weak, causing him to lean against the wall and breathe deeply a few times before he steeled himself to join them in the liwan.

Without wasting a second, detective Mansoor asked him, "When was the last time you spoke with Ahmad Kishat?"

A terrible dread filled his gut, and he hesitated before answering. "Yesterday afternoon, we talked on the phone. We were supposed to meet this morning, but he didn't show up. Why? What has happened?"

"I don't know what happened," Mansoor said.

"What do you mean? What's wrong?" The mullah asked, looking back and forth between Hani and Mansoor.

"You don't know what's wrong with him?" Mansoor asked.

He swallowed. "He seemed ok to me yesterday over the phone."

Mansoor flung several photographs on the small table in front of the mullah, who looked at the first one and then moved his gaze between Mansoor and Hani.

"Yes, he is dead," Hani said in a sorrowful tone.

Mansoor interrupted, "This morning, the cleaning lady found his body on the floor of his office in the factory."

The mullah flipped through the photos, examining them, trying to understand the cause of death. But the images showed only his body sprawled on the floor. No sign of blood or a weapon. "I just can't believe this," he said, then repeated himself. Raising his head, he stuttered, "What happened?"

"The cause of death is not yet known. We are still investigating," Mansoor said.

"We belong to Allah, and to him we shall return," he said. Hani and Mansoor both repeated his words.

"On his cell phone," Mansoor said, "We noticed a few missed calls from you. When we questioned his wife, she mentioned your name, and that you were supposed to meet with him today."

The mullah told the story of the debt

owed and Ahmad's fears that his sister had been murdered. Then he mentioned the court order and the witness they were supposed to meet that morning. Mansoor was scribbling down notes. When he'd finished, Mansoor said, "I understand your concerns and I agree with you. The court order would make anyone suspicious. Nevertheless, without solid evidence, no one can open a closed case. My advice to you is, don't interfere."

"Do you still have the copy of Hadiya's letter?" Hani asked the mullah.

"I don't."

Mansoor looked at Hani and said, "I will ask Ahmad's wife. She probably has it."

Then he asked the mullah, "Do you know who the witness was that Ahmad wanted you to speak with?"

"No, I don't know anything about it."

"Based on what you mentioned, it looks like a dead end. Unless something new comes up while we are investigating the cause of death," Mansoor said.

"What if he was murdered?" the mullah asked.

"We will uncover the truth and punish the guilty," Mansoor said. "But what makes you say that?"

"Is it a coincidence that he died on the same day we were about to get proof Mazen killed his own wife?"

"You are going too far with your reasoning, and these are serious allegations. Especially your inference that Mazen killed his wife. Now you suspect another murder."

"Can't we presume it was a murder and try to find evidence?"

"Justice cannot be based on speculations," Mansoor said. "We will have the coroner's report soon. And since Ahmad didn't have formal proof of his debt with Mazen, there is no motive for Mazen to kill his wife. Plus, Ahmad was the only one who said that he knew of a witness."

"Isn't that enough to suspect he was murdered?" the mullah asked.

"You are the only one he told, about knowing someone with evidence," Mansoor said. "So that makes you a suspect more than Mazen. Just drop it, mullah. A man who can bring a court order while he is outside the country in one day can cause you a lot of trouble."

"If you found out that Ahmad was murdered, and you could prove that Mazen was involved, wouldn't that be enough to suspect that Mazen killed his wife as well?" the mullah asked.

"No, it is not sufficient. Justice doesn't work that way," Mansoor said.

Hani interrupted them. "Mullah, let us not anticipate events. Justice will take its course. Just leave it to us, and we will find out who's guilty."

"Yes, I know you will."

"However, please, don't leave the country," Mansoor said.

"Why? Am I a suspect?" snapped the mullah.

"Just in case we need you. We will be in touch with you," Mansoor said.

"I understand," the mullah said. "Oh, I'm so sorry for my thoughtlessness. I forgot to ask you what you'd like to drink."

"We appreciate your kindness, but we need to move on," Mansoor said. They left him sitting alone in the liwan. His clenched fingers were ivory white and icy cold. His chest felt as if a heavy weight was sitting on it.

CHAPTER 19

Wednesday, May 5, 2010

Ahmad's funeral was held on Wednesday afternoon in the mosque of Shagoor. The enshrouded body was in a wooden coffin covered with black velvet. Qur'an verses were embroidered in gold thread on the velvet. The coffin was at the front of the mosque, and the old building was packed with all of Ahmad's family and friends. An air of shock and disbelief pervaded. Hani was there, his head higher than everyone else in the mosque. Hassan and Hussein, Ahmad's teenage sons, wore black and gazed at the coffin with reddened eyes.

The hearse parked outside the mosque had verses from the Qur'an printed on its sides. Wreaths of Aas -Myrtus Communis and yellow roses covered the front and sides. The back was open, ready to receive the coffin.

Mullah Abdullah led the prayer, and the minute he was finished, the attendees carried the coffin on their shoulders. Right at the front were Hassan and Hussein. The moment the coffin touched their shoulders, a fresh wave of tears streamed from their red eyes.

One mourner yelled, "Wahhiddooh- say Allah is the only one-."

The congregation said, "There is no God but Allah."

The hearse outside played a recording of the Qur'an by a famous reciter with a melancholy voice. All the neighbors were out on their balconies to watch the sad ceremony. The hearse moved slowly, and the congregation walked behind it with the coffin on their shoulders. The driver lowered the volume of the Qur'an recording and used a microphone to announce, "Read Fatiha (the opener of the Qur'an) and grant it to the Prophet's spirit and the family of the Prophet and the spirits of all those who preceded us to the mercy of Allah." Then he restored the volume of the recording, while the congregation recited Fatiha from the Qur'an.

The mullah led the congregation, with Hani walking beside him. The men carrying the coffin switched with others from time to time, but Hassan and Hussein remained with the coffin the whole distance. Along Shagoor Street, pedestrians either stopped and recited the Fatiha or joined the congregation, since many believed they would earn a reward for walking in a funeral procession.

The hearse crept along Shagoor Street toward Bab Sagheer cemetery, one of the oldest graveyards in the heart of the old part of Damascus. It had graves dating back over 1500 years. Some of the prophet's wives and granddaughters were buried there, along with shrines for the decapitated heads of the martyrs in the battle of Karbala.

The tombstones, with their epitaphs, were at different heights and looked like so many white ghosts staring at you all the time. Tombs are supposed to be arranged in parallel lines, but in this cemetery, they were scattered, making it difficult to walk between them. The procession had to wind its way through a maze of tombs to reach their destination. As the congregation arrived, they spread out, trying to find the shortest way to reach the open grave, as it waited to swallow up Ahmad's body.

The congregation gathered around the open grave; a deep hole soaked with darkness, its bottom invisible in the murk. The only one who dared to descend was the undertaker. The sons of Ahmad and the mullah took the enshrouded body out of the wooden coffin and slowly passed it to the undertaker, who descended into the grave until only his head remained visible. He took the body from them and laid it in the grave, carefully arranging it facing towards Mecca. Then he uncovered the face and climbed out of the grave.

The mullah bent over the dark hole to be closer to Ahmad's head, as if he was going to have a conversation with him, and started the ritual. The congregation remained hushed out of respect.

"In the name of Allah, the Most Gracious, the Most Merciful," the mullah intoned in a sad voice. "Peace be upon our master, Muhammad; the best of the prophets and the Seal of the Messengers.

"'Every soul will taste death. Then to us will you be returned'. (29:57)

"'Oh, reassured soul, return to your Lord, well-pleased and pleasing [to Him], And enter among My servants, and enter My Paradise'. (89:27-30)

"Oh, servant of Allah, and the son of his servants, listen.

"Two angels will come and ask you, and you must answer:

"'So, I said, I have accepted Allah Almighty as my Lord. I have accepted Islam as my religion. I have accepted Muhammad as my prophet and messenger. I have accepted the Ka'ba as my hub, and I have accepted the Qur'an as my book.'

"Do not be afraid to utter the testimonies,

"I bear witness that there is no God, but Allah, and that Muhammad is the Messenger of Allah."

The mullah raised his face towards the sky and everyone else did the same.

"Oh Allah, forgive him, be merciful to him, be generous with him, put him in a prominent position, expand his entrance, and purify him of sins. Oh Allah, multiply his virtuous deeds, overcome his evil, and put him at the highest level in heaven. And pray to our master, Muhammad, and his family and companions."

He looked at the men standing around him. "Please read the opening verses of the Qur'an and gift it to his soul."

Then the undertaker disappeared into the grave, covered the face, and stepped out.

The funeral was completed, and the body was buried. The mourners left to continue their daily routine, leaving Ahmad in his dark grave.

The first of three nights of mourning were held on Wednesday night. The male ceremony was at the mosque in Shagoor, under the mullah's supervision and the daily presence of Ahmad's sons. It began after Isha's prayer. The famous Qur'an reciter, Madani, started the recitation in a mournful tone. The men and boys filed in, sat down, and listened with tilted heads, contemplating the profound meaning of the Qur'anic verses. They had entered individually, but when they left, they did so in groups. A server passed around cups of bitter Arabic coffee on all three nights.

Khaled stood with his cousins and Ahmad's relatives at the door to receive the condolences the people uttered as they entered the memorial. He greeted the mullah politely when he entered and left.

On the third night, when Haj Adel came for the first time to give his condolences, Khaled didn't look at the mullah while his grandfather was present, and Haj Adel didn't come close to greet the mullah before he left. He gestured to Khaled and left without looking back. Khaled hobbled out behind his grandfather, also not looking at anyone. Hani shook his head when he saw their behavior.

Hassan and Hussein's pale complexions contrasted with their charcoal black hair and olive-green eyes. They both wore black suits and kept their eyes focused on the ground continually.

***

The female ceremony was held at Ahmad's house in Dommar. It started one day after the men's ceremony started. Rema, the widow of Ahmad, was living in a bubble. She isolated herself from what was going on around her. The women would gather to read the Qur'an to grant to Ahmad's soul, but only her body was with them. Her soul was far away in another world. She wasn't aware of the time or the place or who was around her. She sat on the sofa where Ahmad used to sit and stared straight ahead with vacant eyes. She cried until her sons would come and lead her to her bedroom to sleep. She stopped cooking and lost weight because she stopped eating and drinking. Hassan and Hussein persuaded her to drink a glass of milk by crying and begging her. Ahmad had been her entire world, and she had lost it.

Rema and her two sons continued to wear black for 40 days, as was the custom.

CHAPTER 20

Saturday, May 08, 2010

When Mullah Abdullah awoke, he was confronted by Ahmad's face on the clock beside the bed. The ghostly visage appeared again in the mirror while the mullah brushed his teeth. It reflected in the shop windows along the street on his way to the mosque. The mournful countenance was even reflected in the glass of the bookcases in the mosque.

Ahmad's face seemed to be everywhere.

The mullah opened the door of the ablution area, in which there were three toilets on the left and three faucets on the right. There was a short marble block in front of the faucets for worshipers to sit while performing their ablutions. On the front wall was a row of coat hooks. He took off his cloak and hung it on a hook, raised his white dish-dash, rolled up his sleeves, and sat on the marble cube. He used to mix the hot and cold water before he started ablutions, but this time he turned on the faucet with the red circle. The hot water streamed out and steam ascended. He put his hands under the water, and soon the water covering his hands changed to blood. The blood was boiling.

It was as if a hidden power held his hands there. Soon his face was covered with sweat, not because of the steam, but because of his efforts to pull his hands away. The pain was unbearable. Despite his attempts not to cry, his eyes betrayed him. Tears fell and his throat screamed.

Someone pulled him back and yelled in his ear, "What are you doing?"

He tried to look into the face of the person, but he needed to wipe his eyes with his sleeve to see clearly. It was Fathi, with an astonished look on his face.

"What … why?" Fathi said as he stared at the mullah's hands.

The mullah looked at the boiling water streaming from the faucet and steam filling the air. His hands were scalded. Now he felt the pain, and moans escaped his lips.

Fathi twisted off the hot water tap and turned on the cold. The mullah put his red hands under the cold water to reduce the pain, but the pain only got worse. He avoided looking at Fathi, whose eyes reflected his concern and unspoken questions.

The mullah usually enjoyed the quiet morning hours in the mosque before the afternoon prayers. Today, those hours had become a living hell because of his burns. It was as if his heartbeat had moved into his hands and every beat of his pulse throbbed through them. All of his attention was on them rather than on the prayers he performed.

After the prayer, he was not aware of who was talking to him or what they said. The few minutes' walk from the mosque to his house felt like hours. Amani froze when she saw his shaking hands. She just stared at him as if she didn't recognize him. She ran to the phone. "I will call the doctor."

"No, don't," he shouted.

Amani stopped and looked at him, waiting for him to explain, but he didn't say another word, just went into his bedroom and pushed the door closed with his back. He laid down on the bed without undressing, raised his hands above his eyes and looked at the flaming red skin. Was this the pain of burning in hell? But his burns were only from hot water. What if the burning was from actual flames? How unimaginable such pain must be. Tears flooded his eyes and ran down his cheeks. His mentor, Sheikh Hasan, used to tell him, 'My son Abdullah, in the hereafter, all of humanity will be in hell if they have relied only on their deeds from this life. Only if Allah's mercy covers them will they go to heaven.'

He smiled when he remembered his mentor. It had been the best phase of his life, especially after the hellish time when he'd lived with Sheikh Afeef after his father passed away when he was fifteen. He never felt motherless as a boy, even though his own mother had died in labor. His father filled the roles of both parents during those years until fate tested his patience and took that most valuable person from him.

Sheikh Afeef took him to his home because his father's house had been a rental. He stayed with Sheikh Afeef for only three years. He learned what it felt like to be an orphan. The humiliation of his deep needs, the emptiness of starvation, the embarrassment of poverty, plus the mental and physical pain.

Those three years had been a significant shock to him. Sheikh Afeef was a religious person in public, but a rotten human being in private. He was a person with substantial value in the community, but he'd treated the mullah like a slave when they were at home. He was an influential man who advised people in public to be good and obey Allah, but in his private life, he was a big hypocrite.

Sheikh Afeef continually reminded him that if he hadn't granted him a room in his house, he would have been homeless. Although the mullah paid rent, Sheikh Afeef treated him like a servant. He had to go to the market daily, to buy whatever food and other items the Sheikh demanded. He had to do all the household duties, such as cleaning the house, doing laundry, and cooking. He didn't have a problem doing those things. The problem was the punishment system Sheikh Afeef implemented whenever he made even the smallest mistake, or if Sheikh Afeef didn't like the results. Nothing ever satisfied Sheikh Afeef. Thus, everyday punishment would be meted out. The mildest was being sent to bed without his dinner, and the harshest was ten slaps on the face.

He had been on the brink of rejecting all the high principles his father had taught him if Sheikh Hasan hadn't rescued him.

He had gone to class with bleeding hands that day. Sheikh Afeef had smacked his hands with a metal rod the night before for forgetting to lock the fridge after preparing dinner. Sheikh Afeef had padlocks on the refrigerator and all the cabinets in the kitchen, so the mullah couldn't eat without his permission. When Sheikh Hasan saw his hands, he immediately asked him to move into his house. Never again did he return to Sheikh Afeef's house.

Sheikh Hasan never asked him for details, but he had read his face and understood his suffering. His discretion was the thing the mullah loved most about his new mentor. The first thing Sheikh Hasan had taught him was that nothing is free in this life. He let him rent a small room in his house. It was the room Zahra used nowadays, since Sheikh Hasan had bequeathed his home to the mullah. It was his wedding gift to the mullah, with the only condition being that he, Sheikh Hasan, would continue to live there as a guest until his death.

Sheikh Hasan had been the one who introduced Amani to him, telling him she was from a religious family, and he would not find a better match. As it turned out, she was a lucky choice indeed. The mullah was jubilant, unable to believe there was such generosity in this life. He was more than glad to have his mentor in the house after they were married, as he had always been a reliable source of answers for any obstacle or challenge the couple faced. His daughter Zahra was born two years later. Sheikh Hasan had suggested calling her Zahra after the Prophet Mohammad's daughter. That same year, his mentor passed away and left him in a deep pool of sadness.

He finally fell into a fitful sleep, and when he awoke, a loud moan escaped his throat. He raised his hands to look at them. They were shaking furiously. He didn't notice his wife staring at him silently, her eyes brimming with tears. He turned his head to look at her when she asked, "What happened?"

"I burned them in the mosque."

She asked for no more details, but continued, "Please let me call the doctor."

He smiled despite the deep pain and thanked Allah in his heart for his obedient wife. "Please, be patient."

She couldn't remain quiet. "What are you trying to prove? Why are you doing this to yourself?" Her cheeks were now wet with tears.

"I blame myself for Ahmad's death." He knew Amani wouldn't try to change his mind. From their years together, she was well aware of his stubborn nature.

"How will you atone for this sin?"

"First, I will find out who killed him and be sure they will go to jail. Second, I will find out who killed his sister, Hadiya. Don't ask me how. I don't know yet."

"I will pray for you to find the killers and punish them. But what about your hands? Why do you want to stay in agony?"

"This is nothing compared to the agony in the hereafter."

Amani sighed, kissed him on the forehead, and said, "I will fetch a yogurt drink to help you relax."

***

The mullah's bedroom had become a torture chamber thanks to his pain induced moans, his sleepless nights, and his swollen, blistered hands. By the time Monday morning dawned, he was delirious, with a dangerously feverish temperature. Amani called the doctor and asked him to come immediately. The doctor injected him with anti-inflammatory medication, applied a soothing ointment, wrapped his hands with gauze, and gave him a hefty painkiller. He slept deeply after the injection and stayed home to rest until Friday morning. As was his custom, he prepared his sermon for Friday prayer and went to the mosque to do his duty, even though his hands were not fully recovered.

After the prayer, the congregation surrounded him and heaped questions on him regarding his bandaged hands until he became exhausted. When the mosque was finally empty, he sat down to recite a few verses of the Qur'an before returning home.

That evening, he called Hani to ask about the progress in Ahmad's case. Hani refused to discuss details over the telephone and promised to come to the mullah's house after his shift.

Amani and Zahra went to bed before him, and he remained in the liwan, his head bobbing from drowsiness. When he finally heard a knock, it was already midnight. Startled, fully awake, he hastened to open the door.

As Hani entered wearing his police uniform, he immediately noticed the mullah's hands wrapped in white gauze.

"Just a small accident," he said without waiting for Hani's question.

They sat in the liwan, and with no preliminaries, Hani said, "He was murdered."

The mullah stiffened, his eyes searching Hani's face for answers. "But ... by whom? And why?"

"We have concluded that the cause of death was a sharp blow to the back of his head."

The mullah was quiet for a few long seconds, tasting the bitterness in his mouth. "I believe the person who killed Hadiya also killed Ahmad."

"But we are not confident that Hadiya was even murdered," Hani said. "The only hint we have is Ahmad's suspicions, and suspicions don't count as evidence."

"No, there was more evidence than Ahmad's suppositions. I'm certain that was the reason he was murdered. They don't want him to reveal the evidence."

Hani sighed. "Well, speculation doesn't count as evidence, either."

He looked at Hani, wondering if he really wanted to help or just be an obstacle. "Ahmad wanted to introduce me to someone who would testify that Mazen killed his wife. That wasn't speculation; it was a fact."

He'd known Hani for five years, long enough to know the only language he understood was money. "I want to find out who killed Ahmad and Hadiya. And I want all your help and support. Naturally, your share will be reserved for you."

Hani lifted his eyebrows. "Is there a new client asking you to reveal the reason for Ahmad's death?"

"Ahmad and Hadiya's death," the mullah corrected him. "And I prefer to keep it confidential. I'll let you know at the right time."

"But maybe we are talking here about two different cases."

"It doesn't matter if they were killed by the same person or different people. I am appointed by Allah to find the sinners and bring them to justice. Unless I'm mistaken, you are assigned by the government to catch bad people. Are you not?"

"Not only out of a sense of duty do I pursue this. But Ahmad was also my friend. My priority is to find who killed him and to find justice for him. But in the meantime, don't talk to anyone about Hadiya or Ahmad." Hani smiled sarcastically. "We don't want another murder on our hands."

The mullah didn't smile at the sarcasm. "I get the idea you don't believe Hadiya was murdered? Aren't you the one who brought me the news of the fake report?"

"As I told you before, a police report doesn't always mean there was an investigation. Let's assume Hadiya's death was a crime. I need to find out who the detective was, if there was an investigation in the first place, and try to examine the evidence and circumstances. I need to see if I can find anything that would prove it was a crime."

"So, if there was no investigation, I need you to help me investigate who the killer was." He leaned closer to Hani's face and spoke. "And as I promised, your share is being held in reserve."

"It's not a matter of my helping or not," Hani said. "It is nearly impossible to restart an investigation on a closed case. So, imagine if there is no case at all. It's like asking me to shave a bald head."

Pain pulsed through the mullah's gauze-wrapped hands. "So, am I to understand that if there was no investigation, you won't try to find out what happened to the unfortunate lady?"

"No, I didn't say that."

He wanted to object, but Hani raised his palm and continued, "Please, just let me find out if there was an investigation. Until then, just wait to hear from me."

"Ok, I will await your call."

Hani scratched the back of his neck and said without looking at him, "Do you have any good news for me about Samah, the girl I want to marry?"

The mullah didn't bother to hide his annoyance. "Don't worry. If it is written for you, you will marry her. Just give it more time."

"What is that supposed to mean?" Hani asked, faking a smile.

"It means all of our fate is in Allah's hands."

"I know, but Allah also wants us to make the effort to achieve what we seek in this life."

"Yes, true, and I am doing my best to help you."

"Ok, thank you for your help, anyway."

"Any progress regarding Salah?"

"Oh, I need more time. It seems we will need to scour the entire country to find him. By the time you have an answer for me about the girl, you will definitely hear about Salah."

What a jerk.

After Hani left, the mullah lingered in the liwan, staring at the portraits of his father on the wall. He wondered what he would have done if he was in his position. Would he have kept digging to find the murderer? Or would he have decided to leave it in the hands of Allah and let the murderer receive his punishment in the hereafter?

CHAPTER 21

Wednesday, May 19, 2010

At Wednesday's afternoon session, the mullah and seven of his students sat in a circle. All the students held notebooks and pens.

Today was the first day after taking the bandages off his hands, and for the next few days, he had to continue applying ointment until they healed entirely. He was incredibly careful with his sensitive new skin.

He started by saying, "The necessities of life make certain prohibitions permissible. This principle has a role in facilitating human life in critical situations. When a person reaches the limit of permanent damage or even loss of life, it is incumbent on that person to take any chance or opportunity to prevent the damages in question and save a life without thinking of the legitimacy of the violations. For instance, a man on a ship with women who are not his kin may not touch them at all. However, if the ship is in a severe storm, and one woman almost falls off the ship. If there is a man close to her who doesn't try to catch her and pull her back from the edge, she will fall to her death. In this case, he must act to save her life. In doing so, he would not be committing a prohibited act. Another example might be a person in the desert dying from starvation and dehydration. If he finds a dead dog and does not eat its meat, he will be unable to proceed any further and he will die. Of course, in this situation, he must save his life and eat whatever he finds in the desert, be it dead dogs, lizards, snakes, or whatever."

Some students made faces as he continued, "This allowance is sensitive and a definite exception. People should be careful when implementing it, not to abuse it by evaluating simple actions as necessities such as claiming his or her life is in danger when it isn't." He paused, raised his glass of water, and sipped. Then he asked, "Who can give me an example of the necessities of life that can make prohibitions permissible?"

Fathi raised his hand, and the mullah gestured for him to speak. "Some medicines have alcohol in them."

"Good one. Who has another example?" the mullah exclaimed.

Salem spoke without first seeking permission. "If a person was on a plane with his wife and his mother-in-law, and the engine dies. If they need to lower the weight, it may become necessary to throw out his mother-in-law." The students burst out laughing, and the mullah might have fallen off his seat from laughing if he wasn't in the mosque. He ignored Salem and asked, "Anyone have a better example?"

Saeed raised his hand, and he gestured for him to speak. "If a human is asked to pay a bribe to facilitate his business or prevent his business from failing."

"Such action would not be considered as 'necessities permit prohibited' acts. Can anyone tell me where we would place such an action? Under which category?" The mullah asked.

"The aim justifies the method," Amjad said.

"That is correct. But is the aim really justified here? What do you think?"

The students started mumbling. Five of them agreed the aims would not justify the means, and the other two said the contrary. He said, "It is not an ethical function, and people must avoid acting in this way. We are not allowed, under any circumstances, to commit major sins in order to reach ambitious aims and goals. We are not allowed to give or receive a bribe to facilitate your business. Another example might be someone striving to reach a higher position. A position that would grant him power and authority. His intention is to use the power and authority he gains to help ordinary people, but he could not reach that position without committing sins and disobeying many divine orders. In such a case, his noble intention wouldn't give him permission to go above divine law. Has anyone else got another example?"

"It is not acceptable for a person to blow up his body to kill civilians in order to reach heaven," Alaa' said.

"Excellent example," the mullah said. He paused a moment in case someone had another example, but when no one spoke, he went on. "Allah will not be pleased with our worship unless it is done in the way he has ordered."

Amjad interrupted, "Do you mean there are acts of worship which will displease Allah?"

"As long as the acts of the worship came from Allah, meaning they are defined by Allah as such, then they will please Him. Otherwise, it would be a heresy. Anyway, let us get back to our original subject. There is a narration by the prophet that says, 'Allah won't be worshiped by the disobedient.' For example, if a person wants to build a mosque, which is a form of worship, he must not steal money to enable him to build it, because that amounts to a sin. Thus, he cannot worship Allah by building the mosque if he is going to disobey Him by stealing the money."

Salem raised his hand. The mullah hesitated, afraid that the student wanted to crack another joke. Salem started talking anyway. "Under certain circumstances, a tyrant will appear and kill innocents, and thousands of people will suffer because of him. To kill him is a blessing to humanity, and the oppression will stop. No one will object or say it's not permissible to kill this tyrant, whatever his religion might be."

"First of all, this instance is not in the 'aim justifying the method' category," the mullah said. "Second, in Islam, it is not permitted for a person to kill another person by personal endeavor. To reach such a decision, religion's senior scholars would meet and discuss the issue in all its aspects, and then, if they agree, a fatwa will be published to eliminate such a tyrant. Ordinary people cannot make such decisions, or chaos would spread throughout the community. No man can assign himself as judge and implement divine orders to kill people, claiming they are oppressors. That's why Islam issued Hudood, the boundaries, which delineate punishments for sinners. A lot of restrictions were also issued to keep the enforcement of these punishments to the minimum.

"Because the purpose of the limits is to prevent people from committing sins openly, not to make Allah appear brutal or for people to feel happy at the pain of others. So restrictions are applied to give all sinners the opportunity for repentance and to ask forgiveness from Allah. Because the first cause of a breakdown in social cohesion is the committing of sins openly in society. Thus, only people who commit sins openly would be punished in a prescribed manner.

"Also, the decision to carry out a punishment must be issued by the elders who have jurisdiction. They must be well known for their virtuous and trustworthy character, and most important of all, they themselves will implement the divine orders without hesitation."

After the session, he stayed in the mosque alone, contemplating the things going on in his life. How did he get himself involved in such a situation? There was a murder, and yet the murderer was still free. He felt partly responsible for that. Was he being honest with his students by teaching them something but not implementing it himself? He had told them that the end justifies the means is a prohibited notion. But wasn't he doing just that, by sacrificing an innocent girl like Samah just to know what happened to Salah? Mahmoud's visit to his house the day before had shocked him. The strong, confident man had come to his house dragging his feet and with slumped shoulders. His thinning hair was not combed, the tail of his shirt was untucked from his trousers. He looked ten years older.

"I want my son to come back home," Mahmoud said with a trembling voice.

"I pray to Allah every night to have him back amongst us." The mullah told him.

"Why is Allah doing this to me? Why me? Salah is my only son." Mahmoud's jaw muscles quivered and sweat covered his face. He barely opened his eyelids.

"Allah tests us in a variety of ways in this life, and our reward will be in the hereafter." He wondered if he would ignore spiritual values like Mahmoud, if anything ever happened to Zahra?

"But why does the test have to be my only son? Why not test me by taking my life instead?" Mahmoud's lips were dry, and his voice was shaking.

"Brother, please remember the patience of prophet Jacob-Yaqoob. When his son, Joseph-Yusof, disappeared for many years. He never lost faith in Allah. He simply waited until Allah brought them back together."

"I called Sharshabil," Mahmoud said.

The mullah gasped. "Why would you do that?" Sharshabil, in his seventies, was famous for dabbling in black magic to achieve what his customers demanded of him. He claimed to be the twin of a spirit, and the spirit does whatever he asks. Such actions are absolutely prohibited in Islam, if Sharshabil actually dealt with spirits.

"One of my wife's friends said that when her daughter disappeared, Sharshabil was told by the spirit she had run away to Lebanon with her lover."

"For Allah's sake, don't do that. I suppose he asked you for hundreds of thousands. I beg you not to do it, don't let the wrath of Allah come down on you and your family."

"Please don't tell me what to do or not to do. It is not your son who has disappeared. If your daughter Zahra disappeared, would you not try any means possible to find out where she is?" Mahmoud spoke through trembling lips.

The mullah started to say, "Please calm …" when Mahmoud interrupted him. "Don't tell me to calm down," and moved toward the door, ready to leave.

He followed him and touched his arm before he got to the door. "Brother, please just listen to me."

Mahmoud wept, covering his face with both hands, his body trembling with each sob.

"One of my friends has enough power to gain any information I need. I asked him about Salah, and I am awaiting his answer. Please, just be patient and don't pay Sharshabil. Let's see if my friend can help us first."

With no reply, Mahmoud moved to open the door.

"Please," the mullah begged.

"Ok, but for how long must I wait?" Mahmoud's eyes were a window to a broken soul.

"Less than a week," he lied. After Mahmoud left, he made a call and made an appointment to see Abu-Ahmad, the bean vendor.

CHAPTER 22

Thursday, May 20, 2010

On weekdays, the mullah had no chance to eat breakfast with Zahra because of her schooling. Friday's breakfast was his only chance. Friday is the weekend for the Muslim community. Every Friday morning, families prepare a lavish breakfast. In Damascus, a basic dish often served for breakfast is brown beans and chickpeas. Ordinarily, the man of the house will go out early in the morning to one of the many restaurants which specialized in making these dishes. That's why the career of bean vendors has been so profitable in the region, ever since the olden days.

Every Friday morning, Mullah Abdullah would bring these dishes to his family from Abu-

Ahmed's shop, which is in the historical Medhat Basha market. Abu-Ahmed is well known for his top-quality recipes.

But today is Thursday, his meeting with Abu-Ahmed was to discuss an important matter. When he arrived, the restaurant was busy with customers, so the door remained open. On the left side of the shop is a wide black marble counter. Customers line up behind the counter, waiting for their takeaway orders. Inside, there are twelve tables for customers who may wish to sit down to eat.

The mouth-watering aroma of cooked beans filled his nostril as he entered the restaurant. He found Abu-Ahmed waiting for him, and they reserved the first table on the left. After the typical greetings, Abu-Ahmed said, "Whatever the critical issue might be that you want to talk about, it can wait until we fill our stomachs."

"I don't want to be a bother," the mullah said.

"What are you talking about? I didn't have my lunch while I waited for you and I'm hungry."

A young waiter in clean white trousers and a T-shirt with the logo of the restaurant on it approached their table carrying a tray of food and placed it on the table. Thin slices of hot pita bread and two plates of brown beans, soaked in olive oil. Another plate held pickles, cucumbers, turnips, and pale chilies.

He made a few desperate attempts to prevent the olive oil from dripping from between his fingers while eating, but it was impossible, so he gave up and just devoured his food.

"What a scrumptious meal," the mullah said, dabbing his mouth with his handkerchief in delight.

Hot tea was placed in front of them as they scraped up the last spoonful, slurping noisily.

The time had come to discuss the important matter, so he adjusted his seat and said, "Brother Abu-Ahmed, I have known you for an exceptionally long time. What has it been, twenty years?"

He didn't wait for Abu-Ahmed to reply. "Your reputation is flawless. Members of your family are the sincerest of people, just like yourself."

Abu-Ahmed's cheeks reddened slightly. "Thank you, mullah. But I don't deserve all this praise. Please tell me how I might serve you?"

"Someone has asked for the hand of your only daughter. What's her name?" He pretended not to know her name, despite his wife having repeated it many times.

"Samah. Her name is Samah," Abu-Ahmed said. Then he asked politely, "From which family is this man?"

"From the Farawati family, and his name is Hani."

The smile evaporated from Abu-Ahmed's lips when he heard the name. "Do you think this Hani is from a sufficiently honorable family to ask the daughter of my honorable family to marry him?" Without giving him a chance to answer, Abu-Ahmed leaped to his feet. His metal chair tumbled backward and clattered to the floor. Guests at other tables stopped what they were doing, turning to stare. It all happened in a fraction of a second.

Abu-Ahmed was turning to leave, but the mullah grabbed his icy hand and said in a shaky voice, "Abu-Ahmed, please hear me out." If flames had shot out of Abu-Ahmed's ears at that moment, he wouldn't have been surprised. It was the first time he'd seen his face so stony, and when their eyes met, he was a little frightened by the silent fury he saw in Abu-Ahmed's eyes.

"Please, sit back down, if only for five more minutes." Abu-Ahmed picked up the chair and sat, with his forearms crossed over his chest.

The mullah said in a weak voice, "This man wants to marry in accordance with the laws of Allah and the instructions of the Prophet. If you don't feel any animosity toward him, why not just allow them to get engaged and let them meet and get to know each other under your supervision, of course?" He cursed himself because he knew this trick wouldn't fool Abu-Ahmed. After all, Hani's deplorable reputation was already known by many.

Abu-Ahmed lurched to his feet again, even angrier this time, as if the mullah had slapped him and was talking rubbish. He leaned on the table, throwing his full upper body weight onto it. The table groaned. With his face inches from the mullah's, he said, "This guy is not welcome in my family, and if you want to remain my friend, don't you dare mention his name again in my presence, ever! This cretin has come to me already, asking for the girl's hand, and we rejected him politely. You are the last person I'd expect to try to convince me to give my daughter to him."

Abu-Ahmed strode away, but after only three steps, he turned and asked in a booming voice, "If this guy came and asked for your daughter's hand, would you give her to him?" He strode away without waiting for an answer.

Murmurs from the nearby crowd burned his ears, and he felt their eyes drilling into him. He picked up his cloak and left the shop as quickly as he could.

CHAPTER 23

Friday, May 21, 2010

On Friday, after dawn prayers, Mullah Abdullah went out to buy traditional handmade bread as he did every Friday. Warm steam from freshly baked bread enveloped him as he entered the shop.

The bakery on Shagoor Street comprised one large room with a window overlooking the street. The ceiling was black from soot and smoke. The wall opposite the door was lined with sacks of flour. On the right, a colossal mixing bowl was nearly overflowing with freshly kneaded dough. Two racks held large wooden trays with rows of rising dough balls, waiting their turn to be punched down. To the left stood the large mud oven, shaped like a ball, with a circular opening at the top through which the discs of dough were loaded. A deep bed of glowing embers in the bottom heated the cooking surfaces above.

No matter how old he got, Mullah Abdullah was certain that standing in front of this window observing the graceful movements of the bakers would always be a fascination for him.

Two flour-covered bakers worked together in unison. The one sitting at the tiled counter took the balls of dough one at a time from the wooden trays and slapped them down on the tiles, which had been liberally sprinkled with flour. He then slapped it rhythmically with the palm of his hand to shape it and stretch it. When he was satisfied with the shape, he tossed the flat round of dough in front of the other baker.

The other baker used his bare hands to lay the raw dough over a leather-covered bread cushion. Then he picked up the cushion and inserted it through the opening. Using all his strength, he slapped it against the concave surface so the thin dough would stick. He moved quickly and gracefully to avoid burning his hands or his face. It was like watching an artful dance. No one would fully understand it unless they worked with fire like these bakers to earn their living.

When the tips of the bubbles on the surface of the loaf were nice and brown, the baker removed it from the oven and in one quick motion, threw it towards the marble counter because it was scorching hot. It was still steaming and the customers standing around enjoyed the amazing aroma.

The mullah didn't wait for his four loaves to cool down. He simply pulled his sleeve down over one hand, loaded the hot loaves on that arm, and hurried back home. He didn't stop at Abu-Ahmed's shop, as he did every other Friday. He really needed to calm down before they met face-to-face again.

After breakfast, Zahra went to her room without asking him about her computer again. Amani cleared the table herself since Zahra was preparing for her final exam in high school. The mullah was sitting on a sofa in the liwan when Amani came back from the kitchen and sat beside him. They sat listening to the chirping of the birds and the splashing of the fountains.

"This exam will decide what university will accept her, based on her marks. I'm hoping she will do well." Amani said.

He closed his eyes, took a deep breath and said, "I hope so too."

"Oh dear, I am sorry. It's not your fault you were arrested during her school term." Amani came closer and put a hand on his shoulder.

He looked at her with raised brows. "I am not worried about her studies. She is a smart girl, and if she doesn't get good marks this year, she can always repeat next year. What I'm really worried about is her safety."

"Why?" Amani gasped.

He sighed, "What if Ahmad has really been

murdered? What if his killer …" He couldn't finish the sentence when he saw the level of panic in Amani's eyes.

"You have always trusted in Allah, and whenever anything happened against your intentions, you placed it in Allah's hands. Why do you insist on something obvious this time?"

"How is it obvious?"

"I wish justice for Hadiya as much as you do. I've heard many gossip stories. Most of her neighbors believe she was killed. But after thinking about it for a long time, I've reached the conclusion, if she was killed, none of her family would have remained quiet about it."

"That's why Ahmad is dead now because he tried to speak up," said the mullah.

"Hadiya dedicated her life to bringing up her four daughters and Khaled. I don't think if Mazen killed her, the children would stay silent. I believe we would have heard about two murders. The first would have been Mazen murdering his wife, and the second, her children killing him."

"If I don't fight to learn the truth, I would not be trusting in Allah and leaving it in His hands. It would be the exact opposite."

Amani blinked back her tears. "We almost lost you once. We don't want to take that chance again."

Was he chasing an illusion? Was it possible Ahmad had manipulated his emotions and trapped him? *Oh, Allah … help me … She is right; how could Hadiya have been murdered, and no one noticed? How could Mazen murder her, and her children remain silent?* But then he remembered and said, "Before his death, Ahmad was positive that Hadiya had been killed, and he said he had evidence. I believe that was the reason for his death."

"If Ahmad's killer was somehow involved in the killing of Hadiya, we will know who was involved in her death when the police catch Ahmad's murderer. Do you agree with me on that at least?" Amani asked.

He didn't answer.

"You should allow the experts to do their job and solve both murders," Amani added.

"Yes, I agree with you," he said weakly. But, at the same time, he must strive to finish what he had already started. Then there was the indelible fact: his instinct whispered that Hadiya had been killed. He must warn Khaled, but how could he do that? Especially after the court order.

After their discussion, the mullah was busy preparing for the Jumu'ah prayer and speech when an idea came to him. He decided to give the perplexing issue of Hadiya's death one last effort. He would attend to it right after the Jumu'ah prayer.

***

Dressed in his religious garb, the mullah entered the same room where Ahmad had fought with Lieutenant Hamad Alwasat. Nothing had changed in the office. The same table, same sofas, same cupboard, and the same overweight lieutenant sitting behind the same worn-out desk, writing in a massive book similar to the one he had been writing in the last time. It might even be the same one. He greeted the lieutenant, expecting him to be rude and aggressive as soon as he remembered him.

The lieutenant stopped writing and peered up at him.

The mullah held his breath but was surprised when a smile appeared on the lieutenant's face.

"How can I help you?" the lieutenant asked.

He realized then that the lieutenant didn't recognize him. "Mmmm ... I do not know where to start. I'm not at all sure you can help me." He was embarrassed as his words faltered, but he had promised himself to be honest before he'd entered the station.

The lieutenant rose, stepped from behind the desk, and gestured for him to sit on the sofa. He then took a seat on the sofa opposite. "Say it as if you are talking to yourself."

"One of my friends believes his sister didn't die a normal death, that she was murdered." The lieutenant didn't respond, so he continued, "All the evidence suggests the death was a natural one, except for his doubts and my instincts."

The lieutenant replied in a kind voice, "But it is impossible to start an investigation based on doubts and instincts alone. We need substantial evidence to open the case."

"No, no, I am not here to start an investigation. When the lady died, someone called the police, and a report was written."

"So, you want to see the report?" The lieutenant was quiet for a while, as if debating whether to help him. "It's against the law to show you the report unless you have a court order." He brought out a piece of paper and a pencil and handed them to him, saying, "However, this once I will pretend no one came and asked about it. You just write the name and the date. I will go to the archives and get it for you."

He was overwhelmed by the lieutenant's unexpected kindness. He took the paper with shaking hands and wrote Hadiya's full name and the date she died. He handed it to the lieutenant. "The date is approximate; I don't recall exactly when she passed away."

"No problem, you just wait for me here and don't talk to anyone about what you've asked of me," the lieutenant said as he left the room.

The mullah turned to face the lieutenant when he returned with a paper in his hand. He expected him to close the door behind him, but he didn't. He approached, gave him the paper, then sat back on the other sofa again.

He began reading the report and was soon absorbed in the details.

At 7:45 am on Tuesday 12th of Jan 2010, the fifth territory precinct received a call from a neighbor of Mazen Mis'ed. The neighbor said they had heard very loud screams coming from the apartment of Mazen Mis'ed only minutes earlier. Sergeant Laith Sqoor and Sergeant Milad Kharrat

were sent to deal with the issue. When they arrived at the location, they found the body of Hadiya Kishat, 39 years old, lying on the sofa, covered with a blanket. Also in the apartment were Adel Mis'ed, Mazen Mis'ed, his four girls and his son. The Criminal Security Administration dispatched a telegram to the precinct, informing them that this case would be under their jurisdiction. They sent Detective Mansoor Chait from the Criminal Security Administration to follow up.
Officer Ah MHD.

He kept staring at the paper. Why didn't Mansoor mention anything about handling the investigation when they had met earlier this month? He found it confusing that Mansoor had tried to convince him that no crime had happened that night. Especially when the mullah explained Ahmad's doubts. There were only two possibilities: either there had been no crime and Mansoor was being honest, or Mansoor was the corrupt connection and the one who had covered up the crime in return for a bribe, as Hani had mentioned. What if Hani knew Mansoor was the detective in charge of Hadiya's death report? It would mean he was an accomplice, of course, if Mansoor was the villain and covered up the crime.

Was he a fool? Was Hani using him to further his own intentions? As a man of faith, he should not judge Hani before asking him.

The lieutenant brought him back to reality

when he asked, "Are you satisfied now?"

The mullah looked up, his mind still swarming with questions, and said, "Well, I don't know if I am satisfied. The brother of this woman told me he had substantial evidence she had been killed, but he himself was murdered on the very same day he told me that. This report mentions that the Criminal Security Administration handled the investigation and not this precinct." He expected the lieutenant to be curious, or at least interested in, the second killing.

The lieutenant said, "The Criminal Security Administration is responsible for investigating the matter further. Maybe you should visit them and ask for their help?"

"Yes, I'll do that."

The lieutenant stood and lumbered over to his desk, and said, "Anything else you need help with?"

Despite his confusion, the mullah answered with a bright smile, "Oh no, thank you very much. I will pray to Allah to bless you and your family." Then he rose to shake his hand and left the police station, his head roiling with conflicting thoughts.

The afternoon sun was grilling most of the other pedestrians' heads, but his fez protected him as he rushed toward home. Amani and Zahra would delay lunch so they could eat with him. But first, he must speak with Hani.

Hani's husky voice suggested the call had awakened him. "What is it, mullah?"

"Do you remember when you came with

Ahmad to the mosque and told me about the fake reports? Which precinct handled the report of Hadiya's death?"

Hani was quiet for a few moments before he answered. "I don't know. Why do you ask?"

He ignored Hani's question and asked, "Do you remember the detective who was in charge of the investigation? The one who drafted the report?"

"Not really," Hani said, lowering his voice. "My snitch conveyed the information without mentioning names or addresses for my safety. Again, why do you ask?"

He had to think fast. Should he answer Hani? Tell him he knew the detective's name?

Hani's raised voice came through the phone. "Are you still there?"

If Hani was being honest and he really didn't know the detective's name, he could be in danger, as he claimed. But if Hani was lying, the mullah and his family might be the ones in danger. "Oh, I just thought, maybe if you knew, I could get a copy of the report and read it."

Hani said, "I told you, don't make any moves regarding Hadiya's case. Please, just leave it to me. I promise you'll be satisfied."

Hani is bullshitting me, he said. "Of course, don't worry, I haven't made any move, just waiting for you to update me regarding Ahmad and Hadiya."

"Just don't forget my share," Hani said with a laugh, and the line went dead.

CHAPTER 24

Wednesday, May 26, 2010

"All right everyone, open to chapter 24 of the Holy Qur'an," the mullah demanded. Only three students were attending this Qur'an recitation session, otherwise the mosque was empty following the afternoon prayer. The ceiling fans were barely cooling the air. Very few people had attended the afternoon prayers, either because of the heat or because they were at work.

Fathi, Sa'ad, and Waseem opened the Qur'an, and the mullah gestured for Fathi to start. After Fathi, he motioned to Sa'ad, to continue from verse 31.

"And tell the believing women to reduce [some] of their vision and guard their private parts and not

expose their adornment except that which [necessarily] appears thereof and to wrap [a portion of] their head covers over their chests and not expose their adornment except to their husbands, their fathers, their husbands' fathers, their sons, their husbands' sons, their brothers, their brothers' sons, their sisters' sons, their women, that which their right hands possess, or those male attendants having no physical desire or children who are not yet aware of the private aspects of women. And let them not stamp their feet to make known what they conceal of their adornment. And turn to Allah in repentance, all of you, O believers, that you might succeed."

Fathi looked around the group and asked, "Does this rule apply to both living and dead bodies?"

"Yes, both," the mullah answered. "That's why when a woman dies, another woman is always required to wash the corpse."

"So, she must hide the corpse's private parts when she is washing the corpse?" asked Fathi.

The mullah slammed the Qur'an shut and stood up abruptly, his students watching him open-mouthed. He blurted out, "Sorry, I have to leave now. I have just remembered something very important I need to attend to."

How blind he'd been and how obvious it was to him now. Why hadn't he understood the reason Ahmad asked him to meet in Bab Tomah Square? Murshidah, the woman who washed Hadiya's corpse, lives in Islah alley. The only entrance to the alley is from Bab Tomah.

Murshidah's house is the only one at the end of a narrow alley between Maktab Anbar and Islah Alley, in the heart of an ancient part of Damascus. The alley isn't wide enough for two people to walk shoulder to shoulder. Although it was still daylight, the alley was dark and oppressive. The walls seemed to close in on him from both sides. He knocked on the door and waited. Waleed, Murshidah's husband, opened the door a crack. Of course, the mullah had not expected Murshidah to open the door for him. Waleed was in his usual beige shirt, brown trousers, and black slippers. A man in his seventies, yet he still had the strength to dig graves. He was about the same height as the mullah, with a full head of white hair.

He and Waleed met every time there was a funeral. Not only was he the undertaker but also the person who washed the male corpses. His wife, Murshidah, did the same for the female bodies. This was not the first time he had entered Waleed's house, but he still felt uncomfortable and mumbled the name of Allah under his breath. After all, he was entering a home where a husband and wife spent their lives washing dead bodies. He shivered when he imagined the souls of all the corpses lurking in dark corners. Inside the front door, a short, dark hallway led to a small courtyard. He'd never understood why it was always dark, nor why the courtyard held no plants, no fountains, and no liwan.

The kitchen was a small, shadowy cove in the corner to the right. The sofas were out in the courtyard, under the open sky. He wondered what happened when it rained. He sat down on a sofa, took off his fez, and set it beside him. As he waited for Waleed to finish boiling a pot of coffee for them, he contemplated the grimy walls that were centuries old and very delicate. Even a mild earthquake would cause this house to collapse.

Waleed brought the tray holding two coffee cups, and as Mullah Abdullah leaned forward to pick up his cup, he gazed up at Waleed's face. A map of deep wrinkles told of long years of struggle. He had hardened eyes from decades of dealing with the dead. He lowered his gaze, took the cup, and fixed his eyes on the dark steaming coffee.

"I need a favor, brother Waleed," he said finally.

"Whatever you ask." Waleed's voice was deep and husky. He raised both hands, palms to the sky as if he was waiting for something to fall from the heavens.

"Well, it is not a favor from you. I need a favor from your wife."

Waleed remained silent. Waiting.

"I need to speak with her, if you don't mind?"

Waleed took a deep breath before saying, "Ok, let me call her." He went into the home's only room and closed the door behind him.

From his place on the sofa, the mullah could hear voices humming behind the closed door. In truth, he was not very comfortable sitting alone in the courtyard of this old house. He had the constant feeling of someone or something peering at him. He slipped his prayer beads out of his pocket, feeling their familiar comfort between his fingers, and started reciting the name of Allah.

Waleed came out with Murshidah trailing after him. She wore a black veil covering her face.

The mullah stood and greeted her, politely looking at the ground to avoid staring at her.

Murshidah sat down on the sofa next to her husband.

"I am here to ask you about a very delicate matter, about a corpse you handled recently." Waleed gasped, but before he could object, the mullah raised his palm to stop him. "Brother Waleed, I know the details of your dealings with the corpses are confidential, and Allah, before the law, will punish you for revealing information about any corpse. But the lady I am asking about was probably murdered. You are the last hope for her to achieve justice."

"If she was killed, the police would have been involved," Waleed said, his voice slightly raised. "You don't need someone like us to tell you about it. You must go to the police to find out."

"It's complicated," the mullah said. "The police were there, and a report was written. The official document says the death was from natural causes. That's why I need your wife's help to tell me if she noticed any unusual signs on the body when she washed it."

Murshidah's face remained lowered modestly, but she asked, "Who was the woman?"

"Hadiya Kishat, they called her Um-Khaled." Again, he avoided looking at the veiled woman. Instead, he did his best to detect any sign of surprise on Waleed's face. Unfortunately, Waleed's face remained set like it was made of stone.

Waleed turned to his wife. "There were no unusual signs on the body, were there?"

"No," she said, shaking her head. "There was nothing unusual about the lady's corpse."

The mullah put his fez on his head and stood up to go. But, before turning toward the door, he asked, "Did Ahmad Kishat ask you this same question before I did?"

"Yes, and he got the same answer from us," Waleed replied firmly.

***

Asmar went to meet Hani at the time written on the piece of paper under the Peugeot's window wiper. The location wasn't important, as long as the coffee shop's computers had Skype. At 7 pm sharp, he was online. Hani typed the information he wanted, with no greetings or preamble, then logged off. Asmar folded the piece of paper, wrote Salah's full name on the outside, put it in his jacket's inner pocket, and zipped it up. He closed Skype, cleared the cache, and left to start his night shift.

At his workplace, Asmar greeted his colleagues as usual, then sat at his desk in a massive hall, among twenty-four other desks, all identical and perfectly aligned.

Twenty-four secret agents, just like him, were seated at those desks where they awaited their day's assignments in sealed envelopes. His envelope was already on his desktop. He opened it and claimed he was assigned to the computer lab despite of his mission was to analyze the recorded phone calls of suspects under surveillance. And that was in an entirely different lab.

The data archive was in the same computer lab on the ground floor. Upon arrival, he signed his name in the logbook and stated the reason for this session was to search for details of suspicious activity. The lab held forty computers with the highest specifications available, and access to a vast database.

Sitting at a computer, he quickly typed in his ID number. The computer scanned his face and granted him access. Opening a database he wouldn't normally access, he entered Salah's full name, then stared expectantly at the screen. A red box popped open on a blue background informing him he was about to view highly confidential information. He glanced around nervously, even though his existence in the computer lab was perfectly legitimate.

His finger hovered over the enter button on the keyboard as if a hidden force preventing him from entering such a file. He pressed enter and stared hard at the screen without blinking as if he wasn't looking at words, but at his and Hani's graves, where they would inevitably be buried if their investigation was discovered. Damascus was one of the safest and most secure cities in the world. On the screen were the details of a conspiracy threatening the safety of this country.

It was an accident for him to access such sensitive information, but going through this highly alarming and confidential information to satisfy his burning curiosity was not an accident at all.

He could dig for information up to a certain limit; however, he knew what he was looking at now was definitely beyond his limit.

Why is this file not secured? Why was I granted access? It didn't take long for him to figure it out. They just want to know who would access the file. It would mean there is an internal traitor, and now he would be on the list of suspects.

He exited the database without writing any of the details and left.

With bulky headphones covering his ears, he listened to the recorded calls of suspects, which was his actual assignment. Picking up a pen to write his analysis report, he realized he didn't remember anything from the recorded call. He listened to it again, struggling to focus this time.

CHAPTER 25

Thursday, May 27, 2010

After he finished the longest night shift he could remember, Asmar got in his car and headed for home. After a few anxious glances in the rear-view mirror, he eased any doubts that the yellow taxi behind him was tailing him. He was convinced all his movements were now under surveillance. His mobile phone would be tracked, his home phone bugged, his whole life placed under a microscope.

He parked the car near his building and switched off the engine, but didn't get out. He rested his forehead on the top of the steering wheel. What had he done? Why hadn't they arrested him already? Why had they allowed him to leave the building? He raised his head to look in the rear-view mirror. The yellow taxi was at the end of the alley.

They didn't even bother to conceal the fact they were tailing him. He understood the system well; he is part of it, and this was the last chance for him to lead them peacefully to his accomplices, otherwise he will confess under grilling.

Asmar looked at himself in the rear-view mirror and, despite the danger he'd put himself in, he smiled.

It was time for revenge.

He called Hani and asked to meet him in the evening.

Hamra Street is one of the most crowded and modern markets in Damascus, with many fashionable shops and glamorous saleswomen everywhere.

The smell of falafel motivates pedestrians to stop and buy freshly fried falafel sandwiches. Dozens of people crowded around the stall, enjoying their sandwiches and chatting, but it was still no problem to pick out the massive frame of Hani among them.

Asmar approached Hani and, with no greeting, said, "A secret security operation has been launched against a proliferation of extremist cells among the younger generation in Syria."

Hani snapped back, "I thought you called me to tell me what happened to the guy whose name I gave you."

"Salah is part of that organization," Asmar said.

"Don't mention names, you moron," Hani glanced quickly around, but no one in the crowd seemed to have taken any notice.

"The extremists are planning to start a revolution," Asmar said.

Hani left without another word.

Asmar watched Hani's figure getting smaller with each step and smiled. For him, the three agents tailing him were easy to spot. The pretty girl on the opposite side of the road, talking on her mobile phone, while aiming the camera at him and Hani. Then there was the technician checking wires on the phone box for no apparent reason, and the old packman selling cigarettes on the corner.

When Asmar arrived to start his night shift, his sealed envelope was already on his desktop. Tonight, his task was simple and easy. His instructions were to go to the office of a top-ranking officer to pick up a parcel and deliver it to an address he would be given. Of course, there was no need to remind any agent that such an assignment would be strictly confidential.

He entered the office on the fourth floor and greeted the officer. With no reply, the officer handed him a piece of paper with an address written on it and gestured to a box on the table. He was surprised how light the box was, considering its size. The address was room number eight in the interrogation division, which was in the third-floor basement. The deepest and worst place for a person to be sent, in his opinion.

The light barely lit the corridor between the interrogation rooms. The walls were bare concrete, the steel doors bare and rusty. The air was filled with a mixture of scents; dried blood, rusty metal, and dirt on the floor, which seemed not to have been cleaned since the day it was built.

As he pushed open the door to room number eight, a wave of foul air struck him, forcing him to cover his nose with his hand. The room was empty, the only light coming in from the corridor, cast his elongated shadow across the floor.

There must be some mistake, he thought. But it wasn't his duty to ask. His duty was just to do as he'd been told. Placing the box on the floor in the middle of the room, he moved back toward the exit.

Then an officer appeared in the doorway, holding a notebook. The same notebook he himself used to carry when interrogating a new prisoner.

The officer gestured for him to return to the center of the room and snapped, "Open the box, put on the clothes in it, then put your own clothes and all your belongings in the box." He opened the box and found a pair of orange coveralls. He undressed until he was naked, donned the orange coveralls, stuffed his own clothes and belongings into the box, then stood silently, awaiting further instructions. He wished sincerely that Hani would meet the same fate. The officer took the box and left without a word, locking the door and leaving him cut off from the outside world.

***

Hani darted into his bedroom, pulled a travel bag from under the bed, and opened it on the bed. He threw enough clothes in it for at least a month, called a taxi, and in five minutes he was in the taxi, headed to the central station. He was planning to stay in Beirut for a month.

He was very aware of the government's vehement opposition to violent extremism. The active intelligence and security services made the country an unattractive operating environment for terrorist groups. Thus, the government uses an iron fist to deal with any scenario with ties to extremism or terrorism. If they arrested an innocent man like him, it would be a long, gruesome process until they could be convinced of his innocence. If they suspected his involved in such an organization, it would cost him everything he owned, if not his life.

The central station in Baramkeh is a crowded street, day or night, in the heart of modern Damascus. At the Syria-Lebanon line in the station, only two yellow cars were waiting to take passengers to Beirut. He sat on a bench on the sidewalk, watching cars pass in the street. The noise of car horns was unbearable. It seemed as if the drivers honked every time they took a breath. This spot in the Baramkeh area is always crowded, since it is the point of departure for those traveling between Syrian cities. The people come from different towns, wear a variety of clothes, and speak in many dialects.

Shortly, there were three passengers

gathered, but the driver insisted he needed four passengers before he would move. Hani paid for the fourth and asked the driver to get a move on, so the old yellow Chevrolet headed into Beirut. The air conditioner wasn't working, so all the windows were rolled down the entire time. The other two passengers were young men whom he figured must work in Beirut. The driver was bald, and clean-shaven, and smoked like a chimney all the way to the border despite the stickers in the car proclaiming that smoking was not allowed. Still, Hani remained quiet, not wanting the other passengers to know he was a police officer. He didn't object to either the smoke or the loud music on the radio.

The distance from Damascus to the Syrian border was less than 50 km, and it took less than 40 minutes to cover. The border immigration point was busy despite the lateness of the hour. The driver asked all of them to get out of the car and go inside the immigration building to get their passports stamped. Hani glanced around at the blackness around the immigration building and shivered in the chill breeze.

Inside, four uniformed officers sat behind a long black marble counter. In front of the counter were four queues of people with their passports in their hands. After 17 minutes, Hani reached the front of the line he was in and handed his passport to the young man, who scanned the barcode and stared at the screen. Without a word, he got up from his chair and disappeared through a door at the back, taking Hani's passport with him.

Hani knew precisely why the immigration officer went inside. Now he realized he was too late. He maintained an appearance of outward calm and looked at the other three officers, who were all busy with passengers in front of them. He patted first the back pockets of his trousers, then the pocket of his white linen shirt, pretending he'd forgotten something. Frowning and mumbling to himself, he walked calmly, without rushing, so as not to attract the attention of the other three officers. He exited to fetch whatever he was pretending to have forgotten.

Outside he darted around the corner of the building and let the shadows envelop him as he disappeared into the darkness.

CHAPTER 26

Sunday, May 30, 2010

With eyes still shut, the mullah reached for the little clock on the bedside table to switch off the alarm. He groped for the button on top and pressed it, but the ringing didn't stop. He opened his eyes. It was 6:25, and the ringing was coming from the telephone. He raised the receiver to his ear. "Peace be upon you."

A male voice mixed with a crackling noise, probably because of a poor connection. "Abdullah Al-Allab?"

"Speaking."

"Your presence is required at the State Security Administration in Fairooziah Street at 8 am today."

"What for?" He became alert, pulling himself

up and pressing the receiver to his ear.

"In case you decide not to come, there will be consequences to bear."

"But..." the return of the dial tone indicated the person had hung up. He froze, still clutching the phone.

His wife's voice brought him back to reality when she asked, "What is it?"

He answered in a shaky voice, his hand still holding the phone to his ear. "I must go to the State Security Administration at Fairooziah today at 8 am." He avoided looking at her.

Amani raised her eyes heavenward. "Oh Allah, we don't ask you to overturn the decree, but we beg you to temper it." She hurried to the water jug, poured a glass of water, and brought it to him, then sat beside him on the bed, watching as he drank.

He dialed Hani's number, but it rang several times before a recorded voice asked him to leave a message. He put down the receiver without leaving a message.

He changed into a plain shirt and pants. He decided not to wear his religious attire, as he wished to draw minimal attention to himself as he entered the intelligence agency.

He arrived at Fairooziah at 7:45 am. At the gate of the State Security Administration, the guard registered him and held his ID. Inside, another guard searched his pockets and took his mobile phone from him after he'd switched it off. Following the instructions he'd been given, he went to room number 8 on the seventh floor.

The room was square, with a single desk in the middle. Behind the desk sat a young man in civilian clothes. On the desk was a laptop, a regular notebook, and a pile of photographs. On the wall behind the desk, a large portrait of the president hung between the national flag and the government party flag. An air conditioner provided a cool breeze. The young man approached him politely to shake hands, then asked him to take a seat on the single plastic chair in the middle of the room.

The young man sat down again behind his desk and said in a clear, loud voice, "Mr. Abdullah? Your mother is Salamiah Altahoon?"

"Mister?" the mullah queried sarcastically.

The young man laughed and replied just as sarcastically, "Why? Can't we call you Mister?"

"Please, just call me by my name, Abdullah," he said, irritated. "Surely you know I am the imam of a mosque, so call me sheikh or call me what they call me in my neighborhood, Mullah. And yes, my mother's name is Salamiah Altahoon."

The young man ignored his comment and said, "My name is Malek. You have been called to answer a few questions. Do you have any problem with helping us?" He bent his head and looked at him with raised eyebrows and said, "Mister Abdullah."

"Of course, I have no problem answering, not only a few questions, but as many as you like." *As if I have a choice. Last time you forced me to write out my life story three times and repeat it over and over, at least ten times.*

As if Malek had read his thoughts, he said, "My only task is to ask questions, then pass the information on to a higher authority, who will be the one to decide what the next step will be?."

"The next step?" he asked, without bothering to hide his panic.

"Yes, and please don't ask me why they called you to come in. I don't have an answer to that question."

The mullah's ears blazed with fury.

"Mr. Abdullah, please relax. We don't want this to take any longer than necessary. And don't worry, there's no danger for you here."

"Sure," the mullah mumbled.

Malek busied himself on the laptop for a few minutes, and then he said, "Now, I will play you some recordings. You will hear a variety of people's voices. Your only job is to tell me the names of any individuals you recognize." Without waiting for a response, Malek pushed a button on the keyboard and voices from the speakers echoed in the room.

'I didn't touch her. I just knocked on the door, and while standing behind it, took the plastic bag.'

He thought it sounded like a male in his forties.

'I swear I didn't kill her.'

'I hit her head with a hammer until her brains were all over the marble counter of the kitchen…'.

The same voice, only huskier.

Malek looked up from the screen, but the mullah shook his head. Malek started the next recording.

'You don't feel ashamed to hit a woman?'

It was a coarse voice, but he was pretty sure it was female.

'I didn't kill him; I swear I didn't kill him.'

The words were broken up by her sobbing.

'We added rat poison to the tea.'

'We cut his body...'

'We threw it...'

He didn't know who that voice belonged to, either.

Malek started the next recording.

At first there was the hysterical sobbing of a male who was attempting to say something, but his voice was distorted. There were sounds of something being hit. From the screams, the mullah thought the blows were probably landing on the man's body. With every scream, the mullah's frown deepened. Soon his forehead was so furrowed it looked as if he was the one in pain.

'I didn't go near her...... Ahhh no! Please...... I beg you to stop....... I swear I didn't touch a single hair of her...... he...... Ah...... Ahh...... Ah I didn't touch her.'

The sound of the blows got louder, as did the man's screams.

The recording stopped and then continued. The same guy this time, but calmer, without the screaming.

'I raped her...'
'We were scared...'
'We buried...'

The mullah cried out, "Please stop it. I don't know this monster." His voice came out dry in a much higher pitch than usual.

He knew Malek had been observing his facial expressions throughout the whole exercise. The tongue could lie with ease, but the body could not.

The next recording was the voice of an old man.

'Infidels, we must slay them like goats.'
'The sword is the only solution for...'
'Destroy those...'
'To fight them is a noble...'
'Worse than pagans...'

Malek stopped the recording, waiting for him to speak.

"I have never heard this person's voice before."

Malek started the next recording, which sounded like one side of a telephone conversation.

'Yes....... All the money....... Roger that....... Nothing less than decapitating him.'

He didn't recognize this voice either. By now, he was twisting the ring on his left hand, and his right leg was shaking.

Before starting the next recording, Malek said, "The following recording contains more than one person."

An old man said, *'What evidence do you have to prove their behavior is wrong when they use violence to spread their religion?'*

A chill spread through the mullah's body. He shut his eyes tight as he listened to the recording.

A younger man said, *'The verse from the Holy Qur'an, (there shall be no compulsion in [acceptance of] the religion) chapter 2 verse 256. It tells us we shouldn't force others to follow a particular religion or to act upon it.'*

Another young man. *'The narration says, 'if one of you sees a prohibited action, change it by his hand, if cannot, by his tongue, if cannot, by his heart.'*

The first young man again, *'How did you find out that this narration warned us not to be violent when we spread the religion? Don't you see the terrorists use it as a flag to justify their actions?'*

Then the voice of a new young man asking, *'Mullah, what is your answer to the narration Saeed mentioned?'*

Then the mullah's voice erupted from the speaker. *'I am with Saeed in what he says. This narration shouldn't incite violence, but totally on the contrary. When the prophet said 'If we cannot change it' it means there is a condition. The condition is that the individual wanting to remedy the evil deed of another person must have a mandate over that person. A father has a mandate over his family. A manager has a mandate over his employees, and the president has a mandate over his subordinates. In the absence of that condition, the second option would be the only available choice, but also with one condition. That condition is, that no harm shall come to this person in the event of his speaking to others, trying to prevent evil deeds. With the absence of that condition, the third option would be the last and only available one, and there are no conditions to implement it'.*

Malek stopped the tape and looked at him with a sly smile. "What are the names of the men speaking there?"

He felt a sharp pain in his throat, as if his words needed more time to come out of his mouth. He was not shocked that the secret police spied on his lectures. What shocked him was, the spy was one of his own students.

"I gave that talk a year ago. They were Fathi, Saeed, Khaled, and the lecturer was me."

"Mr. Abdullah, this is the last recording," Malek said. "It is also more than one person, so please focus carefully." He pressed the button to start it.

An angry male said, *'Why are you calling me? I warned you not to call under any circumstances.'*

The mullah's heart skipped a beat, as he could have distinguished this voice from thousands of others.

Then the voice of a young man, 'it's *urgent.*'

The angry man said, *'What is it you want?'*

'I must come and see you to give you the information you asked for about Salah.'

'You son-of-a-bitch, don't mention names.'

'Today. Seven PM, opposite the stall of the falafel shop on Hamra Street,' the young man said.

The recording ended, the mullah said, "Hani

Alfarawati."

"And who was the second man?" Malek asked.

"I don't know him."

Malek held up a black-and-white photograph of Hani on the street, obviously taken without his knowledge. It was hard to tell where it was taken because the area around Hani's body was blurred. The focus was only on Hani's face.

Without waiting for Malek to ask, the mullah said, "Yes, that's him."

"What is your relationship with this man?"

"No relation."

"How are you able to recognize his voice and picture?"

"He has prayed in my mosque a few times."

Malek wrote something down, then held up more photographs, one by one, waiting for the mullah's answers. He didn't recognize most of them until Malek raised the photo of Salah. His heartbeat leaped, and his words came out automatically. "Salah. Do you know where he is?"

"I am the one who asks questions here, Mr. Abdullah." Malek put Salah's photo down separately, wrote something in his notebook, and continued showing other pictures. The mullah denied knowing any of them until he saw his students' photos. When he named them, Malek placed them with Salah's photo and continued. After he had shown him the lot, he raised Salah's photo again and asked, "Tell me everything you know about this young man."

"He is a diligent student, but he disappeared recently, and we don't know where he is."

"You don't know where he is now?" Malek asked to confirm.

"No," the mullah emphasized.

"Would you like to know where he is now?"

"Yes indeed," the mullah said eagerly.

"Why would you like to know?"

"I told you. He is a diligent student. Actually, he is one of the best I've had. Also, his father is my friend and has asked for my help to find him."

"Do you know Allah puts those who tell lies in hell?" Malek said with a chuckle.

"I seek refuge with Allah from lying," the mullah snapped, crossing his arms and gripping his elbows. His cheeks were boiling.

Malek busied himself typing on the laptop for a while, then he held up the photo of Salah in his left hand, and the picture of Hani in his right, and said, "One is a worshipper in your mosque," he said squinting at Hani's photo. "And the other is your student." He squinted again at Salah's photo. Then he glared at him and asked, "Is there any relation between these two guys?"

"I am the only relation that I am aware of."

"How is that?"

He stroked his beard and thought about what the margin of risk would be if he admitted he had asked Hani for information about Salah's disappearance. He decided to speak the truth, whatever the cost, "I called Hani and asked him to find information about Salah's disappearance for me."

Malek resumed typing on the laptop, then asked, while still looking at the screen, "Why Hani?"

"Salah's family had already asked at all the hospitals, the police stations, the immigration ports, even the graveyards, and still no traces of him."

Malek sighed, "I meant why Hani in particular? Why not ask someone else?"

"I had used Hani before," he said and instantly regretted saying it.

"Used him? Used him for what?"

He kept quiet for a moment, worrying that he'd implicated himself even more by mentioning details Malek hadn't asked for. However, he'd promised himself he would speak the truth whatever the cost. "One of my friends was murdered, and Hani brought me the details."

"What friend? Can you elaborate on the details of this murder?"

The mullah informed Malek about Ahmad and his doubts about the murder of Hadiya.

"Did Hani know who the murderer was?"

"No."

Malek silently typed some more on the laptop before asking, "Has Hani informed you what has happened to Salah?"

"Not yet."

"When was the last time you met with Hani?"

"Last week."

"Do you know where he is now?"

"No."

"Would you like to know where he is now?" a sly smile appeared on Malek's face.

The mullah felt a genuine sense of danger creeping up his spine. It added to the fear he'd felt ever since he'd entered the building. *Was Hani working with them, or had he come to them and reported him for asking about Salah? There was no other explanation for why he had been called in for this interrogation.*

The plaintive sounds of the call to noon prayers erupted from a nearby mosque, snapping him back to reality. He asked, "Is there a prayer room in this building?" He had been in this interrogation room for four and a half hours.

"Of course, there is. It's on the fourth floor. After you finish praying, you must come back here. Don't run away," Malek exploded with laughter.

He wanted to ignore the insult, but he couldn't. "Why would I run away? I haven't committed any crime." He went out and slammed the door, not caring what Malek thought of his childish act.

When he returned, Malek was not there. The table was empty, and the air conditioner was turned off. He looked around the empty room, then walked to the window and looked out. Almost the entirety of Fairooziah Street could be seen from this height. Below him, a group of men in grey uniforms stood listening attentively to their leader. A few army trucks were parked along the thick grey wall, and at the two visible corners he could see, there were small concrete cubes with only enough space for a guard and his Kalashnikov.

The door opened, and he turned his head to see who it was. A young man had only come in to warn him he was not to leave the room until further notice.

He sat on the plastic chair, took out his prayer beads and started praising Allah, hoping to reduce his anxiety. His underwear was soaked with sweat, and he was sure the heat was not the only reason. He placed his hands on his knees to calm their shaking. It felt as if his clothes had gotten tighter and he needed more oxygen. What was going on? Why were they doing this to him? Hundreds of questions swarmed in his head. Oh, Allah, when will all this end? Time passed slowly, in contrast to his accelerated breathing. He needed a drink. He stood up and began pacing from wall to wall. It seemed as if the walls were crawling slowly towards him. He froze in place, his hands trembling. Sharp pain in his lungs. He put his shaking hands on his neck, and the room began to spin.

The sound of the third call to prayer brought him back to the empty, silent room. He estimated that over three hours had passed while he'd waited. It must be around 4:00 pm by then. He didn't care if they wanted him to leave the room or not, he must pray. He ran to the door and went to pray the afternoon prayer.

***

When the mullah returned to the room, general Zafer Abyad was sitting on the chair Malek had been sitting on before. When the general saw him, he stood up and walked over to shake hands. The old general's firm grip made him wince a little. He noticed the luxury watch on the general's wrist. The general's white hair was neatly groomed, his face clean-shaven. His rounded face and arched eyebrows only increased the intimidation that radiated from his cruel eyes.

"Where were you just now, mullah?" he asked, once he'd made a call to inform the receiver that the mullah had returned. The general was wearing the same uniform he'd seen him in the previous time.

"I was praying," he said with a shaky voice. He rubbed his temples, trying to ease a headache.

"We ask Allah to accept our prayers," the general said.

The mullah sat down and put his hands on his knees. He tried to smile and remain polite but found it difficult.

"I am here regarding the things that have been happening to you lately." The general sat behind the table. "After a lengthy discussion with higher authorities, we have decided to let you out of the dark and shed some light on your situation." On the table were a few papers, a small notebook, and the general's mobile phone.

He raised his right hand and interrupted the mullah, who was trying to say something, "Please, let me finish, then you can ask me anything you like."

The mullah nodded, and the general continued, "As you know, our community comprises a variety of sects and religions. Every one of them has equal rights and freedoms to practice their rituals. However, some sick ideas have been forming in the minds of a few fanatics. We have information regarding a proliferation of extremist cells among the younger generation in our society, trying to implement their evil plans. Their intentions are to befriend poor people and promulgate their sick ideas in an effort to convince them the Syrian government is secular and does not respect Islam. They're hoping people will come to believe it is their duty to start a revolution against this government. Especially using Arab Spring as motivation.

"Some people were granted huge salaries to persuade them to betray their homeland, their honor, and their religion. The group's sole mission is to recruit youth and prepare them as portable bombs, ready to explode at any moment to disrupt our safe society. Vast tracts of land have been purchased along the borders with Jordan, Iraq, and Turkey, and the buyers are outsiders. They've dug hundreds of tunnels to smuggle people, weapons, money, or whatever they need to support their cause."

The mullah's thoughts were confused. He held his breath. The general said, "The homeland security intelligence agency first revealed the conspiracy and has studied the methods used by the extremist cells. They've found targeted segments of the community are young people between seventeen and twenty. Mostly they would gain entry to study sessions in the mosques, hoping to recruit vulnerable young people. After significant efforts for over a year, we have been able to limit our focus to a select group of suspects and keep them under surveillance until we find out who the ringleaders are and eradicate them."

The general had a deep, authoritative voice. "You don't need to be a genius to guess that we've had your students and your mosque under observation for a while. However, we had concluded that you are not involved in the scheme."

Unable to stay quiet any longer, the mullah cleared his throat to speak, but the general raised his hand to silence him and continued, "Until the day we discovered that one of your students was involved and we arrested him. When he was interrogated, he claimed you were actively involved in recruiting young people to join the organization."

The mullah erupted, "Who was that student?"

"Salah Almawazly."

He threw himself back in the chair, cold creeping into his guts. He squeezed his eyes shut, and said, "Oh Allah, we ask your mercy." Salah was the last person he would have imagined capable of doing such a thing to him.

"We had no choice but to interrogate you, of course. When we first looked for you, you were out of the country, so we arrested you on your way back in. The outcome is, you've been proven innocent conclusively. We now know Salah was bluffing to divert attention from himself." The general was interrupted by the ringing of his phone, but after glancing at the screen, he chose not to answer.

"Lately, we arrested a suspect who had gained access to a top security electronic government database and leaked information related to that same group of fanatics. Upon interrogation, he confessed a police officer had extorted him. We arrested the police officer, who confessed that you had requested information about Salah from him for a generous amount of money."

The mullah said, "But ..."

Still, the general cut him off. "Of course, the official response was to arrest you on the spot without delay. Leaking such confidential information is punishable under the law."

The mullah inserted a finger inside his collar and tugged at it to loosen it.

"Your arrest didn't happen as it would have under the usual security procedures, for two reasons. First, your name had been cleared during the first interrogation. Second, the arrest warrant doesn't go into effect until I sign it. I allowed them to question you, but without an arrest." The general stood up, moved around to the front, and sat on the edge of the table with his palms supporting his weight.

"I ordered them to call you with all due respect

and ask you to come in. Although it was apparent you were not part of this extremist organization, we wanted to know the reason you asked for such sensitive and confidential information. After today's session with Malek, we're satisfied your purpose was to help your friend Mahmoud and his son Salah."

The mullah blurted out, "Are any other of my students involved with the extremists?"

"I can't reveal such details, but I can assure you everything is under control."

"Why didn't you inform Salah's parents?"

"We don't want panic to spread among the public when they find out about the existence of such an organization. The extremist group is managed from a secret headquarters outside the country. They don't reveal their goals, plans, or activities to anyone, even to their team members, unless they are high-ranking. This is to guarantee that information is not leaked if they're arrested and questioned. They have villainous procedures. These people have a military mindset, and they always take the least risk in their operations."

The general crossed his arms over his chest and continued, "Although you are not involved with the extremists, you still need to prove your loyalty to your homeland by choosing the right side. Black or white, there is no grey choice."

"Of course, I choose the safety of my homeland. Who wouldn't?" the mullah said.

"An honest person loves his homeland, but

simply saying it doesn't make it so. Your actions will be the proof."

"How will I do that?"

"By serving this country and helping us," the general said.

"My soul and all that I have are worthless compared to the safety of my homeland. But what sort of services do you require?"

"It's very simple. You remain alert and report any unusual activities to us. Especially among your students."

The mullah frowned. "You're asking me to spy on my own students."

The general raised his hand and said, "Never. On the contrary. We want you to reveal only the spies around you."

He sighed and rubbed his eyes, and said without looking straight into the general's eyes, "OK, I'll do it."

The general gathered up his things. Without looking at him, he said, "Do you have questions?"

"Yes, I do."

The general stopped what he was doing and came back to stand in front of him with crossed arms, waiting for him to go on.

"The authorities took my daughter's computer when they searched my house in my absence. I have tried everything …"

The general interrupted him, "Tomorrow morning your daughter's computer will be at your house. Anything else you need?"

"No. Thank you." The mullah smiled for the first time since he'd entered the place.

***

They released Mullah Abdullah, just as the sun was slowly sinking behind the buildings. At the outer gate, they returned his belongings to him. When he switched on his mobile phone, he discovered it was 7:11 pm, and he had missed seven calls from home. He called immediately, and Amani picked up on the first ring. She was so relieved to hear from him. She said, "Thanks be to Allah. Are you ok? Where have you been? Are you coming home?"

"I'm ok and I'm sorry to make you worry. Is everything ok with you?"

"I'm sorry I called so many times," Amani said, "But Murshidah is here in our house. She insists on talking to you personally. I told her you were not here, and she should come some other time, but she refuses to leave without talking to you."

His heart was beating fast. There was only one reason for Murshidah to ask to speak with him. "Oh, that's no problem. You can disturb me as much as you want as long as we are in the service of people. Did she mention why she wants to see me?"

"No. She's being very mysterious."

"Ok, I am on the way to the mosque for Maghreb prayer. I'll be home after that." He sensed his wife's pleasure from her tone when she said, "May Allah protect you."

He took a taxi and paid no attention to anything outside the car during the drive. He was still in shock from the news that Salah was a member of the extremist group. Had Salah's kindness and obedience been fake? Had he been so blind not to notice Salah's words and actions and not understand he was hiding something?

In one of their sessions at the mosque, he had asked, "What do you like most about our history?"

"I love the unlimited power the Islamic Caliphate had," Salah had answered.

He couldn't remember what the rest of the students' answers were, but he still remembered the pride he'd felt when Salah had said that. How blind he'd been. "Oh Allah, I beg your mercy," he said in a low voice.

The taxi driver looked at him in the mirror without comment.

Who else could be involved with Salah? Fathi or Moneer? Salem or Saeed? Waseem or Amjad? Alaa or Khaled?

Outside the taxi, simple ordinary people walked along peacefully, not realizing the conspiracies that were being plotted against their homeland.

***

Back at home, Amani was sitting with Murshidah in the liwan. He greeted them both, politely averting his gaze. Getting right to the point, he said, "How can I be of service, sister?"

"It is a vital issue, mullah. I believe the wrath of Allah has fallen upon me because of it." Murshidah's voice seemed brittle.

He crossed his arms over his chest and said, "I seek refuge in Allah from his wrath. What is this important issue? Please speak, sister, so I may see how I can help you?"

"I don't think anyone can help me and release me from the guilt I feel every day and night," Murshidah said.

He exchanged looks with his wife, then glanced at Murshidah for only a second. She was wearing black from head to toe. She hid her face in her hands and sobbed. Her whole body trembled as if crying from the depths of her soul.

Amani reached out to Murshidah, her face full of concern.

He rolled his eyes and said, "Sister, let us hear the reason for this guilt."

Murshidah blew her nose and said, "On the day Hadiya died, her father-in-law, Haj Adel, came to our house, with one million Syrian pounds in a black plastic bag. He said they were a very religious family and would not want anyone to know any details about Hadiya's body. He said the million was a gift for us to remain silent. I beg Allah for forgiveness. At the time I thought Hadiya was a drug addict or something worse, and they didn't want people to know. Anyway, I was wrong and …" Murshidah choked back her sobs as she struggled to speak. "She was murdered. Her body showed all the signs of death by suffocation."

A dome of silence seemed to form over them. The mullah was confused. Why were there no tears in his eyes, no lump in his throat, and no pain in his chest? Why no weakness in his legs? He was happy and somewhat relieved? Was it because what Murshidah had just said finally proved he was right? He recalled how his wife had insisted that Hadiya had not been killed; that he was chasing an illusion. Well, she didn't say those exact words, but he had taken them to mean he was being unrealistic. He asked, "Are you sure?"

"The authorities always update us about the signs to look for in a variety of crimes. With a murder, we often have the last chance to reveal evidence if there was no police report. Hadiya's body showed evidence that she died of suffocation. That night, I explained to my husband what I had seen, because he has more experience than I. He came to the same conclusion; Hadiya had been murdered. We discussed the option of going to the police to tell them what we knew, but there was no point. The lady was dead. Telling the police wouldn't bring her back."

"What about the one who killed her? You didn't think that the killer was likely still walking around free and could kill someone else?" he snapped.

"All our lives, we have wanted to go on a pilgrimage to Mecca," Murshidah said in a wobbly voice. "But we've never had enough money. The funds from Haj Adel were enough for both of us to go to Mecca. But the day Ahmad came to us and convinced my husband that if we went with him to the court and gave testimony, he would pay us double what Haj Adel had and he would also ensure we don't go to jail. We were very excited about a way to clear our consciences. Suddenly, Ahmad died. We were devastated and didn't know what to do. Finally, we just kept our mouths shut and didn't tell anyone."

"So, what made you change your minds and speak out now?" he asked.

"I am here without my husband's knowledge." The mullah and Amani both gasped. A good Muslim woman must have her husband's permission before going out. Murshidah continued, "We agreed to go to Mecca together with the money. But then my husband took all the money and married another woman."

Mullah Abdullah gazed at her swollen, tear-stained face. *What woman is crazy enough to accept marriage to an ugly man like Waleed?* "So, it's not because you had an awakening of conscience?" he asked. Murshidah didn't answer, so he continued, "Are you ready to go to the police and tell them what you've told me?"

"I came here to talk to you as a representative of Allah. I will do whatever you advise," Murshidah said, "But I am an old woman, and I'm hoping you won't do anything to harm an old woman."

"Sister, the only way to clear your conscience is to go to the police and confess."

"I have no energy to go anywhere. Why don't you report it to the police? Let them track down my husband and get his explanation."

"There is no power but from Allah." He excused himself and left the liwan without another word.

***

The mullah went straight to his room, closed the door, leaned his back against it, and squeezed his eyes shut. *What a world we are living in. What should I do? Who should I call? Hani, despite all his vices, would have been the ideal person to proceed and put Murshidah and her husband behind bars. However, Hani is in prison. Should I call Mansoor? But Mansoor is the one who wrote the report and probably the one who covered up the crime in the first place. Maybe Mansoor helped Mazen get the court order. If Mansoor was an accomplice to Mazen and Haj Adel, it would be pointless now to report Murshidah to him.*

Should I go to the police station and report Murshidah and her husband? But then they will ask who I am and what is my connection with the crime? Why did Murshidah come to me and not go directly to the police? Will the police take the issue seriously? Of course, they will. It was a crime, after all. They would interrogate Murshidah, and she would confess. No, they won't take it seriously from me because of the court order, unless someone from Hadiya's family is with me. It's clear that Mazen killed his wife. But then, why didn't he bribe Murshidah himself? Of course, his father would have been pleased to help him, otherwise the stream of money from Dubai would stop. Is it possible Haj Adel is the one who killed his daughter-in-law?

Oh, Allah. It's all a big conspiracy, and the real losers are the children. To hell with the court order, I must go see Khaled and his sisters to tell them what happened and take Khaled to the police station to file a report. Maybe the children know but have been threatened to keep them quiet. The unspeakable signs of torture on Zakiya's back were undeniable evidence. If they don't know already, they have the right to know their mother was killed.

He changed to his religiose attire and went to the mosque to lead the Isha's prayer. After the prayer, he looked at the time; it was 9:36 pm. Despite his exhaustion, he strode over to Khaled's apartment.

When Khaled opened the door and saw the mullah, he gave him an 'are-you-stupid?' look, and tried to push the door closed. The mullah shoved his foot in the door and winced when Khaled threw his body weight against the door.

"I need you to come with me to the police station."

Khaled loosened the pressure and stared at him. "Why?"

Facing his former student, now with a throbbing foot, he questioned the instincts that had led him to this moment. *What if I simply turn around and leave? No, Khaled and his sisters deserve to know the truth.* He pleaded, "We need to report that your mother was murdered."

Khaled glanced around uneasily, biting his thumbnail. His hand was trembling.

The mullah remained silent, letting Khaled grasp what he'd just said.

"Did anyone see you?" Khaled asked impatiently. "Did you tell anyone you were coming here?"

The mullah smiled. *How considerate that my student is worried about me.* "Don't worry, my son. I will take all the responsibility if anyone complains. I'm the one who disobeyed the court order."

Khaled put a finger to his lips, signaling for him to come inside quietly. Slightly irritated by this behavior, the mullah followed as Khaled hobbled through the barren living space. The silence in the house was unnerving. The air was dense with the heavy odor of fried broccoli. The only light in the main room came from the doorless kitchen, which made the room look like a dream scene, gloomy and out of focus.

He expected Khaled to ask him to take a seat on a sofa, but Khaled kept hobbling until he reached a door at the far side of the room, opened it, and waited for him to go in.

Mullah Abdullah nearly gagged. The odor of dirty socks and underwear was intense. A tiny bedroom, with a single bed, a narrow closet in the corner, and a single plastic chair and a little coffee table. It was the first time he'd been inside Khaled's own bedroom, and his heart ached seeing the degree of poverty, while their father lived like a prince in Dubai.

The lad took a seat on the edge of the bed,

laying his crutches beside him. His short legs stuck straight out in front.

"Didn't we discuss the murder issue already?" Khaled asked gravelly. "It was because of that you were banned from coming near our apartment. Why do you insist on saying these things?"

"The court order convinced me even more that something strange is going on, and your mother deserves to be treated fairly," the mullah said with a deep sigh.

"What is fairer than going to live in heaven?" Khaled asked.

"I know you loved both your parents, and you are trying to protect your father, but your mother was murdered. She didn't die of natural causes. And if your father had a hand in it, he must be brought to justice."

"What makes you so sure this time?"

"There was a witness."

"That is not true. The night my mom left us, only my father, sisters and I were in the apartment."

The mullah hesitated. *Should I reveal who the witness was? Will Khaled be in danger if I tell him? No, we are going to the police anyway, so he must know.* "The lady who washed your mom's body confessed that she found evidence that your mom was strangled."

Khaled swallowed. He stuttered, "What are you talking about?"

"Your mom's body bore the signs of someone

who died of suffocation," the mullah said.

"So why she didn't report it when she washed Mom's body?"

"Your father bought her silence," the mullah said.

"Really?" Khaled said.

"Yes, she told me."

The bed squeaked as Khaled stood up, gathered up his crutches. Standing with his back to the mullah, he remained silent for some time. "So, you want me to go to the police and report that my father murdered my mother?" Khaled said without turning.

"No," the mullah said, "I just need you to come with me to report what the old lady said. All they need to do is interrogate the lady. Her evidence will lead them to your father and grandfather. Your mom was oppressed. We should not remain quiet. We must act quickly."

"I won't be much help, in this case," Khaled said. "I think it is better if you talk to my sisters. Maybe one of them witnessed something that night or heard something. Plus, I don't like to do anything without consulting them."

"Ok, but let's talk to them quickly." He just wanted this long day to be over.

Khaled hobbled out without looking at the mullah, crutches clacking on the tiles. The noise of the crutches continued marking his passage through the apartment.

The mullah leaned back, crossed his arms over

his chest, and dried his sweaty hands with his cloak. Closing his eyes, he inhaled a deep, calming breath. He wished it was all over with, and the murderer was in prison. Since the day Ahmad had first come to see him, he had been feeling stressed.

The clacking of crutches returned. He got up, ready to leave. When Khaled opened the door, he said, "My son Khaled, please let's get going. You can tell me what your sisters said on the way."

"I think it is better if you hear them for yourself before we go. They are just covering themselves and will be here shortly. I will get you something to drink."

Before the mullah could object, Khaled closed the door and left again. He sat back in the plastic chair and sighed. His head felt like it weighed a ton and his muscles ached with tiredness. He took out his mobile phone. *Wow, it's 10:40 pm already.* He wondered if his legs would ever stop shaking today. He noticed that the clacking sounds came closer and then further away a few times.

It seemed the process Khaled was using to bring him a drink was excruciatingly slow. First, Khaled entered the room and leaned the right crutch against the wall, then went out. He brought in the tray with his free hand and put it on the tea table, then he brought two cups, then he brought a jar of sugar, and last, the teapot. He assembled them on the table, then poured the steaming liquid into the cups. He put sugar in the cups and stirred them. The mullah watched, barely able to control his temper over his lack of urgency. "What is this Khaled?"

"Hot chocolate. Please enjoy while we await my sister's."

"All right, son," the mullah said. "Now, could you please ask your sisters to hurry up?"

Khaled left the room, closing the door behind him.

The mullah started to drink the hot chocolate. However, hot, it was not. He remembered he hadn't eaten or had anything to drink since he woke up. He was not a fan of this drink to begin with. Maybe that's why it tasted weird to him. His empty stomach made him drink it to the last drop.

***

The clacking of the crutches on the tiles seemed loud enough to shatter glass. It echoed in the sad silence of the night, as Khaled hobbled around the middle room, agitated. His hair was wet with sweat. He couldn't concentrate. He stopped. He hobbled. He stopped. He looked at his sister's door. Finally, he decided the first thing he must do was lock them in. He hobbled to the door, turned the knob, and pushed it in slowly, peering in. Only Farah was still awake, reading in the dim light of the single hanging bulb. Marwa, Ro'wa, and Zakiya were asleep. He shut the door quietly, inserted the key in the lock, and turned it with a click.

He stood in the middle of the room, eyes closed, listening to his rapid heartbeat and his heavy breath through his nostrils. There were no other sounds. Not of his sleeping sisters' systematic breathing. Not of the mullah struggling for air around the gag in his mouth. Not the sounds of cars or airplanes or bicycles. Not the voice of his mother or father or grandfather or grandmother, nor his friends Salah or Fathi. The world was utterly silent, as though everyone was watching and waiting for his decision regarding the drugged man in his bedroom. He glanced at the locked door, knowing he needed to decide what to do next?

Hobbling to his parents' bedroom, he took the laptop from under a pile of clothes in the closet and put it on the bed. Leaning his crutches against the edge of the bed, he sat on a chair beside the bed. He booted up the laptop and made a Skype call to his mentor Atturkey. The time in the corner of the screen read 11:57 pm.

He was panting now, his hands sweaty and clammy.

"Peace be upon you, brother," Khaled said.

No response, despite the good connection. He was online, but there was no reply. He said again, "Peace be upon you, brother."

A text message popped up, "Switch the light on."

He made a grab for his crutches, but they slid away from him and crashed to the floor. His hands shook as he picked them up and hobbled toward the wall and switched on the light. Returning to sit on the chair, he said shakily, "Sorry brother, I forgot to switch it on. Please forgive me."

Another message appeared. "Turn the

camera around to show the entire room, slowly."

He turned the laptop slowly to show his mentor that the room was empty, and he was alone.

Another message appeared on the screen. "Close the door. Keep the camera aimed at the door until it's closed."

He aimed the laptop camera toward the door and hobbled slowly over and closed it. He came back and sat in front of the laptop, waiting for his mentor to resume.

A man's croaky voice spoke out, "I hope you have an important reason for breaking all the safety protocols and calling me outside of the scheduled time." It was Atturkey's voice.

"Yes brother, it is a grave matter," Khaled said while looking at the room's door. "Mullah Abdullah Al-Allab is here in my house. He wanted me to go with him to the police station to report that my mom was murdered."

"Is he the hypocrite who is working with the infidel government?"

"Yes, and I have given him the same drug I used to help my mom. He is in a deep sleep."

"Allah said in the Holy Qur'an in chapter 66, verse number 9, 'O Prophet, strive against the disbelievers and the hypocrites and be harsh with them. And their refuge is Hell, and wretched is the destination.'" Atturkey said, "You must get rid of this hypocrite."

"You want me to kill him?"

"It is not killing. You are ridding the world of

an impurity."

"Should I use the gun with the silencer?"

"No. Hypocrites must die in a more sinister way. You will slaughter him," Atturkey said in a flat voice.

Khaled swallowed and stuttered, "O ... OK."

"Don't worry about the body," Atturkey said. "Within 24 hours, we will send a team to get rid of the body. You only need to send me a message saying it's done, and I will handle the rest."

The connection went off.

Khaled suddenly realized that he'd forgotten to insert the USP to hide his address before starting the call.

CHAPTER 27

Monday, May 31, 2010

Mullah Abdullah struggled to open his heavy eyelids. At first, he could see nothing. Everything was pitch black. Then he realized he was wearing a blindfold. He stayed still, listening for any sounds that would give him a clue to where he was. Besides the annoying buzzing in his ears, he could hear nothing. He closed his eyes and concentrated hard, trying to remember how he'd gotten here, but it only made the pain raging through his head more unbearable.

He was sitting on a chair with his hands tied behind his back. Severe pain spread across his shoulders. He tried to move his hands, but it only resulted in pins and needles spreading through his hands and up his arms.

He struggled to get to his feet, then let out a strangled gasp. Something had him around the throat and caused him to fall back into the chair. The rope around his neck had tightened so much he felt as if he was strangling.

The sound of a door opening, then closing again, was followed by a tapping noise on the floor tiles. It was an all too familiar sound. He sensed movement near him. *Why are you doing this to me? Is this how you treat the imam of a prominent mosque? A loving husband and father ...?* That suddenly reminded him of his family, and he choked back a sob. *I am a loyal citizen. I've never harmed anyone. I always help my neighbors, and I teach people how to love ...*

At that moment, he realized he was not talking because of the smelly old rag was tied over his mouth for a gag.

The rope around his neck was unbearably tight. Breathing was becoming nearly impossible as the rope pulled on his neck from above, forcing him to stand on his tiptoes. He was becoming light-headed and was losing all feeling in his arms and legs. He expected to lose consciousness at any moment.

Suddenly, the rope went slack, flopping him awkwardly onto the chair, causing him to draw in a long desperate breath through his nose. The tapping on the floor came closer, and the mask was snatched from his face. The room really was dark. The only light came in under the closed door, barely enough to reveal the lines between the tiles. As his eyes adjusted to the darkness, the features of Khaled's bedroom gradually appeared. The silhouette standing before him was Khaled.

For a few seconds he thought he might be dreaming, but no, the pain was too real in every bone and muscle. He recalled some of the most recent events, but he still couldn't comprehend why Khaled was doing this to him. He tried to speak, but his voice came out like a moan. He shook his head and moaned again, hoping Khaled would take the gag from his mouth if he moaned more. He followed Khaled's movements until his silhouette disappeared from his line of sight.

He was surprised when Khaled loosened the gag. Was he not afraid he might scream for help? Probably Khaled knew he would never scream and yell for help from anyone, except maybe from Allah. It had never even crossed his mind to scream or shout. He was too busy contemplating how he'd got himself into this situation.

Have I been blind to the possibility of wickedness from the disabled person standing before me? Khaled always seemed so sincere; always kind and helpful to others. Did I fail as a mentor and teacher in Khaled's case? Are his actions out of love for his father? Is it all an effort to keep his father out of jail? What about Khaled's mother? The woman who spent all her life caring for him and his sisters. Didn't Khaled have any feelings for her? Maybe Khaled cared about his mother, but feared the scandal if his father became known as a murderer. Surely Khaled could have discussed it with me first without doing this to me.

"You are close to my heart, Khaled, and I forgive you. I will beg Allah to forgive you for your sin. Sometimes we act wrongly out of stress. Please, untie me and let me go. I promise no one will know what happened here. I won't go to the police to report your father, if that's what made you angry." His mouth was dry, and his voice croaky.

Khaled moved back into his line of sight. Eyes like two shiny black olives in the semi-darkness. Khaled whispered, "Are you serious? You will ask Allah to forgive me? Who do you think you are? You think Allah will listen to someone like you?" The sarcasm in Khaled's voice hurt the mullah more than the rope around his neck.

"The door of repentance will never close until we are in the hereafter," he answered. The pulses in his head were stronger now. *Am I dying?*

"I have committed no sins that require me to seek repentance," Khaled snarled.

"Humans are not infallible. All of us commit sins, and we must seek repentance day and night." A sharp pain in the mullah's chest caused him to squeeze his eyes shut.

"I didn't say I am infallible. But I have committed no major sins," Khaled said as he came even closer.

He could see Khaled's facial features clearer now and smell his foul breath.

"My son, Khaled. The narration says, don't look at the size of the sin, but look to whom you are disobeying whenever you commit the sin. When we commit sins, we are disobeying the Lord of glory. Allah created us, and it is obligatory to obey our creator at all times and be thankful for the endless gifts we are given."

"What endless gifts are you talking about?" Khaled asked. "Are you blind? Can you not see me? I am disabled. I live an impoverished existence without a father or mother."

"What Allah doesn't grant you in this life, you will be compensated for in the hereafter."

"Even now, under these circumstances, you continue to lecture me?"

The mullah said with a shaky voice, "You are the last person in this life I thought would dare to treat your mentor this way. What has changed you?"

"I was stupid and naïve, and I misunderstood the religion," Khaled said. "I followed the wrong examples, smiled at the faces of the wrong people. I helped individuals who didn't deserve to be helped. Allah guided me to the right path until I have become the Khaled you see before you now."

Khaled moved back and sat on the edge of the bed. Only his silhouette was visible; just a dark blob perched on the side of the bed.

"I don't see that the new Khaled is better than the old one. I see you deviating from the true path."

Khaled's voice turned from seriousness to sarcasm. "So, the correct way is to pray only in your mosque and attend your classes. Is that right?"

"Every person has the freedom to choose any mosque to pray in, and to attend their choice of classes." Another stabbing pain across his shoulders forced an agonized groan.

"I feel pity for those students who still attend your classes," Khaled said. "They don't know you are not teaching them true Islam. You are teaching them how to be slaves to the infidels. But I will be an obedient servant of Allah when I kill you and stop you from spreading your poison."

The mullah had always bragged about not being afraid of death, so why was he so anxious now? Maybe because he'd never expected one of his students to adopt such extremist views.

"You commit a grand sin when you kill any human being. You may believe it is permissible to kill the soul that Allah has forbidden you to kill, but the authorities won't see it as permissible. They will punish you. Think about it. You can kill me and hide my body, but do you think for a moment the authorities won't find out who killed me?" It was as if he was talking to himself. Khaled's silhouette dissolved in the blackness. *When will this horrible nightmare end? Oh Allah, please help me...*

"Our war began with the authorities you speak of. We will restore the correct laws of Allah, promoting virtue and preventing vice." Khaled's voice was gravelly now. "You should know I am not alone in this. I asked my mentor what I should do with you. He ordered me to sacrifice you so I can be nearer to Allah. After I kill you, a group of believers will come and get rid of your corpse. My sisters are locked in their room as they are every night. They don't even know you're here. I haven't spoken to them about your pathetic theories."

Despite his exhaustion, the mullah said sarcastically, "If you were not planning to kill me, I might have asked to join your group and help in your noble mission."

"Killing you is part of the noble mission," Khaled said.

"How is that?"

"Your hands are tainted because you have been following the teachings of the infidels."

"Who do you mean by infidels?"

"The government. Look around you. Major sins are spilling out into the streets, and yet the government takes no action to stop it. Vices are everywhere. Adultery is spreading, and cheating is everywhere. Bribery has become a necessity for survival. Women are working, while men go jobless. The government is totally corrupt."

A sharp pain attacked the mullah's chest. He wanted to speak, but his voice came out husky and strained. He tried to swallow, but his mouth was as dry as dust. He raised his head and looked into the blackness. Despite the pain in his throat, he said, "There is no power but from Allah."

"We will make the warped straight again," Khaled said with pride. "We will improve our country by ridding it of infidels. We will decapitate everyone who is against the laws of Allah. Soon now, a state of truth will be reborn, and all the countries of the unbelievers will collapse. We are the ones who will send the infidels where they deserve. Straight to Hell."

"So, you will announce jihad in Syria?" The mullah's voice, barely audible now. "Why don't you declare jihad in the occupied lands outside of our country?"

"The enemy inside the country is far more dangerous than the ones outside," Khaled snarled.

"Those people you call enemies are Muslims."

"They are hypocrites, and it is our duty to kill them."

With his eyes closed, the mullah said, "Wouldn't it be better to guide those people to the truth rather than killing them? Doesn't Allah tell us in the Holy Qur'an, 'There shall be no compulsion in [acceptance of] the religion'?"

"Allah said in the Qur'an, 'Seize them and kill them whenever you find them,'" Khaled's voice was gruff.

He almost forgot his pain and said, "Khaled, my son. In which chapter is this verse?" He opened his eyes to find Khaled's face only a few centimeters from his. His heart raced.

"Don't call me your son. I am no son of yours." Khaled spat at him, forcing him to close his eyes and mouth to avoid the flying spittle.

Patiently, the mullah said, "The passage you quoted is not the whole verse. If you read the complete verse, you will find it is speaking of a specific group of people at that particular time in history. It is in chapter 4, verse 89.

"They wish you would disbelieve as they disbelieved so you would be alike. So do not take from among them allies until they emigrate for the cause of Allah. But if they turn away, then seize them and kill them wherever you find them and take not from among them any ally or helper.

"It refers to a treaty between the messenger and a non-Muslim tribe. The messenger was attempting to persuade them not to veto the treaty. If we want to be honest and fair, we need to continue reading to understand that Allah was asking the messenger not to fight those people if they didn't veto the treaty. It is from verse 90 that follows that one.

"Except for those who take refuge with people between yourselves and who is a treaty or those who come to you, their hearts strained at [the prospect of] fighting you or fighting their own people. And if Allah had willed, He could have given them power over you, and they would have fought you. So, if they remove themselves from you and do not fight you and offer you peace, then Allah has not made for you a cause [for fighting] against them.

"You must not ignore that section, *'So if they remove themselves from you and do not fight you and offer you peace, then Allah has not made for you a cause [for fighting] against them.'*" The mullah felt triumphant.

Khaled said, "Allah says in Chapter 8, verse 60, 'And prepare for them whatever you are able of power and of steeds of war.'" Khaled moved back again to sit on the edge of the bed.

Hoping to shake Khaled's confidence, the mullah recited the entire verse "*And prepare against them whatever you are able of power and of steeds of war by which you may terrify the enemy of Allah and your enemy and others besides them whom you do not know [but] whom Allah knows. And whatever you spend on the cause of Allah will be fully repaid to you, and you will not be wronged.*

"Prepare doesn't mean attack or fight. It is obvious in that verse that preparation of the power is just to intimidate their enemies and show them we're not vulnerable. And to be fair, you should read the next verse as well.

"*'And if they incline to peace, then incline to it [also] and rely upon Allah. Indeed, it is He who is the Hearing, the Knowing.'*

"You need to pay close attention to '*incline to peace*'.

"Why don't you and your group follow the steps of the messenger and be peaceful with peaceful people? Those people you intend to fight and kill are Muslims that have made mistakes. Our duty is to guide them, not to kill them." He felt dizzy, his throat screamed for water and severe pain wracked his neck and shoulders.

He closed his eyes as Khaled answered, "That is the style of a coward and a weakling. The sharpness of the sword is the best incentive to persuade people to follow the law."

Eyes still closed, the mullah said weakly, "Allah, in the Holy Qur'an in chapter 21, verse 107, told Prophet Mohammad, *'And we have not sent you, [O Muhammad], except as a mercy to the worlds.'* So, tell me where mercy is in your regime?"

Khaled said, "*'We didn't send you, but with the sword as a mercy to the world.'*"

"I beg Allah for forgiveness. That is an obvious distortion." The mullah words devolved into a spate of furious coughing.

Khaled hobbled and grabbed him, putting the gag back in his mouth and tying it tight.

How naïve and blind I've been. Why didn't I connect the dots? The disappearance of Salah. The Jihad books in Salah's room. Khaled no longer attending the mosque. Zakiya's horribly mutilated back, and the warning the general gave me.

Khaled's face was so close to the mullah's face. The mullah could smell the stench and feel the heat of his breath. In a slow, lethal tone, he said, "You think you're a hero. You wanted to go to the police and tell them my father killed my mom. You have no idea what you're talking about. You didn't know my mom or her circumstances. Do you know how long my mom waited for my father to come back from Dubai and live with us?

"More than fifteen bloody years. She never saw a single good day during all of those long years. My grandparents humiliated her over our monthly expenses. My sisters treated her like a housemaid. My father was always absent and never respected her. Many Fridays, we would go to my grandmother's house so we could talk to him on the phone at a prearranged time, but when we got there, we'd find out he had already called. Do you know how hurtful that is to a wife?

"My mom fought to bring us upright, and remained completely loyal to him, but my father didn't care about her feelings. In the end, he threatened to divorce her if she asked him one more time to take her to Dubai to live with him or asked him to come back to Syria. That night, I could have killed anyone who stood in my way. It hurt so badly, seeing her suffer and knowing there was nothing I could do to help. Many long nights, sleep deserted me while I agonized over my father's hypocrisy, treating a delicate creature like her in such a cruel way.

"And how did she react to all of that? She always responded with a smile and kindness. I could no longer tolerate seeing her unconditional kindness to people who never respected her. Her infinite kindness hurt me more than the cruelty of people toward her. Day after day, I realized that my mom's existence was a mistake in this life. My mom was an angel walking among mere humans. Her rightful place was not among sinners. She deserved a position among the angels.

"Sitting there, unable to help her, created a deep rage inside me; a desire to destroy and burn everything in sight. Until the day I met my new mentor, Atturkey. He was the one who encouraged me to do what needed doing. I knew no one would understand why I did it. No one ever treated me like a normal person. They looked at her body and discussed what they should do; mostly how they should hide the facts to avoid a scandal. They didn't even recognize that I was the one who had committed the noble act. They couldn't even conceive of my being the one responsible. They never even acknowledged my presence. I am the only one who loved her unconditionally. I granted her what no one else in this world could give her. I granted her something greater than love; no one was willing to free her as I have done. I sent her to the place where she belongs."

Mullah Abdullah couldn't believe what he'd just heard. He was no longer looking at Khaled, the disabled boy. He was seeing the devil himself inhabiting Khaled's body. He didn't have the energy to talk or even to follow Khaled's movements. He closed his eyes and listened to the sound of the crutches tapping on the floor. The sound seemed to come from gradually farther away, and his head felt like it was floating. An icy cold sensation settled into his inner organs. *Is my heart still beating?*

Then he heard the faraway sound of Zahra laughing as a child. It was unmistakably her voice from when she used to play in the liwan around him. He would often pick her up and smell her neck, always lavender talc, before he kissed her.

The rope around the mullah's neck became tight causing a gurgling sound to escape his mouth.

Is this the final agony of people on the hangman's rope? Fire in the throat, burning eyes, weakness of limbs, brain going blank, then blackness...

***

When Farah opened her eyes to see Zakiya looking down at her, she needed a few seconds to realize she was only in her room, not with the prince she'd been dreaming of. She sighed. "What do you want?"

"I need to pee," Zakiya whispered.

Farah got up slowly, but the bed made a creaking sound, loud enough to wake up Marwa and Ro'wa. She went to the closet to get the spare key that Khaled didn't know about. It was folded in a stack of her underwear, on the highest shelf, so Khaled couldn't reach it if he searched the closet.

On tiptoes she went to the door, and unlocked it slowly, trying not to make a sound. She peered out. The light was on in the main room, but a glance at Khaled's door confirmed his light was off. She gestured to Zakiya, and they crept silently to the toilet.

While waiting for her sister to finish, Farah stared at the gloomy walls, remembering how her mother used to wash those walls every month and what an exhausting job it was. Had she been punishing herself for not having enough courage to confront her husband? Or maybe she just had a lot of rage inside, and rather than direct it at him, she released the anger by doing physically demanding work. Farah hoped her mother was in heaven now. The only place where she could forget what a sorrowful life she had lived.

Zakiya tapped her on the shoulder, causing her to jump. The light switch was on the wall next to Khaled's door and as she went to turn it off, she thought she could hear the low hum of voices coming from his room. Was she imagining it? Slowly, she crept closer to the door, listening intently. A cold sensation filled her gut, as a ghastly terror crawled from somewhere deep in her memory. Zakiya was beside her now, her face pale and eyes dull, her breathing shallow and rapid.

Grabbing Zakiya's hand, she pulled her into their room before her hyperventilating alerted Khaled, bringing the night to a tragic end. She closed the door without locking it.

Zakiya climbed into her bed, shaking violently, and hugging her knees as she sobbed under the blanket. Ro'wa and Marwa were puzzled. Whatever could have happened? In whispers, Farah told her sisters what she and Zakiya had heard coming from Khaled's room.

Khaled's cruelty to them knew no limits, but Zakiya was very delicate and couldn't tolerate it. Her soul was hurt, far worse than her body.

Farah had cried all night when Khaled had last flogged Zakiya. He'd done damage to one of her ears but wouldn't allow them to take her to the hospital. All because Zakiya had challenged him and told him he was a fake Muslim and Allah would let him burn in hell.

Farah, Marwa and Ro'wa took her to the hospital without his permission. For that, he'd punished them by withholding their allowance for a week so they couldn't go to the university that week. If she hadn't gone to her grandfather secretly and complained, the week could have been extended to a month maybe, or more.

Khaled considered them infidels and continually found new reasons to hurt them. Farah, Marwa and Ro'wa would cleverly bargain with him to avoid punishment. But Zakiya always challenged him and always ended up being punished ruthlessly. They had no way to stop him because their grandfather gave the money to Khaled as the man of the family. Khaled would not give them money if they didn't obey him. Without money, they couldn't go to university, buy books or even food. Thanks to Allah, the universities were free, but with a guardian like Khaled, she and her sisters would end up being uneducated, forced to accept the first offer of marriage.

Farah took Zakiya in her arms and hugged her to calm her down.

"What are we going to do?" Marwa whispered.

"We need to stop another murder from happening in this house," Ro'wa said.

"What can we do without the outside door key?" Marwa asked.

Wiping her wet cheeks on her sleeve, Zakiya

went to the closet and fetched a small piece of paper. Unfolding it, she held it out to the others.

"What is this?" Ro'wa asked.

"The number for the police station. I promised I would get it, and I did," Zakiya whispered.

"And how will we call them? Using our washing machine?" Marwa asked.

Zakiya sighed and gave Farah a look that plainly said, 'tell-them-please'.

"Before Uncle Ahmad died, he bought a mobile phone and gave it to me," Farah said. "He told me to hide it and only use it in case of an emergency. I promised to call him if Khaled ever went near Zakiya again. After his death, I offered to give it back to Rema, but she told me to keep it and call the police if …"

The door to their room flew open and smashed against the wall like an explosion, breaking the silence of the night.

Khaled stood in the doorway with a gun in his hand.

Farah and her sisters froze.

Farah thought, *can this be real? A gun with a silencer? Where did he get such a weapon? Is this the same boy my mother gave birth to and raised despite his handicaps? What is going on in our lives? Can life get any worse than this? Are there families anywhere more unfortunate than our family? Oh, Allah!*

Farah tried to focus, but her heart had been taken over by a crazed drummer. Her three sisters were staring at the shocking scene before them. She knew nothing about guns except what she'd read in novels or seen in the movies they watched at their grandmother's house.

"What are you doing, Khaled? Where did you get the gun from?" Farah wanted to yell but her voice came out like a dry whisper.

"Shut up," he shouted so loud it caused his sisters to jerk back. Keeping his distance from them he said, "Give me the key."

Farah was relieved when she realized he hadn't heard the story of the telephone and, by some miracle, he didn't notice the piece of paper still in Zakiya's hand. Pretending to comply with his demand, she moved toward the closet.

"Don't move," Khaled barked.

"The key," Farah stuttered, "Is in the closet."

Khaled gestured with the barrel of the gun for her to move.

She got to the closet in two steps. Blocking his view with her body, she pulled the mobile phone from its hiding place and slipped it into the pocket of her pajamas. Then she turned around with the key in her hand that she hadn't had the chance to return to its hiding place yet.

Approaching Khaled, she held the key out to him with a shaking hand. He snatched it violently and yelled, "Get back!" She ran back to stand near her three sisters, who were now on maximum alert.

Glaring at Zakiya, he snapped, "Follow me!"

Farah, Marwa, and Ro'wa all gasped, and

Zakiya started panting in short, rapid breaths. Khaled yelled, "Move!" and pointed the gun at her face.

Farah had the phone, but Zakiya still had the paper with the phone number. She lunged at Zakiya, grabbing her around the waist, as if to keep her from going. Glaring at Khaled, she said defiantly, "You're not taking her anywhere."

Khaled pointed the gun at Farah's head and growled, "Back off." At first Farah didn't move, but when she heard the click of the hammer being drawn back, she let go of Zakiya and backed away.

"Move! Go to mom's room," Khaled yelled.

Zakiya ran out, crying and gasping for breath at the same time.

Khaled hobbled out after her, locking the door behind him.

Farah rushed to the door, dropped to one knee, and peered through the skull-shaped keyhole. She could hear Zakiya's crying. She raised her tear-filled eyes heavenward and implored, "Oh, God. Help us." Putting her eye once again to the keyhole, she could see nothing. She wiped the tears from her eyes on the sleeve of her pajamas then looked again. Khaled was standing in the middle of the hall, looking at his gun on the floor. Somehow, he'd dropped it. *Is it possible Allah heard my prayers and made Khaled drop the gun?* Khaled tried to grab it, but it was nearly impossible because he couldn't bend his knees. Suddenly, he looked toward his mom's room and yelled, "Who are you talking to?" Khaled let the gun lie where it was and hobbled after Zakiya as quickly as he could.

Farah turned and looked at Marwa and Ro'wa, both with tears streaming down their faces. "Why is this happening to us?" Ro'wa asked her, but Farah had no answer.

"We must break the door. We have to stop him from hurting her again," Ro'wa said as she started toward the door.

"No, wait," Farah said.

Marwa and Ro'wa looked at her in exasperation, but she quickly explained. "I slipped the mobile phone into Zakiya's pocket when I was hanging onto her just then."

***

Lieutenant Hamad Alwasat's head tottered from sleepiness. It was 4:13 am and today was his last night shift for the month. The part of his job he hated most throughout his ten years of service was the night shifts. They drained his energy and kept him from sleeping beside his lovely, warm wife.

He smiled at the thought as he looked around. He'd spent most of the past ten years in this simple room with his desk, a couple of battered old sofas, and a cupboard. Every day in this boring room doing his boring job, archiving whatever data and reports came through the fifth territory police station. It was seldom that anything exciting happened. There was a time a woman came in to report her husband's loud snoring at night. None of the men took her seriously and joked about it until she left in tears.

It was amusing to watch them. Once an old guy came in to report his missing cat. How hilarious it had been when his colleagues pretended to help and started calling other stations to ask about his missing cat. Oh yes, then there was the time when the mullah came in with another guy and they started yelling and one of them ended up out cold on the floor.

He looked at the clock. 4:18 am. He closed his eyes and imagined his wife and what they might do in the shower this morning before breakfast.

The landline started ringing, and he picked it up. "Hi honey, I was just thinking of you," he said in a smoky voice.

"Please help us ... please," a young female whispered between choking sobs.

His chest tightened. Her panicked voice gave him goosebumps, and he shivered.

"Ok calm down, I will help you," he said. "You need to calm down and tell me the address where you are." He found himself whispering unintentionally. Her sobbing reminded him of his own daughter when she was in pain, when she'd broken her leg last summer.

"You don't understand," she whispered. "He has a gun, and if you don't help me, another crime will take place soon."

"Okay, okay, just tell me where you are now."

"Ah ..." she shrieked in pain.

He heard a loud bang, possibly from the telephone hitting the floor. A shrill scream, then the sounds of blow after blow and more screaming filled his ear.

"Aloo … Aloo …" He said a few times, his heart banging furiously in his chest. His body shuddered with each scream. He was biting down on his bottom lip as he tightened his iron grip on the receiver. In exasperation, he laid the receiver on the table and started pacing the room, trying to think what he could do?

Finally, he picked up the receiver again, only to find the line was dead.

CHAPTER 28

Monday, May 31, 2010

Two black vans made their way slowly up Shagoor Street, breaking the early morning silence. They double-parked, switched off their engines, and the silence returned. Twelve men emerged from the vans wearing flak jackets, communication headphones, and infrared goggles. The men stood in a line, awaiting orders. Their leader, Lieutenant Nader, was expecting official go-ahead from the operation's room for the Ministry of Defense's task force against terrorism.

Finally, the order came for them to take their positions, and remain at the ready until further notice. They sprinted to take up their positions. Two men remained at the gate of building number 11, while two men climbed to the roof of the building. Two snipers with their Remington's locked and loaded lay prone on nearby rooftops, their binoculars at the ready. Five men took their positions at the front door with Lieutenant Nader, ready to raid the apartment. The team had been briefed on the layout of the apartment, and each room in the apartment was assigned to two soldiers.

The leader talked through his clip-on earphone, "Roof surveillance, status update."

"Surveillance to command. Infrared shows three bodies moving around in the front room."

"Do you have a visual on them?" the leader whispered.

"No sir. The shutters are closed."

The lieutenant tried to insert a tube camera under the door, but the door was almost touching the ground. He waved his technical expert in, and he took out a set of tools in a small black zippered case, then worked his magic on the lock with expertly trained fingers. Thirty-eight seconds later, the lock was open. He pushed the door open gingerly and poked the tube camera through the resulting opening.

The screen Lieutenant Nader was holding in one hand showed only blackness, so he switched over to night vision mode. The screen lit up with an eerie green glow, allowing him to see that the room contained two sofas and two closed doors, but no sign of any occupants.

The radio crackled in his earphones, and the

order was given to raid the house and apprehend the suspect. Opening the door slowly, he told the others to be ready and alert, then pushed his way inside. His team members followed close behind. The first thing he spotted was a gun with an attached silencer on the floor. He gestured to one of the team to put it in a plastic evidence bag. All the doors leading out of the room were closed.

They stood in the middle of the dark room for a few seconds, listening intently. From one room, they could hear crying and muffled voices. It could only be the three bodies surveillance had mentioned. The lieutenant signaled for every two to cover a closed door. They stood with their guns aimed at the locks and waited for him to give the order. When he did, all three guns fired at once with small popping sounds because of the silencers. The bullets striking the locks made a louder noise than the firing.

Feminine screams erupted from the room as he entered, and announced, "Three females here."

"One female body," his subordinate announced from the second room.

"One male body," came from the third room.

Lieutenant Nader, in the first room, pointed the gun straight ahead of him, and yelled, "Put your hands where I can see them!" The three young women were screaming and clinging to each other with fear in their eyes. "Stand up against the wall, raise your hands in the air, and don't move. Any movement at all, I will shoot." The three young women did as they were ordered.

One of his subordinates rushed in and reported, "The subject is missing, sir."

"Where is Khaled?" he snapped at the three quaking girls.

The three young women just stared at him. From their confusion, he could tell they didn't know.

"You stay here," Nader said to his escort, then went out to check the other two rooms.

Switching on all the lights, he walked into a bedroom and found a small female body on the floor. Her clothes were torn and soaked with blood, her hair was wet and sticking to the side of her face. One of her eyes was only a slit in her purple, swollen skin. Fresh blood oozed from her mouth. He squatted and with two fingers felt for the vein in her neck. He said, "She's still alive?" Then he stood up and scanned the floor quickly. A smashed mobile phone lay on the floor, so he bent to examine it without touching it. "Secure this evidence," he ordered, then went to check the third room.

In the third room, he automatically covered his nose against the stench. The body of a bearded man was tied to a plastic chair, a gag in his mouth and a blindfold over his eyes. A length of thick rope tied tightly around his neck stretched to a metal ring in the ceiling. The ring, normally used to hang a chandelier, had been used to hang the victim.

He returned to the middle room to confer with the others. They concluded the suspect was still missing.

The leader gave the order for the search and surveillance team to start a sweep of the street. He called the operations room and informed them that the suspect was missing and probably at large. He ordered two ambulances to arrive as soon as possible, and an interrogation team to question the three uninjured females.

The order came from the operations room to raid a nearby apartment, which had also been under surveillance for some time. An individual matching Khaled's description had been spotted entering the building.

Outside, the street was like a circus. Blue and red flashing lights, two ambulances, and three squad cars for the interrogators and investigators. Men, women, and children were gathered on most of the balconies, like so many theater spectators. Screeches of laughter erupted from one balcony. A father shouted at his children from another. A mother called her daughters to come out to the balcony. It was a unique night for the neighborhood, and people didn't want to miss any of the excitement.

The two vans with the assault team moved at top speed to the new address, which comprised three buildings in a triangle with a park full of tall trees in the middle. There was only one entrance to the area between the buildings. The district was called Sahet-Almalaab.

Lieutenant Nader ordered the second van to remain at the entrance to the street to control the movement of cars. His van followed the roadway as it circled the trees. The van was just starting through the gate of the building when the windshield exploded and the driver slumped over the steering wheel in a shower of shattered glass. The van swerved out of control, hitting a parked white car, glass shattered from both vehicles. The white car's alarm system erupted.

The side of Lieutenant Nader's head was throbbing with pain as he'd smashed it against the side glass when the collision happened. He raised his right hand to signal his team to hold fast. He didn't want another dead body if he could help it. He called the driver of the second van and asked him to hide around the back. He called the operation room to update them on the situation and asked for snipers to cover their raid.

The shot that killed the driver, while unfortunate, was confirmation that the subject was on the premises.

The side window shattered, showering them with glass. They hadn't heard an explosion either the first time or now, so the shooter's gun had a silencer. The bullets shattered the right-side windows.

Lieutenant Nader ordered, "Take a cover behind the van." so they dove out the sliding side door and squatted down behind the van.

Two more windows shattered above their heads.

The lieutenant watched as two of his snipers, their bulletproof shields held out before them, quickly vanished into the blackness of a building's front gate.

A few minutes of suspense followed as five guards approached, carrying two shields each. They each handed a shield to the lieutenant and each of his men.

As Nader started toward the building's gate, he felt the tremendous force of a bullet as it struck the shield. He would have fallen backward if he hadn't immediately squatted down.

Shattering glass, a woman's scream, and a man shouting orders at residents to take cover and not leave their building. Nader, keeping low, scrambled for the entrance, when a bullet whistled past, missing him by inches. He entered the four-floor building, similar to Khaled's, the shield clutched in his left hand, his gun clasped in his right. Five of his team members were close behind him, negotiating the lower stairs carefully and aiming their weapons at the upper stairs, where each floor had two apartments. On the second floor, a curious resident opened a door. Lieutenant Nader barked at the sleepy head to close it and not open it again. The apartment they were headed for was on the fourth floor.

They had reached the third floor when a woman's shrill scream erupted from the floor above. Nader sprinted up the remaining stairs, still followed by his five men. At the bottom of the fourth-floor stairs, they came to an abrupt stop and raised their hands in the air. A young man at the top of the stairs, around nineteen maybe, was holding a woman hostage, in her nightgown, aiming his gun at her sweaty head while she wept in despair.

Unable to remain standing, she collapsed on the floor, forcing the young man to fall to his knees. Hoping to use this chance to advance, Lieutenant Nader climbed the first two steps. The young man swung the gun in his direction and squeezed the trigger. The lieutenant was quick to cover his head with the shield. The bullet smashed into the shield, forcing Nader back the two steps he'd taken. His head banged against the wall behind, causing him to moan in agony. His team began to move in, but he raised his left hand to warn them back.

"Get back, or I'll shoot her," the young man snarled.

"Okay, okay," Nader said and waved to his subordinates to retreat. The five men retreated until the lieutenant was the only one visible to the young man.

"You have no way to escape, son," Nader said quietly.

"Shut the fuck up, you shit hole," the young man screamed. The woman, by this time, was weeping hysterically. The young man hit her on the head with the butt of the gun, causing her to scream in pain.

The lieutenant climbed up two steps again, but two more shots forced him back. This time he was better prepared and his left leg stretched out behind him prevented him from falling.

Again, the woman screamed. The young man yelled, "Shut up!"

Nader could see the gun was a 9mm pistol, but it wasn't possible to know how many bullets were left in the magazine. Some of these guns hold up to eighteen bullets.

What's the best way to get the better of this young man Nader wondered? Glass shattered downstairs somewhere. Someone else was clearly shooting from inside the apartment.

His clothes were drenched in sweat, his neck stiff and sore. The crying of the woman was like a nail being driven into his head. The noise outside the building was increasing as well. He was worried this crazy man, in a moment of desperation, could decide to kill the woman. Oh, shit…

He propped his shield on the top step and hid behind it. With his left hand, he signified for his subordinates to descend.

***

Is this the end? Am I going to be a martyr now? Khaled sat, leaning against the wall of a gloomy room in Fathi's apartment. There was nothing on the old dirty white tiled floor except for a few cardboard boxes with postage stickers, showing they'd come from overseas.

Two of Fathi's friends were shooting at the police officers from the windows of the room next to the one he was in, connected by a door on his right. The main door was on his left, at the end of the wall he was leaning against. Fathi was outside, holding a woman as a hostage.

The stickiness of the blood between his toes was disgusting. His feet were bleeding from the run to reach the apartment. Only two blocks, but he had severe pain in his hips and knees, as if they were totally devoid of any natural lubrication. Every breath sent scalding pain through his chest. Every heartbeat was like a nail being inserted between his ribs.

He no longer had enough strength in his limbs to stand and attack the police officers surrounding the apartment, like Fathi and his two friends. What a night! Earlier he'd killed the mullah and now here he was in this apartment with three other men shooting at police who were trying to prevent their escape.

He knew he must be ready to endure any consequences to pave the path for the building of the true state. Atturkey had told him that much. Of course, they must endure sacrifices to be part of the building of the new Islamic Caliphate.

If any of these police officers are good people and get killed while attacking us, they will die martyrs and find their place in heaven. They would just be inevitable casualties. But if they are bad people, they will die and go to hell, and that's what they deserve.

Despite his discomfort from the external hubbub, it wasn't as disruptive as the war going on inside his head. *How long will I keep deceiving myself that I'm walking the path of truth? How much longer will I lie to myself that I joined the organization to build the true state, and not because I desperately wanted a friend like Salah? All I really wanted was to have someone treat me like a human with value.*

When Salah approached him in the mosque one Friday after the prayer and suggested the idea, he agreed without thinking or even listening to everything Salah was suggesting.

Are these actual tears falling from my eyes? Is it depression that's tearing my guts apart? Is this weeping sound coming from me? Is it fear that has my limbs paralyzed?

He hadn't figured out at the time it would be a one-way trip he'd agreed to go on with Salah, but suddenly now he realized it. He hadn't expected so many difficulties, or that it would end like this. The police officers outnumbered them.

If Fathi and his two friends can escape, they won't want a cripple to accompany them. I would only slow them down.

He looked at the shiny chrome of the pistol in his hand. If his father was here, Khaled would shoot the legs out from under him and leave him to die a slow, painful death. He wanted his father to feel the pain he lived with every day because of him. His father was the reason for his painful existence in this life. The sole reason for all his pain and suffering, and now he realized he was also the reason for all the terrible things he'd done.

If it was not for his father's oppression of his mother, he wouldn't have done what he had to stop her suffering and send her to the hereafter to live in heaven with Allah. He could never forget how she struggled for air as he'd pressed the plastic bag over her head and suffocated her in her sleep. The pain shot through him again. A fresh stream of tears sprang from the corners of his eyes. He'd only wanted to end her miserable life and suffering once and for all.

If not for his father's decision to live in Dubai, leaving Khaled as the man in charge of the household in his absence, he wouldn't have been able to impose his control and dominance over his four sisters. He wouldn't have had to flog Zakiya for her perpetual rebellion.

His father's permanent absence made him grow up with a feeling of inferiority, which only increased with every year that passed until he started begging for sympathy and pity of other people. He only wanted to be friends with Salah and Atturkey, who both had led him down this dark path. And where are they now?

Is there anyone on this earth lonelier than I am?

Everyone had left him: his father, his grandfather, his grandmother, his siblings, his relatives, even his friends, if he'd ever had any in the first place.

Is there anyone more miserable or uglier or more crippled than I? Does it make sense to say that Allah gave up on me like everyone else? No, Allah will never give up on His creations. But if Allah didn't give up on me in the first place, why did he put me under such horrible circumstances? No, Allah didn't put me in these circumstances. I put myself in them. My decisions and actions caused me to be in these inescapable situations. But wasn't it Allah who conceived me as a cripple in the first place? Isn't that like giving up on me? How long must I bear this agonizing pain and isolation? This pain must end this moment in this very spot.

He took out the pistol and pulled the hammer back. The click echoed in the room. Placing his finger on the trigger, he looked down the muzzle. He felt like he was looking down a black hole that would swallow him up. Like a window of death. Death, which would transport him from the darkness in which he lived, into a life of brightness beside Allah in the hereafter.

Suddenly, a burst of gunshots from the room on his right, and two masked men in black with Kalashnikovs darted into the room. He felt no fear for their pointed weapons or from their coarse voices yelling and ordering him to drop his weapon. A loud explosion erupted outside the apartment, and a feminine voice screamed hysterically. The two masked men were distracted for a fraction of a second. Seizing the opportunity, he pulled the trigger. The explosion was deafening. A sharp buzzing sound filled his head. He was drowning in a sea of liquid gel. All the surrounding noise disappeared. Only a dull tone in his ears remained constant, like the sound of the cardiac monitor at the time of death.
Is this death?

CHAPTER 29

Wednesday, June 2, 2010

A massive pain thundered in his head. He was having difficulty breathing, his throat was raw, and he struggled to move. His legs were numb.

Is this how death feels? Why is everything black?

Mullah Abdullah opened his eyelids with a massive effort and immediately closed them again when the bright light burned into them.

Is this heaven? If it is, why do I feel pain?

The voices of Amani and Zahra gradually filtered through the loud buzzing in his ears. It was as if he was underwater, approaching the surface slowly.

Are Amani and Zahra with me in heaven?

He struggled to open his eyes just a slit. The

light burned his eyes again, but this time he didn't close them, instead he squinted and looked around. Amani and Zahra were peering at him with mixed looks of joy and consternation. Amani clutched his hand. "What has happened?" Then Amani and Zahra hugged each other and cried.

But why are they crying if we are in heaven?

He tried to turn his head and noticed the pull of the oxygen mask covering his mouth.

I'm in a hospital!

On his right, there was a cardiac monitor with leads attached to his chest. A glance confirmed an IV bottle and drip tube connected to his arm. A machine the size of a small refrigerator was attached to the left side of his neck with tubes.

His wife and daughter's words came to him muffled, as if his ears were full of water. He noticed a lady wearing a white coat entered the room, and both his wife and daughter were talking to her. The white-coat woman approached him and pried open his eyelids with her thumb and finger. Her eyes were red, maybe from the long shift she'd worked. She left the room and returned a few minutes later with a needle, which she injected into his left arm. He drifted off in a cloudy feeling and ...

The next time he opened his eyes, there was no longer any burning in his arm, no headache, no numbness. Even so, every breath hurt a little. Amani and Zahra were still there looking back at him, but wearing different clothes.

Amani's voice was low and far away. The

feeling of water filling his ears was still there. She said, "Thank Allah you are ok." He smiled and thanked Allah, but his words remained locked inside him.

"What's going on? Why am I here?" he croaked.

"You don't remember?" Amani asked.

"Well ..." he was trying to remember, but his brain was still blank.

"They found you in Hadiya's house, unconscious," Amani said. She squeezed his hand. "Thank Allah you are going to be ok."

Staring at Amani and Zahra, his memory slowly returned.

"The lack of oxygen has caused some damage to your kidneys, that's why they have you connected to the dialysis machine," Zahra said and pointed to the refrigerator-like machine, "But don't worry Papa, the damage is not permanent. They will need to keep you here in the hospital for at least a week while they treat your kidneys."

"When did all of this happen? What day is it?" he asked.

"Today is Wednesday. They brought you on Monday. You have been in a coma since then," Amani said.

A nurse entered and announced it was time for his injection. After the prick of a needle in his left arm, he slipped into a deep sleep once more.

**

The beeping of the cardiac monitor echoed like

a message from outer space transmitting into his mind. He opened his eyes to see an old man in a military uniform sitting on a chair, staring at him. He blinked and refocused before realizing the man was General Zafer Abyad.

The general stood up when he noticed he'd opened his eyes and said, "Peace be upon you, mullah. I hope you will feel better soon."

"Am I under arrest or something?"

The general laughed. "No, you are not, sir. I am just here to ensure you are still alive."

He forced his lips to form a smile, "Thank you, general. I appreciate your visit and your interest."

"And I'm here to tell you we found out who did this to you, and we have him in prison."

He frowned, "Khaled?"

"Yes, but we didn't find him when we raided the apartment. Our forces located him at his friend Fathi's apartment, not too far from where he lives. We arrested them both."

"Surely not Fathi too?"

"Yes, Fathi is also a member of the same terrorist organization. Oh, sorry I didn't clarify. We didn't raid the apartment because Khaled was trying to murder you. When we entered, we had no idea you were even there. Our surveillance team finally intercepted a transmission from Khaled's apartment for the first time, although they've been watching him for almost a year now."

"Khaled confessed to me; he killed his

mother."

The general raised his eyebrows. "What?"

"Yes, surely that will be enough to reopen the investigation into Hadiya's death and arrest all those involved?" He told the general about what happened when he went to read the report about Hadiya's death and found out Mansoor was the detective in charge. Then he told him about Murshidah's confession.

"Unless Khaled confesses, we can't reopen the case."

"Isn't it enough that I am telling you he confessed to me?"

"I believe you personally, but if Khaled denies telling you he killed his mother, we can't prosecute him on your evidence alone."

"So, he'll get away with murdering a good woman?"

"No, he is under arrest right now for his terrorist activities. When you recover, you must come to the police station and report what he did to you. Under further interrogation, he will spill the beans."

"If he confesses to killing his mother, will you arrest Mansoor for faking the report?"

"If Mansoor changed the original report, he will be found guilty. But if he was the one who wrote the original report and misjudged the situation, there is nothing we can do to him. We are all human, and we all make mistakes. But if Murshidah confesses that Haj Adel bribed her, we can pull Haj

Adel in for interrogation. If Haj Adel confesses to bribing Mansoor to hide the truth, then we can go after Mansoor."

"I hope everyone involved in this crime goes to jail."

"Leave it to us. We will prosecute all of them. Once you recover, I need you to visit me at my office and file a report about Khaled's and Murshidah's confessions. Will you do that?"

"Yes, of course I will."

The general stood up, ready to leave.

Mullah Abdullah thought of something else. "Is there any progress regarding Ahmad's case?"

"Which Ahmad?" the general said, fists at his sides as if he was ready for an official salutation.

"Ahmad Kishat, the brother of Hadiya."

"What case?"

"Previously, Hani informed me about Ahmad's murder in the factory, but now, as you know, Hani is not around anymore."

"Hani told you Ahmad was murdered?"

"Yesss ...." His jaw clenched.

"I can't find the words to describe this guy. People like him have a malignant way of getting things done. They tell you whatever you need to hear, so you'll give them what they need in return. As far as I can remember, Ahmad's death was a myocardial infarction. It was described as such in Detective Mansoor's report. When you come to my office, I'll show it to you."

CHAPTER 30

Friday, July 23, 2010

The mullah returned from Jumu'ah prayer loaded down with bags of vegetables, fruit, chicken, beef, and birthday candles. He put the supplies in the kitchen, then went to his room to change so he could help Amani and Zahra prepare for the birthday party.

The minute he entered the kitchen and smelled the cake baking, he closed his eyes and smiled dreamily. Amani was preparing the chicken and Zahra was mixing cocoa powder into the cream to cover the cake.

"What should I do?" he asked.

"Wash the lettuce and cut it with the vegetable knife please," Amani said, without looking at him.

"Roger that," he said, causing Zahra to giggle.

He took the lettuce out of the fridge and rinsed it in the sink while thinking how blessed he was by Allah. His gorgeous wife, a healthy, intelligent daughter, an immense house, and a brilliant career. For him, serving in a mosque and being a private detective at the same time was a brilliant combination. His health was better, especially since the horrible experience in Khaled's apartment and the suffering in the hospital with the dialysis machine for two long weeks. Thank Allah the damage to his kidneys wasn't permanent.

His injuries were nothing compared to those Zakiya had endured. Even after he'd recovered and gone home, she was still in the hospital, with a broken arm and multiple bruises and contusions on her back, arms, and head. He could now understand her attitude in the hospital and her rage towards everything when he visited her with her uncle Ahmad, especially after his own experience with Khaled. It was as if Allah had put him in that very situation to learn to be more sympathetic to people like Zakiya, and not to misjudge them.

He was now more determined than ever to prove to her that Allah exists. That only virtuous deeds come from Him, and evil actions come from humans. He'd spent the money Ahmad had given him for the work on Hadiya's case, on Zakiya and her sisters. He paid for an excellent plastic surgeon to work on her face, and a top-notch psychiatrist to be sure that she wouldn't drown in a swamp of depression. He made sure the four daughters had decent clothes to wear for university. He considered himself a godfather to them, and it was the least he could do for Hadiya. The woman who had shown nothing but patience throughout her arduous life's journey. He put the knife down and stretched his arms wide behind his head, and smiled to himself.

At that moment, the doorbell rang and the three of them stopped what they were doing while he went to open it.

The same four young women he'd just been thinking of were standing outside. He avoided looking directly at them and said, "Please, come in."

He left them sitting in the *liwan* and went to the kitchen to inform Amani and Zahra. He inhaled deeply the mouthwatering aroma of the roast chicken. His stomach growled.

"They're here," he told them with excitement in his voice.

"Oh cool," Zahra said, jumping up to greet them.

He looked at Amani with adoring eyes, then came closer and kissed her on the forehead. "You are the best wife and mother any man could ask for." Her hair smelled of lavender.

She hugged him affectionately. "And you are the best husband and father."

His family and Hadiya's four daughters enjoyed a tranquil meal together in the liwan. The only sounds were the clicking of spoons on plates and bowls. After lunch, Zahra took Zakiya up to her room, and Farah, Marwa and Ro'wa helped Amani to clear the table and prepare the surprise.

When the table was finally arranged, the mullah called Zahra to come down with Zakiya.

The look on Zakiya's face was priceless. She froze in the center of the liwan, staring at the birthday cake on the table. Then she looked at him, then at her sisters. She was at a loss for words. Her eyes blinked rapidly, filled with tears, but she quickly wiped them away with her sleeve. Zahra hugged her, and Farah came and hugged her too, followed by the rest of her sisters. They all shared a joyous group hug.

Amani lit the candles and called them in closer.

Looking at Amani with eyes full of love, he smiled. He wanted to excuse himself, but Zakiya surprised all of them and said, "No, please mullah, stay with us." Her voice sounded brittle. She took a small paper bag from her trouser pocket and held it out to him, saying, "This is your gift."

"Today is your birthday, not mine," he said and took the gift with his right hand.

"Yes, I know. But you are the one who put an end to our miserable life. Now we are all living happily without him."

"All the gratitude goes to your mother. The one who brought you up on the true path," Amani said.

"And for your uncle Ahmad," he added.

"And mullah, I apologize for my behavior in the hospital. I certainly didn't mean what I said, but I was angry and felt everyone had abandoned us in this life. I beg Allah for his forgiveness."

"My daughter Zakiya, this life is a short and worthless phase we live in, compared to the eternity of the hereafter. This short phase is full of challenges to prove ourselves worthy of eternal life. Allah put in our hearts all kinds of emotions and ordered us to use the noble ones to help other humans in need, and to tame the unworthy thoughts and avoid using them against other humans. But we, as mere limited humans, will never completely understand the wisdom of the divine system. We expect miracles to take us out of any unbearable conditions, but the divine system doesn't work that way.

"The narration of the prophet says, 'Humans are the families of Allah, and the most beloved to Him are the most beneficial to His families.'

"So, can you tell me what you understand from that quote?"

Zakiya's cheeks were pink, but a gleam appeared in her eyes, as she said without looking at him, "It means we should not expect Allah to come himself and help us, but Allah will employ righteous people to help those in need."

"Exactly, and that is the beauty of life, humans supporting each other," he said with a wide smile and took a tiny dark blue velvet box from his pocket and passed it over to her, "Happy birthday, my daughter Zakiya."

She bowed and thanked him politely. Farah, Marwa, Ro'wa, Zahra, and Amani each gave her their gifts one by one, then encouraged her to blow the candles out.

As Zakiya stood in front of the birthday cake, he marveled at how different she was now from the girl he'd met in the hospital a few months earlier. She wore a new smile, and her face had color in it once more. There was a glow in her eyes and happiness shone from her heart. He couldn't see it, but he could feel it.

Later, when he went to his room, he took a minute to open his notebook, found the last page of notes on the Hadiya Kishat case, and wrote...

Case Closed.

ACKNOWLEDGEMENT

First, I would like to thank you for reading this book. Without readers, writers are nothing. I hope you enjoyed it, and if you did, please consider leaving a review on Amazon or Goodreads. Your feedback is the best gift Ican recieve. This book would not have been possible to be between your hands without the help and support of many people starting with my family and friends and ending with my editor and designer. Their support gave me the strength to keep going. I thank them all. Last and most importantly, I would like to thank Allah for granting me the health and energy to keep writing. I am truly grateful for all Your blessings.

ABOUT THE AUTHOR

Hussin Alkheder

Hussin Alkeder, a native of Damascus, Syria, first drew breath in the vibrant city. His formative years were spent navigating the winding alleys of Al-Shagoor street, where he attended the venerable old primary school, imbibing the essence of his cultural heritage.

Over the span of twenty-three years, Hussin's roots remained firmly planted in Damascus, forging a deep connection with the city's rich tapestry of traditions and history. However, destiny beckoned him to explore beyond his homeland's borders, and he eventually embarked on a new chapter in his life, finding himself drawn to the bustling cosmopolitan marvel of Dubai.

For eight transformative years, Hussin luxuriated in the embrace of Dubai's multicultural milieu, absorbing its myriad influences and forging connections with people from all corners of the globe. Yet, this ceaseless thirst for cultural exploration continued to pull him, propelling him further eastward towards the captivating realm of Shanghai, China.

In Shanghai, Hussin delved into the mystique of far eastern cultures, immersing himself in the vibrant urban landscape and unraveling the secrets of this ancient civilization. As he roamed the bustling streets and serene temples, the profound allure of Asia left an indelible mark on his soul.

Driven by an insatiable hunger for knowledge and understanding, Hussin has now embarked on a new endeavor. He is currently pursuing a degree in Psychology, seeking to fathom the intricacies and dimensions of the human mind.

With an enriching array of experiences and a kaleidoscope of cultures etched into his being, Hussin found himself propelled towards a newfound passion - the art of storytelling. His creative spirit culminated in the masterful creation of his debut non-fiction novel, "The Victorious Blood," a literary testament to the triumphs and tribulations of Imam Hussain 's journey, painted with vivid strokes of truth and wonder.

Thus, the life of Hussin Alkeder traverses continents, cultures, and literary realms, as he pens a literary odyssey destined to captivate the hearts and minds of avid readers across the globe.

BOOKS BY THIS AUTHOR

The Victorious Blood

Non Fiction Novel

Four Ladies

Short Stories